THE REGENCY
LORDS & LADIES
COLLECTION

**Glittering Regency Love Affairs
from your favourite historical authors.**

THE REGENCY LORDS & LADIES COLLECTION

Available from the
Regency Lords & Ladies Large Print Collection

The Larkswood Legacy by Nicola Cornick
My Lady's Prisoner by Elizabeth Ann Cree
Lady Clairval's Marriage by Paula Marshall
A Scandalous Lady by Francesca Shaw
A Poor Relation by Joanna Maitland
Mistress or Marriage? by Elizabeth Rolls
Rosalyn and the Scoundrel by Anne Herries
Prudence by Elizabeth Bailey
Nell by Elizabeth Bailey
Miss Verey's Proposal by Nicola Cornick
Kitty by Elizabeth Bailey
An Honourable Thief by Anne Gracie
Jewel of the Night by Helen Dickson
The Wedding Gamble by Julia Justiss
Ten Guineas on Love by Claire Thornton
Honour's Bride by Gayle Wilson
One Night with a Rake by Louise Allen
A Matter of Honour by Anne Herries
Tavern Wench by Anne Ashley
The Sweet Cheat by Meg Alexander
The Rebellious Bride by Francesca Shaw
Carnival of Love by Helen Dickson
The Reluctant Marchioness by Anne Ashley
Miranda's Masquerade by Meg Alexander
Dear Deceiver by Mary Nichols
Lady Sarah's Son by Gayle Wilson
One Night of Scandal by Nicola Cornick
The Rake's Mistress by Nicola Cornick
Lady Knightley's Secret by Anne Ashley
Lady Jane's Physician by Anne Ashley

AN HONOURABLE THIEF

Anne Gracie

M&B

First published in Great Britain 2001
Large Print Edition 2009
Harlequin Mills & Boon Limited,
Eton House, 18-24 Paradise Road, Richmond, Surrey TW9 1SR

© Anne Gracie 2001

ISBN: 978 0 263 21040 8

Set in Times Roman 15¼ on 17 pt.
083-0609-81408

Printed and bound in Great Britain
by CPI Antony Rowe, Chippenham, Wiltshire

Prologue

*Near Batavia, on the island of Java,
Dutch East Indies. 1815*

"Promise!" The dying man grabbed her arm in a hard-fingered grip. Promise me, damn you, girl!

Kit Smith winced under the pressure. She glanced down at her father's thin, elegant fingers biting into her flesh. Gentleman's fingers. White, soft, aristocratic, seeming too fine even for the heavy ring he wore. Refined hands, good for lifting a lady's hand to be kissed. For gesturing in an amusing fashion to illustrate a sophisticated story. White-skinned, blue-veined hands. Hands which had never done a hard day's labour in their life. Hands which excelled at the shuffling and dealing of cards...the clever, extremely discreet dealing of cards...

Kit bit her lip and tried to ease her arm from under

the punishing grip. He did not know his own strength, that was Papa's trouble.

People didn't when they were dying.

"Promise me!"

Kit said nothing. With her other hand she picked up a linen cloth and wiped a trickle of blood from the corner of his mouth.

"Dammit, girl, I want that promise!" He searched her face angrily. "It's not as if I'm asking you to do anything you haven't done a hundred times or more in your life!"

Kit gently shook her head. "I cannot, Papa."

He flung her hand aside in disgust. "Bah! I don't know why I bothered even asking you. My daughter!" The scorn in his voice lanced through Kit. "My only living child! She, who has refused to help her father since she turned thirteen!"

"Hush, Papa, do not try to talk. Save your strength."

"Be damned to it…I'm dying, girl…and I'll not…be hushed. By sunset tonight—" He spat blood and lay gasping for breath before he could continue. "Dying, curse it…and without a son to…" He rolled his head away from her, muttering, "Nothing but a daughter, a useless daughter—"

Kit did not respond; she told herself she was inured to the pain of his tirade on the uselessness of daughters. She'd heard it all her life.

Her maidservant and companion, Maggie Bone,

bustled in, carrying a pile of clean linen and a bowl of fresh water. Kit nodded her thanks and, as Maggie removed the blood-soaked wad of linen, Kit pressed a fresh pad against the wound in his chest.

"Done for, curse it." He gave a snort of bitter laughter. "And by some clod of a colonial lout! Me! In whom the finest English blood flows…"

Kit pressed harder, willing the flow to stop.

"Not so hard, girl!"

Kit eased the pressure slightly. In moments fresh, bright blood seeped through it. Her father's life blood, draining inexorably away into a napkin.

"Blasted stiff-necked Dutchman. Accusing me of cheating! Me! The Honourable J—" He broke off in a paroxysm of coughing.

"Hush, Papa, you will only make it worse if you try to speak. And besides, you are not the Honourable Jeremy Smythe-Parker here. That was in New South Wales. The name you are using now is Sir Humphrey Weatherby, remember?"

Not that it mattered any longer, she reflected. The Dutch doctor had left, the Javanese servants could not understand English and Maggie's loyalty was unquestioned. There was nobody to pretend to any more. But one could not break the habits of a lifetime so easily, and keeping track of her father's many identities was such a habit.

Her father ignored her. He lay gasping for breath

for another moment of two. "Felled by a grubby tradesman, in a dirty foreign village in the middle of nowhere. If the blasted Pittance hadn't been late—"

The Pittance was what he called the money which arrived so mysteriously from time to time. It seemed to come, no matter where they were, though it was often late. Kit had no idea where it came from, or why. Her father refused to discuss it.

She glanced through the window at the sea sparkling under the sunlight. It was so blue it almost hurt her eyes. To be sure, there were the swamps and the mosquitoes were very bad—malaria was a serious risk—but on some days, Kit had thought they had landed in paradise.

Yet in her father's eyes, everywhere they had ever lived, no matter how wonderfully exotic or beautiful, had soon been declared grubby or obscure or provincial. Nothing compared with England.

He was, he had always been, a most bitter exile.

Kit reached for a fresh pad of linen. He was growing paler by the moment.

Her father coughed painfully. "Dammit…why could not Mary have given me a son who lived…sons…"

She tried not to listen. She pressed the linen pad more firmly against his wound. Was it her imagination, or was the blood flow slowing?

"A son would understand about a man's honour."

"I understand honour very well, Papa," said Kit.

"Even if I am only a girl." If her father was unaware of the irony of a card cheat and swindler lecturing his daughter on honour, Kit was not. But it was not the card game or the recent duel with the Dutchman he was referring to. No, it was about what had happened in England all those years ago.

"Don't take that tone with me, girl! If you understood anything at all about a man's honour, you would make me that promise." He lay back, wheezing with the effort of his outburst. "Females have no understanding of honour. Their minds are too clouded with emotion… If only my bonny boy had lived."

Her mother had died giving birth to a little stillborn brother when Kit was six, but her father still spoke of her brother as if he was a person he had known and loved.

"If only he had not died. Now…" He looked at her with bitter grief. "My son would not let me die refusing to promise to avenge the great wrong done me."

There was a long silence. All that could be heard in the room were the far distant noises of life going on outside the cottage: the chattering of monkeys in the jungle behind the house, the laughter of children in the nearby village, the squawking of a chicken.

And inside the cottage the sound of laboured breathing.

Not for the first time, Kit wondered about what had happened back in England, before she had even been born. He had always been bitter about it, and yet un-characteristically silent about the details. He'd always vowed revenge, but on whom and for what, she'd never known.

Whatever it was, it had never stopped festering in him.

If it hadn't happened, he'd said over and over—generally when he'd been drinking—he would be a rich man, respected, living in a beautiful big house in England. His beloved England.

She'd never quite believed it. But now she wondered. Had she been too quick to dismiss it as another one of Papa's fantasies?

Had that—whatever it was—truly been the cause of her father living the sort of life he had? Drifting from one place to the next. Living from card game to card game. Arriving in obscure corners of the far-flung empire as Sir Humphrey This or The Honourable Mr That; leaving as a reviled card cheat and scoundrel...as they had just a few weeks ago from Sydney Town in the colony of New South Wales. An ignominious exit, tossed on the first outgoing ship... arriving in the Dutch colony of Batavia.

If the Great Wrong—as he put it—had not been done to him, would he have lived as a decent, con-tented man in England?

She would never know. But he was her father. She ought to give him the benefit of the doubt.

Kit bit her lip. He was her only living relative. And he was dying. Who was she to deny him peace on his deathbed? Her scruples suddenly looked a little like selfishness to her.

She looked down at him. His face was grey, his lips had an ominous tinge of blue. His eyes were closed, but he was not asleep—the tension in his body testified to that.

He looked like a man drained of all hope.

All her life Papa had always had a new scheme, a new horizon, plans…

Who was she to say no to a dying man's last wish?

Kit sighed. She leaned forward and took his hand gently in hers. "I will do what a son would, Papa. I will retrieve your honour for you. Tell me what I must do."

The heavy-lidded eyes opened, wary at first, then suddenly sharp with triumph. The long-fingered hand tightened convulsively and painfully as he pulled his daughter closer to whisper the instructions in her ear.

At last he finished, closed his eyes in exhaustion and sank back against the pillows.

The heat of the afternoon pressed on them. A hot moist wind lazily stirred the leaves in the trees outside. The only other sound was that of a man fighting for every breath.

Suddenly he opened his eyes. "Sent a letter to Rose from Sydney Town. Told her—" He choked suddenly and went into a long paroxysm of coughing.

He subsided shaken, grey and immeasurably weaker. Kit wiped his face with a cool, damp cloth and wondered who this Rose was.

"Hush now, Papa, do not worry yourself. I will do what is necessary. Just lie still and try to save your strength."

A ghastly smile settled on his lips. "My son…" he muttered, so low, Kit could hardly hear him. "My beloved son…"

And with that, her father died. On a low pallet in a simple Javanese cottage on the other side of the world from where he belonged. Killed in a duel for cheating at cards. The final blow in a life that, according to him, had contained nothing but blows.

He died without a word of love or farewell to his only child, his daughter, the companion of his exile for the whole nineteen years of her life.

"Never mind, Miss Kit," said Maggie Bone comfortingly. "He did value you, really. Some men never can say how they feel."

Kit accepted the lie with a nod and a tremulous smile. "I know, Maggie."

"I wish you'd never promised him, though."

"Yes, but I did, so there's no going back on it now." Maggie sighed. "London, is it?"

"Yes, London. To stay with someone called Rose."

Chapter One

London 1816

Mr Hugo Devenish made his way through the quiet streets of London, his eyes on the faint, unnatural glow in the sky over the city. Gaslights. Twenty-six miles of gas mains had been laid around London, he had heard recently. Everyone was rushing to install the new miracle.

Sultan's hooves clattered and echoed on cobbled stones. Hugo leaned forward and patted his mount on the neck. He'd carried his master gallantly for a long distance. Horse and master were pleasantly weary.

He passed the homes of several acquaintances and cast a casual eye over the dark and silent buildings.

Suddenly he stiffened. A shadow moved out of one of the tall mullioned windows on to a small balcony jutting from an upper storey of a large grey mansion nearby. There was something furtive, stealthy in the movement that attracted Hugo's attention. He reined Sultan to a silent halt.

It was Pennington House, the home of Lord and Lady Pennington. Hugo knew the family slightly: Lord Pennington was a member of the Government, a stern, slightly pompous man in his early sixties; Lady Pennington was a prominent member of society. Their son, Hugo believed, was an intimate of his nephew, Thomas.

Shadowy figures ought not to be appearing from darkened windows of the homes of Government members at three in the morning, thought Hugo. This could well be a matter of national security. The war was over, but that did not mean there were no more Government secrets to be stolen and sold. There were always secrets.

Hugo watched intently, his eyes squinted against the glow thrown out by the gas lamp in front of the house. He cursed it silently. The bright glare made it very difficult to make out the figure behind the lamp—all he could see was a silhouette.

As he watched, the figure climbed on to the carved stone balustrade, paused for a moment and then leapt out into the air. Hugo's breath caught—the thief would surely plummet to his death—but no. He clung to the next balcony like a monkey and climbed up. He was an agile little devil, thought Hugo.

He ought to go and rouse the household, to pound

on the front door until someone came. But by that time, the thief would be gone. No, he would try to catch the scoundrel himself.

He watched as the miscreant shimmied skilfully up one of the shallow carved columns which graced the front of the house—not at all an easy task, as a man who had spent his boyhood climbing around the upper reaches of ships and masts well knew. He admired the agility and skill of the rascal, even as he resolved to foil him.

The thief clambered onto a low roof and disappeared around a corner. Hugo followed, wincing at the slight clatter that Sultans hooves made on the cobbles. He hesitated, then slipped off his horse, tied him to a nearby lamp-post and ran into the narrow alleyway which bordered the house.

It was difficult to see the scoundrel. There was only the occasional flickering of movement against the grey stone of the house, the faint scrap of a foot on a slate tile. Then a shadow moved swiftly and lightly along the roof that ran along the back part of the house and for a moment, the scoundrel's silhouette was clearly visible in the soft golden glow the gas lanterns cast against the night sky.

Hugo frowned at the silhouette; it was strange and yet somehow familiar. The intruder wore loose baggy clothing, shapeless pants and a baggy tunic. He wore some sort of cap on his head, and something flapped against his back. An elusive thread of memory twitched in Hugo's mind, but he was entirely focussed on the thief's actions and did not pursue the thought.

The thief leapt lightly off the roof and landed cat-footed, on all fours, balanced on the high stone wall which surrounded Pennington House. He swung his legs over the wall and prepared to drop down.

Hugo raced to intercept him. Just as the thief hit the ground, he threw himself forward in a tackle, catching the thief around the legs.

"Aiee-ya!" The thief kicked out, hard, breaking Hugo's hold.

"Oof!" Hugo, winded, but determined, grabbed again at the intruder. They rolled on the filthy cobblestones and as he clutched at the loose baggy clothing, he caught a whiff of a scent: strong, foreign, familiar.

The thief was wearing a black skull-cap pulled down over his head and dark muffler wrapped around the lower part of his face. All Hugo could see were his eyes, glinting fiercely in the gaslight. He caught hold of a skinny arm and—

"Aiee-ya!" It was as if a blunt axe had landed on his wrist. Hugo swore and let go, and in a flash the thief pulled free, rolled away from him on the cobblestones and raced swiftly along the alley. A long black pigtail bounced lightly against his back as he ran.

Hugo scrambled to his feet and gave chase.

As he rounded a corner there was a flurry of hooves. He threw himself against a wall as a brown horse bore down on him, a small figure clinging nimbly to its back. Horse and rider passed under the gaslight and Hugo gasped in surprise.

The thief was a Chinaman. The cry he had used was peculiarly Chinese. Hugo had heard coolies use it abroad. He'd not expected to hear it in London. And the clothes were unmistakable—the typical loose baggy dark indigo pants and tunic, a round black embroidered cap and most obvious of all, the long black pigtail hanging down the length of the thief's back, bouncing and flying as the horse rounded a corner and disappeared.

Of course! No wonder the silhouette had looked odd and yet familiar. And that was where he'd smelt that scent before—in a Chinese joss house! It was some kind of incense, sandalwood perhaps.

But good God! What would a Chinaman want with the secrets of an English Government member?

Panting slightly, rubbing his sore wrist and feeling rather foolish for having been bested by a man so much smaller and lighter than himself, Hugo limped back to the front door of Pennington House and braced himself to rouse the household.

He glanced up at the gas lamps at the front of the house. They were supposed to reduce crime in London; all they'd done was make it more difficult for him. The scarf had hidden most of the rascal's face, but those damned gaslamps distorted everything. He'd caught a glimpse of the thief's eyes—but in them he'd seen only the reflected blue flames of the gaslight and whoever had heard of a blue-eyed Chinaman!

He gripped the knocker and pounded on the Penningtons' front door.

"Miserable blinkin' weather. I'd forgotten about the miserable blinkin' weather. That's London for you!"

Kit glanced at the sour countenance of her maid, who was peering gloomily out of the window.

"Rain, rain all the blinkin' time—and then, when it does finally stop, what do you get?—blinkin' fog! However did I stand it when I was young?"

Kit tried not to smile. "Never mind, Maggie dear, we need not stay here forever, you know."

Maggie snorted and picked up the woollen stocking she had been darning. "You can't gull me, Miss Mischief. You've always hankered after a home of your own, and now we're finally home in England—"

"But that's just it, Maggie," Kit interrupted, frowning. "I'm not home. I wasn't even born in England. I don't belong here, any more than—"

"What do you mean, you're not home? O' course you're home!"

Kit smiled a little ruefully. "No. I'm not. I have no

family here—no family anywhere. I'm living amongst strangers here, just as I always have."

"Nonsense! No family? What about your auntie? Miss Rose is—"

Kit blinked in surprise. "Maggie, I thought you realised."

Maggie frowned. "Realised what?"

Kit pulled a wry face. "Rose is no aunt of mine. Papa had no kin. She is—or was—one of Papa's *friends*. You've met a dozen of my 'aunts' before."

Maggie frowned. "I dunno, Miss Kit, Miss Rose doesn't seem like one of those types. Your pa was always interested in more, more…"

Kit smiled. "More glamorous females? Yes, but it has been more than twenty years since he last saw Rose. Much can change in that time and Rose may well have been quite a dasher in her youth—"

Maggie stopped her with an emphatic gesture. "We'll not discuss your pa and his hussies. Scandalous, it was!" She lifted a long white frock in delicate muslin and carefully laid it on the bed. Come on, missie, let's have you into this." Tossing the gown over Kit's freshly coiffed head, she turned her around, twitching the fabric into place, examining every inch of her critically. Her eyes softened at the sight of the young woman's flushed cheeks and sparkling eyes.

"You're enjoying this, ain't you, Miss Kit?"

Kit blushed and looked a little self-conscious. "Yes, Maggie. I never dreamed it would be such fun to be a young girl again. To have nothing more to worry about than what to wear and who to dance with. And Miss Singleton is so very kind. I do not care what she may have done in the past, I have not experienced such kindness in…" She sighed, shook her head and drew on her gloves briskly. "Yes. It is very agreeable."

Maggie looked at her searchingly. "You don't think you might like to take the opportunity to get yourself a husband, lovie?"

Kit shook her head firmly. "It's not what I came here to do."

"Yes, but—"

"No, Maggie. I am here under false pretences. I couldn't possibly deceive any man into offering for me. It is one thing for a man to offer for Miss Singleton's poverty-stricken long-lost niece—though money seems to be so important here that I cannot imagine anyone doing such a thing. But to offer for a poverty-stricken unknown adventuress daughter of Miss Singleton's former—" She broke off hurriedly. "Well! That's a very different matter, at any rate. Any man knowing my true background is more likely to offer me a *carte blanche* than a ring, and you know I wouldn't accept that."

"I should hope not, indeed!"

Kit laughed. "Yes, Maggie dearest, your stuffy strait-lacing has certainly rubbed off on me." She caught Maggie's look and amended her statement. "Well, in most areas, at least. I cannot be expected to have inherited nothing at all from Papa, now can I?" She planted a light kiss on her maid's rosy cheek.

Maggie bridled in pleased disapproval. "Oh, get away with you, Miss Baggage! I don't approve and you know it—and I hope I know better than to try to change your mind after all these years, so dratted stubborn you can be—but you do know they hang people here, Miss Kit. Or transport them."

"Yes, and they chopped people's heads and hands off in China, but I still have both my bits, don't I?" said Kit. "You need not worry," she added soothingly. "It is only a small commission from Papa, and not at all dangerous."

Maggie snorted. "Don't try to gammon me, Miss Kit. I wish you'd just forget whatever it is your pa asked you to do. He never was careful enough of your welfare. Can you not forget all that nonsense now His Nibs has passed on?"

"Nonsense? Family honour is not nonsense," said Kit. "In any case," she added hurriedly, having almost forgotten her resolve to keep Maggie ignorant of her doings, "I have no idea what you are talking about. I am merely preparing to attend a ball. Now—"

Maggie sniffed. "Won't break a promise, will you?

And he knew it, drat the man!" she added under her breath. "I'll say no more, for I was never one to waste breath in trying to change what can't be changed."

"Yes, and we must hurry, or I shall be late for this ball. Now, where is that shawl, the embroidered gauze one? I have a mind it will go perfectly with this gown."

Grumbling under her breath, Maggie fetched the embroidered white-on-white gauze shawl and draped it carefully around her mistress's shoulders. She stood back, examined Kit with a critical eye, and sighed heavily. "Aye, 'tis bonny you look, right enough, though I wish you'd wear something other than white. It does bring out that dratted brown colour in your skin."

Kit laughed. "Oh, pooh! I am no longer brown at all—in fact, I think I look sadly pale. But there, that is the fashion, I suppose. And my gown must be white, dearest Maggie. I am supposed to be a girl just emerged from the schoolroom—naturally I must wear white."

She ignored the maid's snort and searchingly examined her face in the looking glass. "I do look like a young girl, do I not, Maggie? My twenty years do not show too much, do they?"

"No, Miss Kit. T'aint natural," the maid said gloomily. "You look barely eighteen—even younger when you smile."

"Good," said her mistress briskly. "I must remember to smile more often then. Now hand me my cloak, if you please, or I will keep this new 'aunt' of mine waiting in the hallway, and that would never do."

Kit hurried down the stairs. She found Aunt Rose patiently waiting in the hallway below.

"Ah, there you are, dear," called Rose. "I hope that cloak you are wearing is warmer than it looks. The evening is chillier than I expected and, you know, that mausoleum of Fanny Parsons's is as cold as a tomb, and she never heats it properly. I blame that husband of hers," she added darkly. "The Parsons have always been shocking pinch-pennies, but he is by far the worst of them. I have had to put on three petticoats—three!—and I am sure I shall still catch a chill." She shivered and hugged a slightly tatty fur cloak around her.

Kit could not help smiling down at the middle-aged woman as she descended the stairs. It was a little cool, but to hear her speak, one would think it about to snow.

"Aunt Rose' was slender, almost wraithlike, with a pale, faded sort of prettiness about her—rather different to the bold good looks her father had favoured in women. And, far from being fashionable, she was generally dressed rather dowdily and, being so susceptible to drafts, always with a great many scarves and shawls trailing about her person.

And yet, despite the faded looks, despite the dowdy clothes and the vagueness, there was a definite sort of something about Rose Singleton, a certain unconscious air of *ton* that even the best looking and most fashionably dressed of her father's other female friends had lacked.

Kit supposed that this was why her father had chosen to send her to Rose Singleton instead of anyone else. The surprise was that Miss Singleton had agreed to take her. In fact, she must still have harboured some warm feeling towards Kit's father, for she had embraced Kit on her arrival in England quite as if she really were her long-lost niece.

"Ah, you are wearing pearls, my love. Very suitable," said Rose. "I must remember to compliment your maid. So many girls in your position would be quite unable to resist the temptation to drape themselves with stones until they look exactly like a chandelier and I do so think diamonds are unsuited to a young girl. Pretty, of course, but so hard. Pearls, now, are much more suitable for an *ingenue.*'

"Diamonds, Aunt? There is no danger of me wearing diamonds, I assure you!" Kit could not help the choke of laughter that escaped her. Diamonds! It had been as much as Kit could manage to purchase one set of good quality fake pearls before her arrival in England. Diamonds, even paste ones, were beyond her budget.

Miss Singleton looked her over approvingly. "Yes, my dear. Very wise of you. One would not wish to appear vulgar."

"No, Aunt Rose," said Kit demurely. What on earth did she mean, *girls in your position*? A vague allusion to her imposture? If so, it would be a first. Rose Singleton could be quite determinedly vague at times, particularly when it came to avoiding subjects she did not wish to discuss. But she had been so kind and generous, Kit would not for the world distress her by referring to anything the lady wished to avoid.

She assisted the footmen to hand Rose into the coach, tuck a fur rug around her and adjust the heated bricks under her feet and then sat back, agreeably warm herself, while the coach rumbled over the cobblestones. She had learned to enjoy small pleasures while she had them.

Outside, the night was clear and bright. The coach pulled up outside the Parsonses' town house, a grand old building, a little on the fantastical side and much embellished with Corinthian columns and odd Gothic gargoyles. It was lit, not only by gas lamps, but by flaming brands held aloft by liveried men.

Kit stepped from the coach and turned to assist Rose down. She felt a thrill of pleasure and anticipation. Tonight she would not think of anything except the ball. Tonight she would let herself be the carefree young girl everyone thought her and enjoy all the pleasures London society had to offer.

No doubt she would pay for it later, but then, that was life.

"Is this not delightful?" whispered a young girl sitting next to Kit. "I never thought there would be so many people. I have never been to a ball in London before," she added confidingly.

Kit smiled. "Yes, it is quite new to me also."

"Are not the ladies' gowns beautiful?"

"Yes, very," Kit agreed. "So many beautiful colours."

"Kit, my dear, here is Lord Norwood, wishing to be allowed to dance with you. Give him your card, my dear," said Rose, smiling meaningfully at Kit.

Thomas, Lord Norwood, bowed punctiliously over her hand. His fair hair was elaborately pomaded and carefully coaxed into the "Nonpareil' style. He wore knee breeches of a nice shade of biscuit, a heavily embroidered waistcoat and a coat which fitted tightly across narrow shoulders; his shirt points were so high and so heavily starched he could barely turn his head. His neckcloth was a complicated affair involving several knots and loops. Added to this was a collection of fobs, pins and a quizzing glass. All in all, Lord Norwood appeared the very epitome of a dandy.

Kit handed her card over, hiding her reluctance. She had been hinting Lord Norwood away for several days now, but he seemed utterly impervious to her hints. She was not sure whether it was impregnable self-consequence which enabled him to overlook her indifference, or whether he had some other motive for making her the unwilling object of his attentions—a wager or some such. For unwilling she was: her plans did not allow for friendships of any sort, male or female. Her promise to her father was her paramount concern.

Lord Norwood scribbled his name on her card, bowed gracefully and handed it back, saying in world-weary accents, "Miss Singleton, my night is complete. The joy of securing my name on your dance card is all I have hoped for, or even dreamed of."

Kit smiled sweetly. "Does this mean we do not actually need to dance, then, now that your name is safely on my card?"

He blinked in surprise, then laughed indulgently. "Such pretty wit," he murmured. "I look forward to our dance." He bowed again and disappeared into the throng.

"You are so lucky," whispered the girl next to her. "He is very handsome."

"Mmm, yes," agreed Kit. "He is handsome."

"And he dresses so beautifully."

"Yes."

"I think he likes you," the girl whispered coyly.

"No," said Kit thoughtfully. "I don't think he does.

I must confess I am quite at a loss to know what he sees in me at all." She frowned as she noticed Lord Norwood disappear into one of the anterooms. It was one of the rooms reserved for those who wished to play cards, rather than dance.

"Oh, but—" began the girl.

Kit smiled quickly. "No, no. Take no notice of my foolishness," she said. "I have a touch of the headache, that is all. I am sure Lord Norwood is everything you say he is. And I am very lucky to have been asked to dance with him. Now, I have been meaning to say, ever since you sat down, what a very pretty dress you are wearing. And such an interesting reticule. Wherever did you get it?"

Successfully distracted, the girl entered into a discussion of clothes and the various shops she and her mama had searched to obtain just the right fabric. As she extolled the delights of the Pantheon Bazaar, Kit's attention wandered.

Lord Norwood was not the only man who had shown Kit a degree of flattering attention and her unexpected popularity disturbed her. It was not as if she was anything out of the ordinary—at least, she was, but nobody in London knew about her unconventional background, so as far as appearances went, she looked very much the part of any young lady making her come-out.

And it wasn't as if she was beautiful or anything;

there were many much prettier and more attractive girls who had been brought out that season, not to mention several diamonds of the first water. Kit had planned to move through London society with barely a ripple, attracting little notice. Anonymity was vital to the success of her plans. To this end she had tried to ensure that her personality, in public at least, appeared fairly bland and colourless. And she had certainly made no effort to attract male attention; in fact, she had tried very hard to deflect it.

And yet almost from the date of her arrival in London, she had been solicited to dance, invited to go driving, had flowers sent to her, and so on. Even the ladies had been exceptionally friendly, inviting her to soirees, musical afternoons, for walks in the park, to balls, routs and pleasure expeditions; in short, to all the many social events on the calendar of the London *ton*.

All this, for an unknown girl, sponsored into society by her not particularly distinguished "aunt". Perhaps this was the reason people referred to "polite society"…?

"He's just come in and don't you think, Miss Singleton, that he's the most elegant-looking man you've ever seen?"

Kit glanced across to where her young friend was looking. A knot of people stood in the entrance, exchanging greetings. Only one man stood out of the crowd, as far as Kit was concerned; a tall dark man in severely cut evening clothes. Elegant would certainly describe the clothes, Kit thought, but as for the man himself...

He stood out like a battle-scarred tomcat in a sea of well-fed tabbies. Tall, lean, rangy, sombre. Detached. A little wary and yet certain of his prowess. His eyes ranged over the colourful throng. Kit wished she could see the expression in them. His very stance expressed the view that he could not care the snap of his fingers for the lot of them.

He looked more like a predator than a guest.

His hair was dark, midnight dark and thick, she thought, though cropped quite brutally close; not quite the Windswept, not quite the Brutus. A style of his own, Kit thought, or perhaps he disdained to follow fashion.

She wondered who he was. He did not seem to fit in this colourful, pleasure-seeking crowd. He stood, a man apart. Indifferent.

His face was unfashionably bronzed, the bones beneath the skin sculpted fine and hard. A long aquiline nose, just slightly off centre. A long lean jaw ending in a square, unyielding chin.

Not elegant: arresting.

His mouth was firm, resolute, unsmiling. She wondered what it would take to make him smile.

A woman hastened to greet him: their hostess,

Lady Fanny Parsons. Kit watched him bend over her hand. He was not a man accustomed to bowing—oh, he was graceful enough, but there was a certain hesitation, she noticed, a careless indifference.

Lady Fanny was laughing and flirting. As Kit watched, the man shrugged a pair of very broad shoulders. The hard mouth quirked in a self-deprecatory grimace. She wondered what they were discussing.

"Miss Singleton?" came the youthful voice at her elbow. "Is he not the most divinely beautiful man you have ever seen?"

Kit blinked. Elegant she could accept. Striking, certainly. Even a little intimidating. But divinely beautiful? Never.

She turned to her young friend, only to find her looking at some other, quite different man, a very pretty young fellow in a pale blue velvet coat, striped stockings and pantaloons of the palest primrose. Sir Primrose had been standing beside her man of darkness, Kit realised. She wanted to ask her young friend if she knew who the dark stranger was. Such a distinctive man would surely be well known.

"Who is—?"

But he had disappeared.

Just then, Lord Norwood came to claim his dance with Kit. And soon the music started and Kit was too

busy dancing to think of anything except the delightful sensation of being a young girl at a fine
London ball.

She would think about the tall dark man later.

"Hugo Devenish! How very unexpected," gushed
Lady Fanny Parsons, surging forward in a froth of
satin and lace. "I was certain you would ignore my
invitation as you usually do, you wicked man."

"Ignore you? Never, Lady Fanny." Hugo bent over
the hand she offered him. "'Tis just that I am so
rarely in Town."

Lady Fanny laughed and rapped him playfully with
her fan. "And I hear you have been doing battle with
frightfully dangerous criminals, you hero, you! So
brave, such a risk you took. I heard the latest fellow
was a desperate great ruffian armed to the teeth!"

Hugo quirked an ironic brow. "Rumour does me too
much honour. It was a small, unarmed Chinaman."

"A Chinaman! Good Heavens! I hadn't heard that!
What on earth would a Chinaman be doing breaking
into the Pennington house—?"

"Black pearls are highly prized in the far east, I
have heard."

"Of course, the famous Pennington Black Pearls!
Poor Eliza is just devastated, you know, and her
husband is furious! An heirloom. Worth an absolute
king's ransom!"

Hugo nodded. "Yes, I was unable to save them, unfortunately."

"Oh, but think how much worse it could have been if you hadn't disturbed the blackguard!"

Hugo shrugged, but said nothing. He had already explained to Pennington that he felt the thief had already completed his depredations when Hugo arrived.

"Oh, you are so wonderfully modest, dear Hugo. I am so glad you are here—you can protect me tonight, in case any nasty Oriental thieves break in." Lady Fanny giggled girlishly and rapped his arm with her fan again.

Hugo bowed again, then took his leave of Lady Fanny and made a leisurely way across the crowded room to where a lady had been glaring at him since his arrival.

"What the devil has brought you to London just now, Hugo?" said Lady Norwood, leading him into a small anteroom.

Hugo observed her coolly. "I was under the impression that you had written me no fewer than eleven missives, stating in terms of utmost urgency that you required my immediate attendance."

"Yes, but I wrote you at least six more after that telling you most expressly *not* to come!"

He smiled and raised a glass of champagne to his lips. "Yes, that is what decided me. I arrived this afternoon and when I presented myself in Portland Place, your butler informed me you were attending Fanny Parsons's ball. And since Fanny had sent me a card…"

Lady Norwood stamped a foot. "Well, it is most inconvenient of you. I beg you will return to Yorkshire tomorrow morning without delay. Your presence is not needed here any longer, and to be frank, Hugo, you are very much in the way."

Her late husband's half-brother did not seem at all perturbed by her hostility. He shrugged. "You wrote to me that you were in grave distress."

"Oh! Yes. Well, I was. I have been so frightfully worried about Thomas, you see."

"About Thomas?" He regarded her with faint disbelief.

"But I have, Hugo, you have no reason to look at me like that." She pouted winsomely in his direction. "You know what a doting mother I am, and oh! the cares of motherhood." She sighed soulfully.

Hugo, displaying a lamentable lack of gallantry, did not respond. She peeped a glance at him through her downcast lashes. His expression was cynical.

"Dibs not in tune, eh, Amelia? Too bad. You'll not get a penny from me, so you may as well give up the play-acting."

Amelia abandoned her soulful mien. "You are nothing but a penny-pinching clutchfist, Hugo!"

Looking bored, Hugo strolled to the doorway and observed the dancers currently engaged in a cotillion.

His sister-in-law was not fooled by this apparent interest in his fellow guests. She glared at his back. The sight he presented did not at all meet her fastidious standards. His hair was cropped far too short and was not coaxed into a modish style, but simply brushed back from his brow. His shirtpoints were starched, but not high enough to be fashionable; his neckcloth was so plain as to be an affront to any person of taste. His coat fitted him perfectly, but it was of such a dark shade that it made him look almost as if he was in mourning, particularly in combination with his black pantaloons.

The entire effect was too sombre for words, but Amelia was forced to concede that his attire, at least, did not disgrace his family. It was the man himself who was the problem.

Those shoulders… She shuddered. More suited to a labourer than a gentleman. And his skin, which he'd carelessly allowed the sun and wind to darken to an unfashionable brown colour. She glanced at the hands holding the wineglass and sniffed. He could have worn gloves, at least! Those hands—tanned, and covered with nicks and scars—a shameful testament to a youth spent in manual labour.

She averted her gaze from her brother-in-law's offending person and concentrated on his miserly habits.

"Not everyone enjoys a life of monkish isolation and deprivation, Hugo. We have expenses, Thomas and I. The life of a fashionable person costs a great deal. You—" She cast a disparaging glance over his plain clothing. "You would have no idea of the demands on a gentleman's purse."

The faint, disparaging emphasis on the word "gentleman" did not escape Hugo. But these days he was indifferent to it. His mother had been old Lord Norwood's second wife, an heiress, with the stigma of trade attached to her. And Hugo was only the second son, after all, and with the blood of "dammed tradesmen" in his veins.

Lady Norwood continued, "In any case, as Lord Norwood, Thomas has a position to maintain, and he has every right to the fruits of his inheritance! You have no business denying—"

"Thomas's *inheritance,* madam," interrupted Hugo in a blighting tone, "was a shamefully neglected estate, a crumbling manor house, mortgaged to the hilt and falling apart with disrepair and a mountain of debts to go with them! The fact that Thomas was left anything at all was no thanks to my father and my half-brother, but to whichever far-seeing ancestor of ours established the entail which prevented them gambling away every square inch of land."

Amelia squirmed, uncomfortably. "Yes, I know, but that is all in the past, after all. And everything has changed now, and you have returned and can—" She broke off as she glanced at him and saw the look in his eye.

She pouted and fiddled with her rings. "Well, I'm sure I am sorry about what happened to you, but it is not as if you suffered too badly—"

"You know nothing about it, madam."

"Possibly not, but I can see you are very far from purse-pinched, after all. From all I have heard, I'm sure you could pay Thomas's debts, and mine, and barely even notice it. We are family, after all." She did not meet his eyes.

His lips thinned, and he inclined his head. "Indeed. Such…belated…family feeling does you honour, I am sure. But I am not going to pay Thomas's debts. Nor yours."

"No, you will not assist us in any way—"

"I towed this family from the River Tick, madam, if you care to recall. And I have expressed myself more than willing to teach Thomas how to manage his estate and—"

"Oh, yes—you would make of him a tradesman like yourself!" Amelia sniffed scornfully. "How Thomas would ever find himself a decent bride with the stench of trade about him I declare I don't know!"

Hugo stared indifferently at the wall above her head.

"If you truly wished to help Thomas, you could settle a sum on him and then you need never worry about us again, but no! You will do nothing so straightforward! I think you enjoy having the power over us that you do!"

Hugo's brows snapped together. There was an element of truth in her accusation, he realised. Not that he wanted power, but Thomas and Amelia's constant requests for money gave him some faint feeling of being part of a family. It was a pathetic thing to realise about oneself, he thought.

"It would please me very well if I never had to see you or Thomas again." Hugo drained his glass of wine. "I would be delighted to be able to wash my hands of the boy, but he is my only relative, after all, and I have a duty to him."

"Well, then, why will you not—?"

"My duty is to ensure that Thomas learns not to get himself into the same spiral of gambling and debt that his forebears did!"

"How dare you sneer at my son's forebears—they were, at least, all *gentlemen born*!"

"And gentlemen born live in debt, is that it? Thank God I had some common blood, in that case. No— we shall not brangle over the past." He stood up and made for the door. "You have my last word on it, Amelia; you and Thomas must learn to live on your income, or find someone else to frank your vowels."

"Well, and so we *shall* if only you will go back to Yorkshire!" hissed Amelia waspishly. "You could not have come to London at a worse time!"

Mr Devenish turned. "What do you mean?"

"Thomas and I have found a solution to all our difficulties, and if you would just take yourself away, we will bring the whole thing off."

"What solution?"

She did not reply, but concentrated instead on examining a small, dark oil painting.

"What solution, Amelia?" he repeated in a deep, commanding voice.

Amelia tossed her head and looked mutinous. Her half-brother-in-law waited, his silent gaze boring into her.

"Oh, very well, if you must know, Thomas is taking the same solution as your father did for his difficulties. But the girl is proving very lukewarm and he will *not* be able to bring it off if you blunder in with your jumped-up tradesman's blood and your ugly labourer's hands, trumpeting your connections with us. You know they *always* want titles and the bluest of blood!" She sat down on her chair again in a flounce of silk.

"*Who* always want titles and the bluest of blood?" Hugo's rather hard grey eyes narrowed. "You don't mean Thomas has decided to marry an heiress?"

"Yes. Of course, he is far too young to have to make such a terrible sacrifice, but if you *will* persist in being so frightfully clutchfisted…"

Hugo considered her announcement. It may not be such a bad solution, he thought. With the right bride, Thomas may be induced to learn to control his ruinous habits.

As his financial advisor and uncle, Hugo could reasonably be expected to have an influence in the drawing up of the marriage settlements. He would ensure that the bride and any children she had would be protected from the results of Thomas's extravagance. It might work, he thought. It all depended on the bride.

"So, who is this heiress?" he said mildly.

Amelia, obviously relieved by his calm acceptance of the news, sat forward excitedly on her chair. "Well, of course, nothing has been settled yet—and it probably won't be unless you go back to Yorkshire immediately and not breathe a word to a soul!—but she has a diamond mine! She is—" Amelia's smooth complexion glowed in triumph "—a nabob's daughter!"

Hugo frowned. "Which nabob? I've heard of no new nabob in town."

Amelia rolled her eyes at him. "It is not generally known. Anyway, there is no nabob—"

"But I thought—"

"He is dead, at any rate, and a good thing too, I say, for nabobs are invariably loud and vulgar—the stench of trade is alwa—" She broke off. "Not that there is any question of vulgarity—the girl is quite sweet and demure, but it is providential that she is an orphan, at any rate. Thomas will have complete control of all her money from the start."

Hugo's frown remained. "I have heard of no new heiress. Who is she?"

Amelia pouted. "Well, but if you must know—not that it is at *all* your business!—it is the Singleton girl."

"The Singleton girl!" Hugo looked appalled. "You cannot be serious!"

She nodded.

"Good God! I had no idea the boy was so desperate! Rose Singleton is as old as you are!"

"Rose Singleton? She is *not*! She's forty, if she's a day!—you forget I was the veriest child-bride! Why, Rose has been on the shelf for years and years. But what has Rose Singleton's age—you don't mean you thought—?" Amelia stared at him in stupefaction. Then she burst out laughing. "*Rose Singleton? And Thomas?*"

"To my knowledge the only unmarried female among the Singletons *is* Rose," said Hugo, with some asperity,

"You have forgotten the long-lost Singletons," said Amelia matter-of-factly, applying a wisp of lace to her eyes.

Hugo frowned. "I didn't know there *were* any long lost Singletons."

"No, nor did I. But then this girl arrived, and Rose is bringing her out, and oh, Hugo, with a diamond mine, she is *exactly* what Thomas was looking for!" She tucked the handkerchief back in her reticule.

Hugo ignored that. "A long-lost Singleton, and a nabob's daughter… You did say she was a lady?"

"Well, naturally there is the trade connection, but of *course* she is a lady, Hugo, else Thomas would not wed the girl!" Amelia said indignantly. "The girl herself is an orphan and the father is safely dead, so he cannot return to embarrass anyone. And there is a diamond mine!"

"Yes…the diamond mine," Hugo murmured. "You've had her investigated, of course."

Amelia shrugged. "She is bound to have vulgar connections, so what is the point?"

Hugo sighed. "Her financial background, I meant."

"Do you never believe a thing anyone tells you?" Amelia snapped crossly.

He bowed over her hand and strode towards the door. "Not usually. I find I prefer to ascertain the truth for myself, wherever possible. If she is as wealthy as you say, it would be an obvious solution for Thomas's difficulties. I have numerous connections with the East India Company, so—"

"Not India. New South Wales."

Hugo came to a sudden halt. He swung around, staring at his sister-in-law in blank disbelief. "*New South Wales?* What do you mean, New South Wales?"

"The mine is in New South Wales."

"*A diamond mine in a convict settlement?*"

Amelia looked puzzled. "And what is wrong with that, pray? I have heard tell New South Wales is very large."

He snorted. "A diamond mine in a penal colony! Lord, imagine the problems—every rag-tag thief and criminal would be committing crimes in the hope of transportation to Botany Bay and a fortune in diamonds. The courts would be even more flooded than they already are. No, no, you are mistaken there, Amelia."

"No, I am not. She quite definitely came from New South Wales—I am not stupid, you know Hugo!"

"A diamond mine in New South Wales!" he repeated scornfully. "Such a thing could not exist."

She pursed her lips in annoyance. "Obviously you wish it did not!" she said waspishly. "But apparently they have only quite recently crossed some impossible mountain range into the unknown interior, so who is to say there are no diamonds there? Certainly not a man who buries himself in rural fastness for most of the year and is odiously selfish the rest of the time!"

"The whole tale sounds too smoky by half to me." Amelia shrugged pettishly.

"I would be very interested to meet the owner of a New South Wales diamond mine," Hugo said slowly.

Amelia glared at him. "This is *nothing* to do with you, Hugo! If you want Thomas to be settled comfortably, then take yourself back to Yorkshire! I won't have you meddling and putting the girl off our family."

"I gather she is here tonight."

Amelia hesitated, then shook her head in dramatic emphasis. "No, no, she didn't come."

"That little dark creature Thomas was attempting to hide from me on the dance floor?"

"No, no, no! It is not her at all—that is some other girl! A completely different girl."

Hugo smiled. Her feverish denial confirmed his suspicions. "I think it is incumbent on me, as Thomas's only male relative, to meet the girl, at least." He strode towards the door.

"Hugo, you will *not* approach this girl, do you hear me?" Amelia shrieked. "I forbid it! You will ruin everything!"

Chapter Two

"Miss Singleton."

Kit jumped and hurriedly turned. There was still the odd occasion where, if distracted, it slipped her mind that she was now Miss Singleton.

A tall dark-haired gentleman stood at her elbow, frowning thoughtfully down at her. The impressive-looking man she had noticed earlier. Heavens! Up close he was even more impressive. Bigger. Darker. Colder. Examining her with a curious mixture of frigid intensity and detachment.

Kit's heart started beating rapidly. She swallowed.

The grey eyes met her gaze coldly. A frisson of *déjà-vu* passed through her.

Who was he? Why was he staring at her in that way? Did he know her from somewhere?

"Will you honour me with a dance, Miss Singleton?"

It was not a request, but a demand, snapped out in an arrogant, care-for-nobody tone. Kit did not care for it. She lifted her chin and rewarded the gentle-man with a frosty look and a disdainfully raised eyebrow. She was not supposed to talk to anyone she had not been introduced to.

"Yes, of course she will," Aunt Rose responded for her. Rose must have introduced them, Kit realised belatedly, but she hadn't caught it. Rose smiled, nodded approvingly at Kit and drifted off towards the card room.

Kit silently held out her card. His dark head bent as he scrawled his name on it, and she peered sur-reptitiously to try to catch the name, without success. His hands were large, square, long-fingered and well-shaped. Oddly, they were scarred and nicked in a number of places. London gentlemen took great care of their hands; some had skin almost as soft as Kit's—softer, in fact, for she'd had occasion to work hard at times.

Interesting. This man seemed to flaunt his imper-fections…no, not quite flaunt, he seemed indifferent to them. Or was it people's opinion of him he was indifferent to?

She leaned back a little and allowed her gaze to run over him.

Up close he still retained that aura of aloneness. He made no small talk. He simply claimed her for a dance. He was either a little shy in the company of women, or very arrogant.

His eyes flicked up suddenly, as if aware of her scrutiny. He held her gaze a long, hard moment, then he dropped his gaze back to the card. Kit fought a blush. Whatever else he was, he was not shy of women.

His eyes were grey, though of such a grey as to be almost blue, although that could have been caused by the dark blue coat superbly cut to mould across his equally superb shoulders.

Kit had not seen such shoulders on a London gentleman before. Like the mandarin class of China, the pashas of Turkey, and the highest castes of India and Java, the members of the *ton* strove to appear as if they had never had to lift anything heavier than a spoon—and a gold or silver spoon, at that.

Fashionable London might believe a gentleman should not have the build of a stevedore, but Kit could find no fault with it. London gentlemen padded their shoulders to achieve the correct shape, but if she was given the choice between muscles or padding… Unfashionable it might be, but such shoulders could rather tempt a girl to…to think thoughts she had no business thinking, she told herself severely.

He had not the look of a man who'd had an easy life, not like many she'd met in the salons of the *ton*. He was not old—perhaps thirty or so—but lines of experience were graven into his face, and his mouth was set in an implacable unsmiling line. It was rather a nice mouth, set under a long aquiline nose and a square, stubborn-looking chin.

Kit wondered again what he would look like if he smiled.

His manner intrigued her. There was a faintly ruthless air about him, and the thought crossed her mind that he might be the sort of man Rose Singleton had warned her was dangerous to a young girl's sensibilities. Certainly he was most attractive, if not precisely handsome. And yet he was making no effort to ingratiate himself or to fascinate her. Kit was fairly sure that a rake would try both, else how would he succeed in his rakishness?

He had made no effort to charm her. His manner was more... She searched for a word to describe it and, to her surprise, came up with the word businesslike. Yes, his manner towards her was businesslike. How very odd.

A thought suddenly occurred to her. Was he doing the rounds of the Marriage Mart in search of a wife? Some men did approach marriage as a business...

Kit swallowed and firmly repressed the thought. She was not here, like the other girls, to find a husband. She was here to fulfil her promise to Papa, her vow to retrieve the family honour. She was not interested in so much as looking at any man, unless it furthered her plan.

Still, this man was most impressive, most intriguing. And she certainly looked forward to dancing with him. She had spent the evening dancing with effete aristocrats and an occasional elderly friend of Rose Singleton's—this man was like no man she had ever met before.

He looked up, frowned, thrust her card back into her hand and strode off, very much with the air of a man who had done his duty. She glanced down. His thick black writing dominated her dance card, claiming not just one dance but two. The second one, the waltz, was the supper dance. So, he wished to take her in to supper, did he?

It was all most intriguing. She still had not the faintest idea who he was. What *was* his name? His name stood out against the others pencilled on the white card. A heavy black scrawl. She frowned at it. It looked uncannily like the word *devil*. How very melodramatic.

She watched his retreat across the ballroom with narrowed eyes. He still looked, to her eyes, out of place in a ballroom, but she wasn't quite sure why. His attire was severe but extremely elegant and obviously expensive, from his dark blue, long-tailed coat to his black knee-breeches.

Fastened in among the snowy fold of his cravat was a cunningly wrought gold tie pin; an exquisitely crafted bird, resting in what looked like a nest of flames, its ruby eye glinting. It was a phoenix, the fabled bird of ancient Egypt, who was destroyed by fire. But then a new bird rose, fully fledged, from the ashes of the old.

A most unusual piece. She wondered whether he had chosen the pin for the significance of the design, or merely because it was pretty. He didn't look the sort to be attracted by the merely pretty.

Who was the man? Why did he feel somehow familiar to her? And why, out of all the young girls arrayed in white, had he asked her to dance? For she had seen him ask no one else.

If he had approached her with an eye to a possible bride, he was surely unique, for he'd barely glanced at her, except for that one icy, searing glance. Kit knew from her past experience that whatever the culture, men generally showed a great deal of interest in the physical attributes of the women they took to wife. In some places she had lived, even the woman's teeth were inspected as a matter of course—not that Kit would stand for being inspected like a horse at market! But a little interest would not have gone astray.

Kit watched as he inclined his head ironically to someone on the other side of the room. She followed the direction of his gaze. An elegant woman in an exquisite lilac silk gown glared at him, stamped her foot and turned her back on him. Kit recognised the woman: Lady Norwood, the mother of Lord Norwood.

Kit wrinkled her brow in perplexity as Lady

Norwood, exuding indignation with every step, stamped away to join her cronies, leaving the tall dark man to saunter away into the crowd. What on earth was all that about?

Lady Norwood was a widow, notorious, according to Rose, for keeping company with rakes and ne'er-do-wells. Was the tall man one of her companions? Had they had a falling out?

Rake or ne'er-do-well? He did not seem to fit either description. He seemed more like a big dark arrogant watchdog; a little fierce, a little harsh, a little cold. But watchdogs guarded things. And people. Who or what was he guarding?

And why was Lady Norwood so angry with him?

She was not quite sure how she felt, but there was no doubt about one thing; she felt more alive than ever. The simple evening of pleasure before her had suddenly turned into a most intriguing event.

"Devenish, old fellow. Didn't think to find you in Town. Thought you preferred rustification— know I do."

The blunt, loud voice came from just behind Kit. She turned her head but could not observe the speaker. She was resting between dances, sipping a glass of sweet ratafia, while her partner went to fetch her an ice. Her seat was next to a pillar draped with netting and twined with drooping greenery; on the other side of the pillar, two men stood talking.

"Shockin'ly dull affair, ain't it? If I'd realised there was going to be so many of the infantry invited, I wouldn't have come. Lord! When did marriage-bait get to be so young—tell me that, Dev?"

The other man laughed wryly. "I'm afraid it is not the debutantes who are getting younger, Marsden, but—"

Marsden! Her father had mentioned a Marsden… Kit wriggled closer, eavesdropping unashamedly.

"Devil take you, don't say it, man! Bad enough to realise I've been fifteen years leg-shackled—fifteen years—can you credit it?" Marsden sighed audibly. "Reason I'm come to the Metropolis—promised the lady wife I'd escort her, celebrate the event in London—celebration! At one of Fanny Parsons's balls—commiseration more like!" He added coaxingly, "I say, old man, you wouldn't care to slip out for a while and pop in to White's for a rubber of whist?"

His companion laughed. "A tempting thought— but no, I cannot. I am engaged for the next waltz."

"Good Gad! Who with?" asked Marsden bluntly. "Never took you for a caper merchant, Dev." There was a short pause. "Never say you're going to dance with one of those fillies in white—don't do it, man! Don't get yourself leg-shackled!"

His companion snorted. "Were I in the market for

a wife—which I am not—I would not put myself down for a waltz with a dreary little chit with more hair than conversation."

Kit listened to the two men laughing and frowned. Many of her fellow ingenues were a little dull but it was not their fault. It must be very difficult to be one moment in the schoolroom and the next expected to entertain sophisticated men of the world.

"Then what possessed you to ask one o' these chits to dance? And a waltz, too. You'll set the matchmakin' mamas in a devil of flutter you know, and—"

"Calm yourself, Marsden. I am here on a matter concerning my half-brother's boy."

"Young Norwood? You mean he is—? Oh, well, that's all right then. Probably suit him, marriage. Chasin' a fortune, no doubt, if you don't mind me sayin' so."

Kit stiffened. *Norwood!* If Norwood was his heir, then who was this Devenish she had been listening to? She pressed closer into the flowers and peered around the column. It was her tall watchdog! Not Devil, but Devenish—of course! She should have realised it sooner.

Then it dawned on her. His name was down in her card for the next waltz. *She* was the chit with more hair than conversation! Kit unclenched her teeth and took a sip of her ratafia. It tasted flat and oversweet. She set the glass aside with something of a snap. It was one thing to masquerade as a naïve young girl—it was another to be called a *dreary little chit with more hair than conversation*! She stiffened further as she caught the tail end of a sentence.

"…I'm still the boy's trustee for a few more years, so if he is considering marriage, it's wise to look her over."

Look her over! As if she was a horse or something! If he tried to inspect her teeth, she'd bite him!

"It won't take me long to ascertain what I need from the girl…"

Oh, won't it, indeed! Kit thought rebelliously. So Lord Norwood was chasing a fortune, was he? And his mother was sending the family watchdog to inspect Kit Singleton—ha! Well, they were certainly barking up the wrong tree if they thought Kit Singleton would bring anyone a fortune. She could set them straight in a moment on that!

But she wouldn't! That description of her rankled. She had an irresistible desire to teach the Watchdog a lesson about judging books by their covers. If Mr Devenish had decided Kit Singleton was a dreary little chit with more hair than conversation, then who was Kit Singleton to contradict him?

She felt a pleasurable frisson at the prospect of their dance. It would be quite soon.

* * *

"So, Miss Singleton, are you enjoying your come-out?" Mr Devenish swung her around masterfully.

Kit kept her eyes demurely lowered. He was by far the best dancer she had ever danced with and his shoulders more than lived up to their promise—the sensation of twirling in his arms was delicious.

It was very clear, however, that he was unused to conversing with very young ladies; he had made no attempt to charm her and his version of polite small talk was rather like being questioned by customs officers at the border. And as the dance continued, his tone, to Kit's immense pleasure, was progressing rapidly towards that of one addressing a simpleton.

"Your come-out, Miss Singleton," he rapped out again with a faint touch of impatience. "Are you enjoying it?"

She murmured something indistinguishable to his waistcoat, managing, just, to keep a straight face. As a chit with more hair than wit, she was making him work very hard for his conversation. She'd barely responded to his questions, and such responses she had uttered were given in a shy whisper.

Her tactics quite forced Mr Devenish to bend his head continuously towards her simple but elegant coiffure. Thus, he was well able to compare the amount of hair she had with the meagre wisps of conversation which had drifted up to him from the region of his waistcoat. And her hair was very short—she'd cut it all off in the heat of Batavia. Still, definitely *more hair than wit*...

"Did you say you were enjoying it, or not? I didn't quite catch your response."

"Oh, yeth," murmured Kit. She was not certain where the lisp came from, but it seemed perfect for the character she had adopted, the simpleton he thought her. She had not yet looked him in the eye. Innocent debutantes were often bashful and shy. Miss Kit Singleton was the shyest and most bashful imaginable.

It was working beautifully. Mr Devenish had very good, if brusque, manners, but there was a growing note of asperity to his questions.

"You have not been in London long. I understand you arrived recently from New South Wales?"

So far she had offered him no fewer than seven "yeths" in a row. She expanded her conversational repertoire dramatically. "Oh, New Thouth Waleth ith a long way from here," she murmured to his phoenix tie-pin. He really was very tall.

"And was your father an officer there?"

Kit managed a quiver and a sob without losing her step. "My papa ith...ith...dead."

Above her head, Devenish rolled his eyes and danced grimly on, silently cursing the length of these wretched Viennese dances. It was worse than he had expected—getting information out of this little dullard was like getting blood out of a stone. Lord knew what his nephew saw in her. A man needed more in a wife than a pretty face or a fortune.

Not that she was all that pretty—oh, she was well enough; small, dark-haired, which was the fashion just now, and passable enough features—a straight little nose, a curiously squared-off chin and slender arching dark brows set over a pair of very speaking blue eyes. Yes, the eyes were her best feature…so very blue…

But Lord! If he had to look at that vapid smile and listen to those simpering "yeths" over the breakfast table every morning, he would strangle the woman inside a month! Less. He would infinitely prefer that he never had to speak to her again.

But he had promised her another interminable waltz, he recalled gloomily. And then supper. At least there might be crab patties at supper to compensate. He was very fond of crab patties.

"Well, Hugo?" Amelia glided up to him, a beaded silk scarf trailing behind her in elegant disarray. "What do you think? Have you learned all about the diamond mine in New South Wales? I hope you didn't tell her you were Thomas's uncle!"

He glowered at her from under dark eyebrows. Five minutes' conversation with the Singleton chit had caused him more frustration and annoyance than he had experienced in a long time. But he was not going to give in so easily. He was loath to admit he had discovered almost nothing about the wretched girl.

Yet.

Hugo Devenish was not a man who would let himself be defeated by a pretty widgeon. *Defeated?* He blinked in surprise, and caught himself up. An odd word to use.

Amelia tugged his sleeve impatiently. "Hugo! What did you tell her? If she discovers your tradesman's blood…"

He withdrew his arm and smoothed the crumpled fabric in irritation. "The girl is a dead bore."

"But—"

"In fact, much more of Miss Singleton's company would drive me to Bedlam. Thomas must be desperate indeed to consider wedding such a dreary little simpleton, rich or not."

Amelia looked at him in surprise. "Simpleton? I do not think she is simple, Hugo."

He shrugged. "Well, either she is simple-minded, or so shy that it cannot make any difference." He rolled his eyes. "And that lisp! Infuriating."

"What lisp?" said Amelia, confused. "Are you certain you have the right girl, Hugo? Miss Singleton has no lisp. And I've never thought her shy."

Hugo frowned down at his cousin. "No lisp? Are you deaf? All I got out of the wretched girl was a dozen 'yeths'—addressed to my waistcoat."

Amelia's eyes narrowed. "Did she indeed? How very intriguing." A faint worldly smile curved her discreetly painted lips. "Hugo, you've flustered the poor little creature. How very, very interesting. She has never once lisped in my hearing, and Thomas has certainly never mentioned it—and I do believe he would have." She frowned suddenly. "So…Miss Singleton is not immune to the charms of an older man, then—"

"Older man!" snapped Hugo. "I am barely two and thirty, Amelia, as you very well know! And you, sister-in-law, have the advantage of me by more than ten years."

"Nonsense, it is barely seven!" retorted Amelia instantly. "I am not yet turned fort—no, I cannot even say it. It was most ungallant of you to raise such an unpleasant subject." She waved away his objections. "The point is, Hugo, that I know how overwhelming a man of your age and experience can seem to a chit just out of the schoolroom."

Hugo opened his mouth to argue, but Amelia continued, "She must have a *tendre* for you, else why would she lisp and behave shyly? Take it from me, she is not shy with anyone else. Quiet, pretty-behaved, yes. But I've found her perfectly ready to converse and not a hint of shyness. No, if she is developing a *tendre* for you, it is yet another reason why you must certainly stay away from her."

"Oh, do not be ridiculous! How the devil can I investigate her background if I cannot go near her? You and Thomas would soon find yourselves in the suds if her fortune was not as large as it is reputed to be."

"We will find ourselves in the suds if the girl decides she prefers you to Thomas, too!" responded Amelia crossly. "Stop it Hugo! There is no need to roll your eyes at me in that disagreeable manner. I am merely stating a fact."

"Rubbish! Believe me, there is no danger of me succumbing to her simple-minded charms."

"The girl is no more simple-minded than you or I!" Amelia stamped her foot. "She is young, yes, and innocent, but she is not the least bit stupid or shy."

"But—"

"And she does *not* stutter—"

"Lisp."

"Lisp, then." Amelia hurried on, her eyes narrowed with ambition. "But she's clearly smitten by your masculine charms, Hugo, and thus all our problems are compounded. I *knew* you would ruin everything! You must leave this girl, and take yourself back to your rural wastes and your horrid ships. Thomas and I will see to securing this fortune ourselves. I'll not stand by to see you dazzle the girl with your elegance, your worldly address and your—"

"Steal my nephew's bride from under his nose?"

interrupted Hugo with asperity. "Apart from being ridiculous, I have no intention—"

"She is not his bride yet; they are not even betrothed. And—"

"Oh, well, if she's not even betrothed," he said provocatively. "Oh, don't look like that! I have no interest in the girl, or her purported riches. I merely wish to investigate her background—as Thomas's trustee! And that is all! Put those ridiculous suspicions from your mind! I have no need of a fortune, let alone a diamond mine of unproven provenance. And there is not the slightest danger of my succumbing to the charms of the younger Miss Singleton. Far from it! I am more like to strangle the girl!"

Kit frowned as she adjusted a curl in the mirror of one of the withdrawing rooms set aside for ladies. It was a puzzle as to why Mr Devenish was so interested in her. All those questions about her father. And New South Wales.

Perhaps Lady Norwood and Mr Devenish thought Kit a fortune hunter, out to snabble a lord for a husband.

She would have to allay their suspicions. It would be disastrous to her plans if Mr Devenish investigated her background too deeply and discovered that Miss Catherine Singleton was in fact Miss Kit Smith, actually christened Kathleen, and not a member of an aristocratic family at all. And that her father had been thrown out of New South Wales and a number of other places for cheating at cards. And worse.

If that came out, there would be a frightful scandal, and poor Rose Singleton would be the one to suffer for it. Kit would not permit such a thing to happen, not if she could prevent it. Whatever she had done in the past, Rose was an innocent, a kind and generous-hearted innocent, and Kit would not allow such a sweet-natured woman to suffer on her behalf.

She would have to speak to Thomas as soon as possible and make it clear she had no interest in him. And if he did not listen this time she would be more firm; once Thomas was out of the picture, Mr Devenish would have no reason to enquire into her background.

Foiling Mr Devenish's brusque, penetrating en-quiries was much like fencing with rapiers—exhil-arating but dangerous. To see much more of him would be dangerous not only to her plans, but to her peace of mind, she suspected.

So she would allow herself one more encounter with the big dark watchdog and then—

"Oh, I'm sorry!"

Kit's thought were interrupted as a young girl came blundering into the withdrawing room and crashed into her.

"Are you all right?" she asked.

The girl, who was very young and very pretty,

stared a moment at Kit, then burst into tears, clearly overwrought.

Kit seated the young girl on a padded velvet bench and set herself to calming her. She had noticed her at a number of social events; like Kit, the girl was only just out.

"Miss…Miss Lutens, is it not?"

The girl nodded tearfully. "And you are Miss Singleton. I met you last week at Mrs Russell's recital. How do you do?" she sobbed, politely holding out her hand.

Kit smiled at such well-drilled manners. She patted the girl's hand and took out a handkerchief. "Tell me what is distressing you?" she said after Miss Lutens had calmed a little.

"Oh, I cannot," she wept. "It is too mortifying, too foolish of me. I am just…" She wiped her eyes with Kit's handkerchief.

"Come now, splash some cold water on your face and you will feel better. Would you like me to fetch your mama?"

"Oh, no!" gasped Miss Lutens in distress. "Mama would be so cross."

Kit stared. It had been her impression that girls always turned to their mothers in distress.

"It is nothing. I am being silly, that is all. It is just that Sir Bar—no! No, take no notice. It is nothing."

Sir Bar— Kit frowned. She recalled seeing this girl

in the company of a certain Sir Bartlemy Bowles. Quite frequently, of late.

"Has Sir Bartlemy Bowles been bothering you?" she asked bluntly.

Miss Lutens gasped. "How did you know?"

"I saw him with you earlier. My aunt warned me about him. He is reputed to have the hands of an octopus, is that not so?"

Miss Lutens blinked.

"Too many hands, too much touching," explained Kit.

"Oh!" Miss Lutens gasped, blushing. "Yes, exactly! And *clammy*!" She wrung her hands together in distress. "I simply cannot bear it."

"Tell your mother," recommended Kit. "She'll soon send the clammy-handed old roué about his business. From what my aunt says, he's notorious for pestering young girls. And though he is rich, he's also married, so there is no need to worry that your mama plans to wed you to the horrid old slug."

Miss Lutens giggled at the description, but shook her head. "No, that is the trouble, for I did mention it once, and Mama did not believe that Sir Bartlemy could be so ungallant. She told me not to be so silly."

Her hands twisted the damp handkerchief into a rope. "He used to be a beau of hers, you understand, before she married Papa, and I think she still has a *tendre* for him." She bit her lip. "I think…Mama thinks he is paying me so much attention for her sake…"

"Ahh," said Kit, understanding her dilemma at last. "Well, then, you must get rid of the fellow yourself."

Miss Lutens stared at her with large brown eyes. "Get rid of him? But how?"

"Be firm, be bold," said Kit decisively. "Tell him to keep his hands to himself."

Miss Lutens's mouth dropped open in surprise. "Oh! I am not sure I could… And what if he does not?"

"Then slap him! Good and hard."

"Oh, I could not possibly slap him!" gasped Miss Lutens. "It would make a scandal, me slapping a man of his rank and years. I truly could not!"

Kit frowned. Miss Lutens had a point. "Well, try being firm and speaking to him about it, and if that does not work, let me know. I shall think of something. We women have to put up with enough in life without having to endure furtive caresses from a slug!"

"Oh, yes! Thank you!" Miss Lutens beamed. "Oh, I am so pleased to have met you. I was not looking forward to this ball, you know, with Sir Bartlemy escorting Mama and me, but now I have made a friend and I am so happy!" She clasped Kit's hand in an eager grip.

Kit smiled, her heart sinking. It was not part of her plans to make friends. If she allowed people to get too close to her, they would see through her deception. Already with Miss Lutens she had not behaved as an unworldly innocent would—she had dropped her role to rescue an innocent child from a nasty groping octopus.

It was a foolish move. But Kit could not help herself. She had learned very young to protect herself from unwanted attentions—she'd had to with the life she'd lived.

Kit hesitated. She'd been watching the other young girls with envy in her heart, envying them their doting parents and protective chaperones and wondering wistfully what her life might have been like if Papa had doted on her like these parents did on their daughters.

But now she realised that their very protectiveness had made these girls quite vulnerable to the unscrupulous attentions of persons like Sir Bartlemy Bowles. Without her mother's support, Miss Lutens was like an oyster without a shell; soft, exposed and utterly unable to protect herself.

But Kit did not have had the benefit of a protected upbringing; she had more than a few tricks up her sleeve. She resolved to help Miss Lutens.

"You need not simply put up with things, you know. You can take action on your own behalf."

"How?" said Miss Lutens, eagerly.

"You must do something to give Sir Bartlemy a disgust of you."

"But what? And what would my mama say?"

"It will be too late for your mama to prevent it. And if you are clever and subtle enough, then you won't have to be in her bad books for long." She gave Miss Lutens a significant look and added with a faint smile, "Much can be forgiven of a young girl who is nervous about making her come-out."

Miss Lutens looked at her blankly. Kit winked. "Do not worry about it. Do I understand that Sir Bartlemy has already had two dances?"

Miss Lutens nodded.

"Good, then you shall not have to dance with him again tonight. Shall you be at Almack's on Wednesday?"

Miss Lutens nodded. "Yes, Mama has procured the vouchers."

"I shall also be there and no doubt we shall see Sir Bartlemy too."

"Yes," said Miss Lutens dolefully. "He is very fond of Almack's."

"Then I shall show you what I mean on Wednesday," said Kit. "And when you come, bring your sharpest hatpin, just in case."

Miss Lutens's eyes widened. "My…my hatpin? But, but I shall not be wearing a hat at Almack's, you know."

Kit wondered what it would be like to be so innocent, so sheltered, so trusting of the world. Vulnerable, she told herself firmly.

"Yes, it is not for a hat. You must keep it in your reticule, but poke the end into a cork, so it does not prick you. And then, if you are bothered by such nasty creatures as, let us say, octopuses, you may take it out and…" She mimed the thrusting of a pin and winked. "Very useful things, hatpins."

Miss Lutens gasped, put a hand over her mouth and giggled.

"That's right," said Kit cheerily, "and even if you do not use it, it will make you feel much more confident, knowing you have your hatpin on hand. In the meantime, take heart. There are plenty of nice, handsome young men who will take one look at you and fall instantly in love. Your mama will soon be so busy keeping track of all your suitors, she will have no time for clammy old horrors like Sir Bartlemy."

Miss Lutens blushed and giggled again.

"That's better," said Kit bracingly. "Now, let us return to the ballroom," she said. "Our partners will be awaiting us."

"Thank you for the dance, Miss Singleton," said Lord Norwood stiffly as he escorted Kit back to where her aunt was seated. He was a little annoyed from having been treated with cool lack of interest all through the country dance.

"You are welcome, sir," responded Kit coolly. "I

do enjoy country dances, though they can sometimes leave one a trifle breathless."

Lord Norwood frowned. There was not the faintest hint of breathlessness about Miss Kit Singleton. Lord Norwood, on the other hand, was hot and still puffing slightly.

"Hmm, yes," said Thomas with determined civility. "Ah, here is my—er, Mr Devenish awaiting you. I believe he is next on your card." He nodded brusquely at Mr Devenish, bowed very correctly to Kit and left.

Mr Devenish had clearly heard Kit's last comment. "Perhaps you do not wish to dance, Miss Singleton." He bowed politely and suggested in a bored voice, "No doubt you are a trifle weary and would prefer to sit the next dance out."

"Oh, yeth, of course, if you wish it," Kit agreed instantly, then added sympathetically, "I forgot how it was with elder—um, mature gentlemen. My poor old papa used to find dancing very tiring, too—ethpecially the waltz—such a long dance, ith it not, and tho energetic."

The strains of a Viennese waltz filled the air. She smiled sunnily up at him and looked brightly around the room. "Now, where shall we find a comfortable chair tho you may retht your poor feet?"

Mr Devenish's lips thinned. An arctic look came into his eyes but he did not reply. Taking her waist in a firm, not to say ferocious grip, he whirled her across the room in a dazzling display of virtuosity and youthful masculine energy, twirling her and twirling her until she was quite dizzy with pleasure and delight.

Kit had danced the waltz several times before, but now, suddenly, she realised why it had been regarded as so scandalous and had taken such a long time to be accepted in polite society.

When danced like this, caught up hard in the grip of a strong, masterful man, twirling in his arms until you lost all awareness of anything except the music and the man, the experience was utterly intoxicating.

Kit simply gave herself up to the magic of the dance. And the man. The world blurred around her in a glittering rainbow, the music spun through her brain in a melody of magic, and all that anchored her to the ground was the hard, strong body of a tall dark man.

After a few moments he looked down at her as if surprised. His grip tightened, his cold grey eyes seemed to bore into her soul and Kit felt herself staring up at him like a mouse mesmerised by a cobra. They danced on, staring into each other's eyes.

Kit felt suddenly breathless; a breathlessness that had nothing to do with the movement of the dance. She longed to simply let herself go, to float wherever he wished to take her, to dance off into a new dawn. The temptation was irresistible.

But she could not. She'd made a promise. It was her honour at stake, as well as her papa's.

She blinked to free herself of Mr Devenish's spell and closed her eyes, shutting out the thought that here was a man the like of which she'd never come across before…

Abruptly he loosened his grip and she stumbled slightly. He caught her up smoothly and she realised he was very strong. He was the sort of man who would never let a girl fall. The sort of man a woman could depend on.

But Kit could depend only on herself. It had always been so. It was the only possible way. She had to break this spell.

"Oh, dear, it ith a long dance, ith it not? Are you getting tired, Mr Devenish?" she murmured, a young Katherine Parr to his aged King Henry.

Insulted, he snapped, "Do you reverse?" and before she had a chance to reply he was twirling her in reverse around the circumference of the ballroom with great, if furious, vigour.

Again it was utterly intoxicating and Kit had to battle her own senses to retain a safe distance from him.

The supper, despite the gloomy predictions of some, turned out to be surprisingly good—a triumph of Fanny Parsons over her husband's penny-pinching ways. She had provided a substantial spread: turtle soup, a number of pies—pigeon, pork, veal and ham—oyster fritters, lobster salad, eels in aspic, sliced roast duck, tiny quails in pastry baskets, dishes of tender green peas, braised capons, a mountain of shaved ham, bread and butter, fruits, jellies, fruit custards, trifles, pastries glittering with a frosting of sugar, and ices in several flavours.

There were even, to Mr Devenish's satisfaction, crab patties. He placed several on his and his partner's plate.

"So, Miss Singleton," he said as they ate, "I believe you have lived a good deal of your life in…New South Wales, was it?"

Kit smiled at him, still exhilarated from the dance. "Oh, no," she said serenely, and popped an oyster fritter into her mouth, thus making further conversation impossible for a few moments.

Mr Devenish frowned. "But I thought you came from New South Wales."

Kit chewed her oyster fritter slowly and thoroughly. Mr Devenish gave up for the moment and devoured a crab patty. "I understood your father had, er, some business in New South Wales?"

Kit smiled. "Papa always had many different interests, yeth."

Mr Devenish noted the way the lisp came and went. Could it truly be a sign of nervousness, as Amelia had suggested? The thought was a little unnerving, especially after the waltz they had shared.

Something had happened during that waltz…she had seemed somehow differ— No! He was not going to think about the implications of that dance. The breathless young sprite he had twirled in his arms had reverted to the idiot widgeon.

He was here to investigate her. On his nephew's behalf.

"Your father was a landowner, no doubt? I do believe land grants—to the right people, of course—are easily come by in the Colonies."

"Do you?" said Kit politely and chewed meditatively on a mouthful of green peas.

"That is my understanding, yes," Mr Devenish persisted. "Did your father operate a farm? I believe wool is said to be doing well there. Did he own a lot of sheep?"

Kit giggled inanely and shook her head, but inside, she was appalled. He was very well informed about a fledgling penal colony that almost no one in London knew anything of, she thought. He may well have visited the colony—that could explain the fleeting sense of familiarity she felt in his company. She had best be very careful. It would not do to be recognised as a card-cheat's daughter.

Mr Devenish decided to take a different angle. "I have heard that vast areas of new country have been opened up since they found a way through some mountain range, is that right?"

Kit nodded emphatically. "Oh, yeth."

Mr Devenish leaned forward.

"I had not heard it myself, of courth, but gentlemen are invariably right, are you not?" she added, and nibbled daintily on a slice of chicken breast. What was it he was trying to get her to reveal? Knowledge of New South Wales? Her father's business?

Mr Devenish gritted his teeth and helped himself to another crab patty. "Do you not know what—er, um." Under those innocently questioning eyes he stuttered to a halt. Then grimly, he tried again. "So, your father did not discuss business affairs at all with you," he said bluntly, shuddering inwardly at his lack of subtlety.

"Oh, no," she said firmly, "for it ith not at all ladylike to talk of such things. In any case, Papa said to be forever talking of money ith horridly vulgar." She smiled beatifically at him and batted her eyelashes gently. "Don't you agree?"

There was a short, strained silence. Mr Devenish reached for the dish of crab patties.

Kit laid a small hand on his, and said earnestly. "Should you really be eating tho many crab patties? They are very rich, you know, and my papa found they did not at all agree with his constitution—"

"I have eaten and enjoyed crab patties all my life," he snapped, and reached towards the dish.

Kit tactfully moved the dish away from him with

an understanding smile. "Yeth, but after a certain age, I believe, gentlemen are not able to do all the things they used to enjoy in their youth. Would you care for a ruthk?" She offered him a rusk, maintaining her demure expression by biting hard on the inside of her cheek.

"No, I would not!" he snapped explosively. There was another short silence while Mr Devenish fought to control his indignation at being treated as an octogenarian.

Kit placidly examined her nails, ninny fashion.

He stood up. "You seem to have finished your supper, Miss Singleton." He held out a commanding hand to help her to her feet.

Kit, relieved not to be pushed further on the question of her background, offered him an artless smile and allowed herself to be drawn from her seat.

"I believe Sir Bartlemy Bowles was hoping to take you on a short promenade around the room," he said, his eyes glinting.

Oho, so the Watchdog stooped to low tricks, did he? How dare he deliver an innocent young girl such as she to a creature like the Octopus!

She turned to leave, but her hem appeared to be caught under the chair. She stumbled and fell against him, quite awkwardly, and floundered against him momentarily, trying to regain her balance. He gently took her upper arms and lifted her upright; she avoided his gaze and babbled hasty thanks and apologies for her clumsiness.

Mr Devenish frowned blackly. At the first touch of her body against his, a surge of awareness had passed through him like wildfire. He thrust her small, firm body resolutely away from him. He was *not* attracted to this little widgeon! He was damned if he would be attracted to *any* respectable female of the *ton*, let alone a complete simpleton!

"Thank you very much for the dance and for escorting me to thupper, Mr Devenish, but my Aunt told me not to go on to the terrace without her, tho, if you don't mind…" She smiled a last smile at his waistcoat, enjoying the sight of his pristine white cravat, the smooth folds of which were quite unmarred…not by a crumb or a scrap of crab. Not even by a tie-pin, phoenix or otherwise.

Chapter Three

Kit joined a group around her aunt, and was soon taken to dance by a very young gentleman, a young gentleman who was rather less subtle than Mr Devenish.

Kit's heart plummeted as he blurted out his question. *"A diamond mine!"* she gasped. "Everybody knows I own—!" She stopped in mid-step. "Oh, good God! You cannot mean it?"

Young Mr Wollborough stared back owlishly at her.

Yes, Kit realised. He did indeed mean it. She ignored his dismay at her reaction and sat down on a nearby bench. Whatever am I to do now!

Mr Wollborough looked dismally at her. "Drat! Mother did say it was a secret, that you did not wish to be courted for your fortune."

Courted for her fortune! Kit closed her eyes and tried to repress a hysterical bubble of laughter. A penniless adventuress, courted for her fortune!

"I'm dashed sorry to have distressed you like this, Miss Singleton! I'm a tattle-tongued fool! You don't need to fret about me knowing. I'll not mention it to a soul. In any case, I'm sure very few people know about it. I know I was told it in the *strictest* confidence."

She stared at him blankly. Very few people indeed! Everything clicked into place: Miss Singleton's comments about her wearing pearls instead of diamonds; Lord Norwood and other men's determined courtships; Mr Devenish's equally determined questioning about her background.

Mr Wollborough hovered, awkwardly. "Can I get you a glass of something? Er, do you want me to fetch your aunt?"

Kit took no notice of him. Her mind was in a whirl. Virtually the entire *ton* must believe her to be rich. *That* was the reason so many people had been so very friendly and welcoming towards an unknown young woman. It wasn't "polite society" at all—these people were no different from others she had encountered all over the world. Money smoothed all paths, honeyed all tongues, welcomed all strangers.

They imagined her to be a great heiress! It would be laughable, if it were not so disastrous to her scheme. But however had such an outrageous rumour started? Such a ridiculous one, what's more—a diamond mine! How could she ever get out of this one?

She glanced up at the crestfallen young blade who hovered awkwardly, looking crushed and miserable. Kit repressed another bubble of half-hysterical laughter. Young Mr Wollborough was only too aware that he'd blown his chance with the great heiress.

"Take me to my aunt, if you please, Mr Wollborough," said the heiress. "I find I have the headache."

As soon as they reached home, Kit broached the matter with Rose Singleton. "Young Mr Wollborough asked me about a diamond mine, Aunt Rose."

"Hmm, yes, dear?" said Rose, retrieving a trailing scarf which had almost slipped to the floor.

"He seems to believe—a number of people, in fact, seem to believe that I own a diamond mine."

"Yes." Rose's brow wrinkled at the look on her niece's face. "What is the matter? I know you did not wish it to be generally known, but these things have a way of coming out."

"But why would people believe I own a mine full of diamonds?"

"It was diamonds, was it not? I'm sure it was—I would have remembered if he'd said rubies or emeralds. Or sapphires—sapphires would go so beautifully with your eyes. But no, I was certain he said a diamond mine."

"Who said?"

Rose frowned. "Your father, of course! Who else?"

Kit closed her eyes briefly. Papa! Who else!

"My papa told you he owned a diamond mine?"

"Wait, I'll fetch the letter." Rose wandered into the front withdrawing room where her small Sheraton writing desk stood. She rummaged through the pile of papers in the desk, then turned and peered around the room, annoyed. "Now where has it got to? Things move in this house, there is no denying it."

"Oh, never mind," said Kit. "It will turn up sooner or later. Now just refresh my mind, will you please, Aunt dearest? Where did my papa say this diamond mine was situated?"

Aunt Rose looked at her in astonishment. "Don't you *know* where it is situated? How very odd. But I suppose…"

"Where is the diamond mine, Aunt Rose?" Kit prompted gently.

"Why, in New South Wales, of course. Where else?"

New South Wales? A *diamond mine* in New South Wales? Kit closed her eyes for a brief second. Of course. It was just like her father to throw in a last-minute embellishment like this. A quite impossible, ridiculous, ludicrous embellishment.

Kit took a deep breath and unclenched her fists. It was, after all, improper, not to say unfilial, if not downright impossible, to strangle the dead!

"Did I get it wrong, my love?" said Rose anxiously.

"But where else would it be, for that was where you were living, was it not? My friend Mr Harris thought it an exceeding odd place for a diamond mine, too. Oh, where *is* that wretched letter?"

"You told your friend Mr Harris I owned a diamond mine in New South Wales? Oh, Aunt Rose! How could you? As if anyone would ever believe anything so fantastical. And ridiculous! New South Wales is a tiny, struggling convict settlement. A *penal* colony, for Heaven's sake!"

Kit took a deep breath as she considered her situation. Everything had been going so smoothly, so well—quite as if it were not one of Papa's schemes. Now, suddenly, she had an impossible diamond mine to somehow incorporate into an already impossible plan! It was quite like old times. Suddenly her sense of humour got the better of her. Kit collapsed in a chair and peals of laughter rang out.

"But was that not correct, my love?" ventured Rose uncertainly. "Only I could have sworn that is what your father explained to me. And his letter did most certainly come from New South Wales." She looked round her distractedly. "If only I could find his letter. It is quite mystifying to me, how so many things seem to disappear in this house." She lifted a blue satin cushion and peered hopefully under it, but no letter appeared.

"No," said Kit, the laughter dying from her eyes. "Papa started to tell me he had written to you, but he was dying. I knew only what he asked me to do. I might have known there would be other aspects to his scheme."

"Scheme. What an odd name for it," said Rose curiously. "I suppose all parents make plans for their daughters' come-outs, but to call it a scheme—how very odd. But then your father was never one to take the simple straightforward path, was he?" She sighed pensively and smoothed the cover of the cushion she was still holding.

Kit regarded her aunt curiously, wondering whether Rose still retained some affection for her father. After a moment or two she said, "Aunt Rose, have you told many people?"

"Oh, Heavens, no," said Rose. "It would be terribly vulgar to boast of such a thing. No, no. I only mentioned it—in confidence, of course—to one or two very discreet friends."

Kit regarded her dubiously. "Well, perhaps it will be all right, but if anyone asks me—"

"Heavens, child, you must not fret yourself about any such thing. No one would dream of asking you." Rose was shocked. "Ask a young girl? As if you would have any idea of your father's business matters!" She laughed. "The very idea!"

Kit bit her tongue. She had spent an entire evening parrying questions about it. But she would not distress Rose by telling her so.

It was a mystery to her why society people seemed to think an interest in business was something to be ashamed of. It seemed to Kit that business, or trade as it was more commonly called, was the way to achieve safety, security and prosperity. But even her father had regarded it as vulgar. And he was a card cheat.

Rose leaned forward and patted her on the knee. "Do not distress yourself about it, my dear. If I was wrong about the diamond mine in New South Wales, I shall simply inform my friends that I was mistaken, and all will be well."

Kit opened her mouth to argue. She may not have moved in the rarefied circles of the Polite World before, but if she knew anything about people, she knew that people who claimed to be discreet almost invariably were not. A diamond mine in a penal colony was a ludicrous concept...

"Yes, that is a very good notion, Aunt Rose," she said decisively. "And if anyone mentions it, I hope you will deny it most vigorously and explain you were mistaken. It would be dreadful if people were to think we had deceived them."

It would change nothing, Kit knew. People would believe what they wanted to. The diamond mine was a fact in their minds, which no amount of denial would budge. But when the truth came out, as it inevitably would, at least Rose would be remembered to have denied all knowledge of it.

"Yes, my dear. I will. I'll make everything quite clear." Aunt Rose beamed and replaced the satin cushion. "And now, my love, it has been a busy evening, and we ladies must get our beauty sleep, must we not? Sweet dreams, my dear." Rose kissed her affectionately on the cheek and floated upstairs, trailing several scarves behind her.

Kit woke early. It was still dark outside, the faint tendrils of dawn only a hint of a shimmer over the dark rooftops.

She knew what had woken her. Anxiety. She always woke before dawn when she was worried about something. This morning she had more than her share of worries.

The problem that leapt to her mind first should have been the diamond mine problem, but for some reason the first thought in her waking brain was of Mr Devenish's face when he discovered the loss of his phoenix tie-pin.

She closed her eyes. Why on earth had she lapsed—with such a man? And in such a situation. It was wicked, it was foolish, it was far too risky. But it was done, and too late now to undo it.

And besides, she had other concerns. Somehow she had to decide how to ride out the disaster of this wretched diamond mine rumour.

She pulled the covers over her head and groaned.

She had planned to enter London society with barely a ripple, to move through it virtually unnoticed and to leave it the same way, having completed her task. She had planned to be inconspicuous. Now she was a diamond heiress. From a prison colony on the other side of the world! Diamonds in a prison! Who wouldn't find that combination fascinating?

She groaned again. It was the sort of ridiculous embellishment her father had delighted in; his way of laughing up his sleeve at those less well-informed. But he'd sent her to avenge him. With such an aim in mind, he would surely not jeopardise the outcome for a silly joke. No, Rose must have got some old letter, where Papa was doing his usual face-saving story-telling, and confused it with the letter from New South Wales, telling her to expect Kit.

Whatever the source, the damage was done. Kit would have to deal with it. It wasn't as if she had a choice.

In the meantime, she needed to clear her head. She needed fresh air, and exercise.

Mr Devenish was in a bad mood. He had slept but a few hours and awakened with a splitting head—no doubt a legacy of the brandy he had consumed. He was cross with himself for doing so—it was years since he had woken with a drink-induced headache.

The headache was exacerbated by the further realisa-

tion that he had spent the evening in a singularly prof-
itless fashion—the information he had gathered about
the Singleton chit had amounted to precisely nothing.

It had seemed so simple and straightforward: speak
to the girl, find out where her father had been based,
and then investigate from there.

But the girl was the vaguest, most irritating scat-
terbrain he had come across in an age; he hadn't got
a single useful fact out of her. If she hadn't been so
brainless, he would have…would have…

Mr Devenish swore and pulled the bell to
summon his valet.

That was another, utterly infuriating aspect of
the wretched evening! How on earth had he
become aroused by a brainless ninny in the middle
of a ballroom?

It must have been the brandy.

That cheeseparing Parsons, serving his guests
inferior brandy! Yes, that was it. It was all the fault
of second-rate brandy: the headache, the bad
temper…the girl.

His glance fell on the collection tossed carelessly
on to his bedside table and his expression darkened
even more. His gold watch with the phoenix design
and the winking ruby eyes. There should have been
two items on his bedside table, not one, dammit! A
perfect ending to a perfect night! He had lost his ruby
phoenix tie-pin!

He had noticed it missing as soon as he had arrived home and removed his cravat. He'd sent a servant with a note around to the Parsons immediately, and was informed an hour later that the servants had searched, but had discovered no sign of the pin. He must have dropped it in the street.

Lost forever, dammit! It was his favourite pin, too. He'd designed it himself, as a reminder that no matter what was destroyed, he could always rebuild his life.

He lay back in bed and tried to recall when he had last noticed his pin in place. Instead, he found his mind wandering to thoughts of Miss Singleton… He sat up hurriedly.

To the devil with her! It was embarrassing, being aroused at thoughts of such a little simpleton!

He could recall each and every time his body had touched hers, from the first moment when he took her dance card from her, to each time their hands met briefly in a dance. And as for that waltz where he'd actually found himself being aroused…

He groaned, thinking of it. Such a thing had never before happened to him—not since he'd been a green youth…

He closed his eyes. Curse it, his body still recollected the imprint of her small, slender body against it when she'd stumbled and fallen against him after supper.

He put the thought firmly out of his mind.

And found himself recalling the first time his

pocket had been picked in Marseilles when he was a very young man. And of attempts since then…

He tensed at the thought which had suddenly popped into his brain. He considered it for a moment, then shook his head.

No! It was nonsense! Genteelly brought-up damsels of the *ton* did not steal their supper-partners' tie-pins. It was not possible. For a start the girl was not bright enough…

Only…she had managed to have two dances and supper with him and avoid giving any information about her background. Would a brainless widgeon have done that? He did not have much experience of brainless widgeons, but on consideration, it seemed more than likely that a truly brainless widgeon would have prattled non-stop and blurted out all sorts of dreary details about her home and family. But perhaps the lisp made her self-conscious about prattling.

Oh, it was ridiculous. His tie-pin had simply fallen off.

Mr Devenish was disgusted. His head was likely to split. He had a sour taste in his mouth in more ways than one. Ridiculous to imagine a young lady making her come-out was as skilled a pickpocket as a Marseilles wharf rat. He needed some exercise in the cold morning air to clear the cobwebs away.

His man arrived, and was dispatched to fetch a tankard of ale, to lay out Mr Devenish's riding buckskins and to send for a groom to saddle up Sultan and bring him to the door. Mr Devenish was going for a ride.

Despite the very early hour of the morning, the streets were busy and full of life as usual; carters with loads of cabbages and potatoes, handcarts laden with flowers, barrows full of old clothing, porters carrying baskets of corn or mysterious boxes, a pieman with fresh hot pies balanced on a tray on his head, servants bustling out to run their masters' or mistresses' errands, beggars rattling their tins, urchins scrambling underfoot, racing thither and yon, an occasional late returning gambler and a carouser or two returning unsteadily to their lodgings.

Mr Devenish took little notice. His mount, Sultan, a big black stallion with a gleaming coat and a proud arched neck, demanded most of his attention. The horse caracoled and danced with high spirits and too many oats, taking offence first at an urchin here, shying at a butcher's boy and his cart there; he reared in apparent fright as a dog ran close to his hooves; he danced sideways along the cobblestones, tossing his head in disapproval at the flapping skirts of a couple of maidservants, clutching baskets.

Mr Devenish smiled, enjoying Sultan's mischievous antics. His stallion was well under his control; the horse needed a run as much as the master.

The park, in contrast to the streets, was almost deserted. The leisured classes had not yet arisen, and the rest of the world had little time to dally in parks. The morning air was fresh, crisp and cold. Mr Devenish took a deep breath, enjoying the bite as it hit his lungs.

Sultan pranced and snorted, eager to get moving. Mr Devenish urged him into action and then, as no one else was around, he gave Sultan his head, relishing the contrast between the warmth and power of the spirited beast under him, and the whoosh of cold air through his body. Sultan's hooves pounded on the turf, echoing in the near silence.

He passed a couple of rabbits nibbling on the sweet, damp grass. He scattered some birds feeding off breadcrumbs left by some child the day before. He passed a couple of men in frieze overcoats lurking by a clump of rhododendrons. They looked out as he came towards them but stepped back in a hurry as Sultan thundered down towards them. He idly wondered what they were doing there, but soon forgot them as he swerved to avoid a gaggle of indignant geese.

After a time, man and mount were breathing hard, and Hugo could tell that just as the ride had swept the cobwebs from his brain, so his horse had raced the excess energy from his body. He allowed Sultan to slow to an elegant canter. Hugo smiled. One of the things he loved about this particular horse was the way he moved so smoothly from one gait into the next. Hugo breathed deeply. He was feeling refreshed, invigorated, alive. And hungry. He could hear another horse galloping in the distance. Galloping hard and fast.

He looked around and saw another rider, a lady in a plain dark blue habit with a black hat crammed low over her hair. Another early riser. Soon the park would begin to fill with others, who, like him, preferred the relative quiet of the early morn to the crowded fashionable hours of the afternoon.

He watched the lady rider. It was unusual for a female to rise so early, but he soon perceived that this was no ordinary female. Most females he knew preferred to walk their horses, or, at most, to canter. This woman galloped. Hard and unfashionably, like he and Sultan had. The mount she rode was undistinguished; that much was obvious, even from this distance, but she rode magnificently. He had never seen a better seat on a lady. She had certainly almost grown up on horseback. He wondered briefly if she was a lady—there was no groom accompanying her that he could see.

He shrugged and turned his horse in a slow circle and headed back, much the same way he had come.

Suddenly he noticed the regular beat of the other horse's hooves had come to a halt. He glanced back over his shoulder, idly, then swore. He wrenched Sultan around and thundered back the way he'd just come.

The two ruffians in frieze overcoats he had seen earlier had accosted the woman. One of them had grabbed the horse by its bridle and was fighting the lady for its control. She was giving as good as she got, beating him over the head and arms with her riding crop, all the time urging the horse to move. Her horse reared and snorted but could not pull away. The second man grabbed the skirt of her habit and pulled at it, trying to unseat her.

Hugo let out an oath and urged Sultan to gallop faster.

The woman unhooked the leg which gripped the pommel of the sidesaddle and kicked the second scoundrel hard in the face. He reeled back. Hugo heard the man shout in pain. He also heard the threats the man made towards his female attacker and his blood boiled.

"Belay that, you villains! Leave that woman alone!" he shouted, wishing he had worn spurs.

Both men glanced around. The woman took instant advantage of their momentary inattention, and wrenched her horse's head away. Giving a final vicious swipe with her crop across the head of the first attacker, she forced the horse into action and broke away.

"Well done, madam," shouted Hugo and, pointing Sultan straight at the two ruffians, he urged his horse at them in a thunderous gallop. The men scattered and ran.

For a second Hugo wanted to pursue the villains, but his first priority was to see the woman was all right. She would no doubt be totally overset by the incident, brave fighter though she had been. He would offer her his escort to her home.

He followed her. She was galloping fast towards the nearest exit, but her horse was a commoner and Sultan easily overtook it.

She glanced quickly over her shoulder as he came near, and to his surprise, she urged her horse into greater speed.

"It is all right, madam," Hugo called, "I mean you no harm."

She answered him by digging her heel into her horse's flank, urging him to greater speed.

"I am a friend," Hugo called, deciding she was probably in a panic. "My name is Devenish, madam. I merely wish to satisfy myself that you are unharmed."

"I am perfectly well, thank you so much. Please do not concern yourself," she flung over her shoulder in a cool voice.

Hugo brought his horse abreast with hers. "I have every intention of escorting you safely to your home and nothing you say will alter that," he responded firmly.

He glanced across at her, wishing he could see her

face, but he could not. She wore a fine dark veil—to protect her complexion, no doubt. Many ladies did. It also protected her from inquisitive glances. Hugo found the aura of mystery the veil created very intriguing. In any case she was taking no chances; she kept her face averted. He rode beside her, a small smile on his lips.

She was not of his own class, he thought, or if she was, she had come upon hard times. Her habit was plain, old-fashioned and a little shabby, though immaculately clean and pressed. She was small and slender and her hair was dark; curly wisps of it escaped from the base of her brown curly brimmed riding hat. She was young too, and possibly good-looking, judging by the grace and delicate creaminess of her neck, a small amount of which was all the skin she had bared.

He could not see whether she wore a ring; she wore gloves of York tan, but her hands seemed small and gripped the reins tightly—more tightly than was warranted—too tightly for such an experienced and skilled horsewoman. He looked closer. Aha, her hands were shaking, just a little. She had been frightened after all, but was determined not to show it. A spurt of admiration went though him. She had courage, this woman.

"You need not fear any importunities from me, madam," he said softly. "I simply wish to see you safe."

She did not slow her pace at all.

Hugo was a little irritated. He was her rescuer—or would have been had she not rescued herself. The least she could do was thank him. Well, his conscience reminded him, she had thanked him, perfectly politely, but it was not enough. He wanted a face-to-face encounter. Yes, he wanted, quite desperately, to see her face.

"My name is Devenish," he repeated. "And I *shall* escort you home, madam."

She made an irritated sound, but otherwise did not respond. Her face remained averted.

Hugo urged Sultan forward a little closer, trying to catch a glimpse of her face under the flimsy veil. She urged her mount forward too and kept her face turned away. Hugo's lips twitched at her determination. Was she playing a game, or was she in earnest? A virtuous woman, quite properly refusing to speak to a strange man, or a clever vixen, enticing the hound…?

With her seat, she would hunt magnificently, he thought.

"You ride very well," he said.

She did not respond. They reached the park exit and immediately it became necessary to slow the horses because of the amount of traffic on the streets. At a walk, conversation was easier.

"I imagine you have ridden most of your life. I do not think I have seen any other lady ride as well as you," said Hugo. "I am most impressed at your managing to stay seated with two ruffians trying to pull you off."

She shrugged and kept her face turned.

"Do you know what they were after? Was it money, do you think? Did they say?"

Silence.

"I shall report the incident to the park trustees."

She seemed to hesitate.

Hugo added, "I shall speak to them as soon as I have seen you safely home."

She made a small noise in her throat. Annoyance? Or resignation?

Hugo repressed a smile. He was quite determined to see the lady's face, and to hear her speak again and the sooner she realised it, the better for both of them. She was brave and stubborn and wilful and spirited and, he thought, probably very attractive.

He felt a surge of interest, man to woman. Yes, that was it, he thought. It had undoubtedly been too long since he had taken a mistress. That was also, no doubt, why last night he had felt so unaccountably attracted to a chit just out of the schoolroom, with no conversation, a frightful lisp, no social skills and the infuriating habit of treating him like an octogenarian.

He glanced speculatively across at his silent and unwilling companion. She wasn't acting like a light-skirt; she had certainly made no attempt to attract him. On the other hand, she was playing cat and mouse very skilfully; a clever courtesan would know that most men preferred the role of hunter. Was she a respectable woman trying to protect her identity from a stranger, or was she deliberately setting out to engage his interest by behaving mysteriously?

Respectable woman or not, Mr Devenish was extremely interested.

"There is no need to concern yourself," she said finally. "I am almost home. Thank you again for your assistance." She still refused to look at him.

Hugo smiled. She was annoyed with his persistence. And if her speech was any guide, she was also a lady. "It is my pleasure," he said smoothly. "But I am not one to abandon a lady so recently in distress. I will see you to your door."

She made another small sound—this time unmistakably one of annoyance. "There is no need to see me anywhere. I am not the least upset. I have encountered robbers before, and have survived much worse experiences. I am not in need of assistance, I thank you. And I will thank you to leave me alone!"

He briefly glimpsed part of her profile as she spoke, and though he did not recognise her, a *frisson* of familiarity passed though him.

"You have encountered robbers before?" he said, and reaching across, he caught her rein.

"Yes," she snapped. "In Jaipur once when I was

fourteen! Now have the goodness to release my horse immediately!" He made no move to do so, and before he realised her intention, she raised her crop and to his amazement, brought it down smartly on his hand. With an oath, he released her rein, and heedless of the traffic, she galloped away.

Hugo stared down at the livid red mark on his wrist. It didn't hurt all that much, but dammit! The girl had hit him! She'd actually hit him. Quite as if he was just as big a ruffian as those two in the park.

He would have laughed if he wasn't so shocked. Because as she'd turned to hit him, he'd glimpsed her face through the veil, just for a second.

His damsel in distress was Miss Singleton, Miss Catherine Singleton, schoolroom chit with no con-versation—well, she'd been consistent in that at least, he reflected ruefully.

But what the deuce was a young girl like Miss Singleton doing riding unescorted in the park at dawn? On a morning after she'd danced the night away, what's more. And wearing a habit that was more suited to a servant than herself.

One thing, though, was clear. The motives of the men in frieze coats was no longer a mystery—their target was reputed to be the owner of a diamond mine. The fools must have expected her to carry diamonds on her. Or perhaps their motive was ransom.

He rode slowly on, frowning in thought, avoiding

barrows and pedestrians and hand-carts without consciously noticing them. The robbers had been waiting for her. That meant she must make a habit of riding in the park at that hour of the morning.

Odd behaviour for a chit just out of the schoolroom. Even odder for an heiress. Possibly that was why she wore such a shabby riding habit—to deter possible robbers. But she really ought to have taken a groom at least to protect her. It was all most peculiar.

He reached his home and called for hot water, and for breakfast. Over a sirloin steak, he mulled over the situation. What the devil was a rich young woman doing riding an ill-favoured job-horse from a hired establishment? Someone with a seat like hers surely knew horses enough to demand the best.

And Rose Singleton had always been a stickler for the proprieties—so why had Rose not arranged an escort for her niece? Miss Singleton might encounter robbers again—good God! He suddenly recalled what she had said. She *had* encountered robbers before. *In Jaipur once when I was fourteen!*

Jaipur! He was fairly sure Jaipur was a kingdom or sultanate somewhere in India. And if that was the case…India was famous for its precious stones. Perhaps the fabled diamond mine was not in New South Wales, after all, but India…

But what was she doing being accosted by robbers in India at an age when she should still have been

safely in the schoolroom, sewing samplers and prac-
tising her pianoforte?

He pushed away the remains of his breakfast, and
drained his tankard of ale. Now, suddenly, his suspicions about how he had lost his tie-pin did not
seem so ridiculous.

He'd gone out for a ride to clear his head, but instead
had returned with it chockful of unanswered questions!

And the central question was—who the devil was
Catherine Singleton? Because he was now certain to
his bones that she was not the simple little chit she
appeared to be.

No chit fresh from the schoolroom could fight off
an attack with such courage and then be so cool
about it only a few moments later. That kind of self-
possession came with age…or experience.

And there had been no sign at all of a lisp. An af-
fectation, after all.

It was all very annoying. He'd planned to go for a ride
and blow all thoughts of the inconvenient and irritating Miss Catherine Singleton out of his head, and hang
it! She was more firmly ensconced there than ever.

And worst of all—his park encounter with her had
done nothing to diminish the attraction he had felt!

On the contrary!

He was more intrigued—and, yes—more attracted than ever.

Blast it!

Chapter Four

Kit tossed the reins of the hired horse to the waiting stable lad, pressed a coin into his waiting palm and slipped into the side door of Aunt Rose's house. She silently closed and bolted the door after her, then leant against it, her eyes closed.

Of all people to run into at the park, why did it have to be him? Such bad luck, to find the very man who had been disturbing her concentration, appearing out of the mist, riding *ventre à terre* to her rescue. Wretched man! He had almost ruined a very successful morning.

The footpads were a worry. She had been so careful to establish her routine, to account for her absence from home in the early hours. It had not occurred to her she might become a target for thieves. Kit Smith! A target for thieves! She laughed, wishing Papa was alive for her to share the joke with.

She would have to vary her routine now, for it wasn't only footpads who'd discovered her.

Who would have thought Mr Devenish would ride at dawn?

Had he recognised her?

If only she'd worn a thicker veil. Only she hated the thick one. It made her feel trapped, a little as though she was suffocating. She hated the feeling of being shut in.

And how stupid to have spoken to him—to have spoken at all! And in her own voice, her own accent!

Would the lisp she had adopted in his company be a sufficient disguise?

Kit took a deep, steadying breath. There was no help for it after all. What was done was done. She'd learned that lesson young.

There was never any going back.

So Mr Devenish had caught her riding alone in the park, unescorted. If he had recognised her, it would be a blot against her reputation. But he could not prove it was her.

And if she had fought off her attackers in a less than ladylike manner, what was that to say to anything? Many ladies she knew were not always ladylike.

And if she'd failed to act like an innocent young girl just emerged from the schoolroom… Well, not all schoolgirls were innocent.

Kit shrugged as she took the servants' stair to her

room. He could make of it what he would. She had
no control over what he would think anyway, so
there was no point in brooding.

Kit tugged off her gloves. The worst damage
would be that a slur would be cast on Rose's reputation as a chaperon. Regrettable, but not so very bad,
in the larger scheme of things.

She peeped into the small dressing room attached
to hers. Maggie was still fast asleep in her truckle
bed. It was only just after dawn, after all. Only the
most menial of the servants were stirring yet, and
their hostess, Rose, would be abed for another four
or five hours. She rarely arose before eleven.

Kit stripped off her habit and hung it neatly in the
closet. She quickly tossed on the nightgown that
she'd discarded an hour or so earlier, and shivering
in the cool air, climbed into her high, still faintly
warm bed. She could catch a quick, refreshing
catnap, and no one would be any the wiser about her
dawn excursion.

She was well used to interrupted sleep, after all.
Another lesson she'd learned as a child was that the
most productive hours were often the hours when the
rest of the world slept or were at their most vulnerable—the hours just before dawn.

The Watchdog rode magnificently, she thought
as she watched the early morning sunlight play
across her window. She'd noticed him in the

distance before those footpads had accosted her...not that she'd realised who was riding that splendid black horse.

Horse and master were perfectly matched.

It was odd, how strongly he appealed to her. He shouldn't. He wasn't at all what most people called handsome—his face was harsh, almost saturnine. And he stared at her so coldly and made no attempt to charm her. In fact, it seemed to be a strain on his temper merely to be agreeable towards her.

She'd met many men in London who were much more personable and good looking, and yet she wasn't nearly as attracted to their practised compliments than to his barked-out interrogations. Why was that?

And yet...when he thought he was dealing with an unknown woman in the park, he'd acted quite differently. He'd been quite gallant in her defence and, afterwards, solicitous and protective.

Towards a stranger.

Why so brusque and businesslike towards his young nephew's supposed intended, and yet so charmingly protective and, and—yes—flirtatious towards a stranger whom he must have known, from her horse and habit alone, was not of his station in life?

A Watchdog indeed.

It was all most intriguing.

She sighed.

* * *

"Whatever are ye doing, Miss Kit?" said Maggie, later that morning.

Kit pulled out a white muslin dress from the large oak wardrobe, examined it closely and tossed it onto a pile. "No, that won't do either," she muttered and pulled out another one, also white, but worked in fine pale blue embroidery around the hem and sleeves. She scowled at it a moment, then tossed it, too, aside. "Insipid, insipid, insipid! Why is everything so insipid?"

Maggie let out a small cluck of annoyance. "Oh, will ye stop tossing those dresses around so carelessly, Miss Kit! Gowns like that don't grow on trees, ye know! Whatever is the matter, now?"

"They won't do, Maggie. Not at all."

Maggie stared at her a moment. "What do ye mean, they won't do? You mean somebody said something to ye at the ball about yer gown? Drat! That dratted dressmaker—I knew she couldn't be trusted. Her little black eyes were too close together! The woman swore to us that they were the very thing for a jern fee only just out!"

"But I'm not a *jeune fille* only just out."

"Ye are too—" Maggie broke off. She stared at Kit a moment. "What d'ye mean, ye're not a jern fee?" Her eyes narrowed shrewdly. "What are ye then?"

Kit sighed. "I'm a diamond heiress."

There was a short silence broken only by the ponderous ticking of the grandfather clock out in the passageway.

"A *diamond* heiress?"

Kit nodded. "Apparently Papa said something to Rose in a letter and..." she shrugged "...it's all over London."

"Drat!" said Maggie. There was another short silence, then she said, "Typical of yer pa. He never did like to keep things simple, rot his bones!" She sighed heavily and smoothed the fabric of a dress. "A diamond heiress. Are ye sure?"

Kit nodded glumly. "Everybody says so."

"Drat!" said Maggie again.

They gloomily surveyed the pile of simple white dresses which had been purchased for the *jeune fille*. They were fresh and simple; not at all the sort of thing a diamond heiress would wear.

"Ye cannot afford a new wardrobe, I suppose. No, silly question. Oh, Miss Kit, what a thing to—"

"A diamond heiress might prefer simplicity," said Kit slowly. "Don't you think so?"

Maggie snorted. "Well I hope so, because simplicity is all this diamond heiress can afford!"

"Yes," Kit continued. "I think I very much dislike ostentation—"

"Just as well!" Maggie busily began to sort clothes into two piles: one, obvious "jern fee" clothes, the other with heiress possibilities.

"—and, of course, I *never* wear diamonds! Nor any other stones."

"That's right." Maggie started to enter into the spirit of things. "Nasty vulgar things, diamonds. Especially for a jern fee."

"Yes, Papa would never have allowed me to wear diamonds. Not even tiny ones as earrings."

Maggie made a rude noise. "No, he'd have had 'em out of your ears and off to the nearest card game before you could say Jack Robinson!"

"Maggie!" said Kit reproachfully.

Maggie stopped her sorting and directed a sceptical eyebrow in Kit's direction.

Under that gimlet gaze, Kit capitulated. "Oh, very well, yes, he would have. But *not* if I were a diamond heiress. Which I am, apparently. And I cannot think that a diamond heiress would wear such….such insipid garments as these. It was one thing when I was merely an obscure, long-lost niece…but a diamond heiress."

They both stared gloomily at the pile of clothing.

"Perhaps a diamond heiress—of the becomingly modest variety—would wear some of these…only not quite such commonplace things," said Kit. "What about…?"

She reached down and dragged a small trunk from under the bed. A quick rummage secured the piece she sought, a brilliant blue length of Indian silk, bordered with exotic embroidery. "How about this?" She draped it around herself and posed.

Maggie regarded her critically, then sniffed. "Not bad. Matches your eyes. What else have we got?"

Kit rummaged around some more and drew out several gorgeously coloured, exotic small hats—caps they were, really, and not designed for women. She placed one at a rakish angle over her dusky curls. "A new fashion, perhaps?"

Maggie adjusted the angle of the cap, frowned and nodded. "It'll do. And what about the young prince's jacket?"

"Oh, yes!" said Kit excitedly. She went to a large chest of drawers and took from it a heavy dark red silk jacket, which she slipped on over her white muslin gown. The jacket was cut short, just to her waist, with long tight sleeves and a high collar of unusual cut. The thick silk gleamed with subtle richness. It was densely embroidered in a stunning black and gold design on the collar, cuffs, down the front and around the base.

She gazed at herself in the looking glass. The white of the muslin gown did not look so insipid now; in fact, it provided the perfect background for the heavy gorgeous red of the jacket. She fetched one of the caps, a black one with a small tassel of gold, from her trunk, put it on and frowned critically at the effect. "If we got some slippers to match, and perhaps embroidered a reticule with the same design… What do you think Maggie?"

Maggie pursed her lips for a moment, then nodded. "Might be the sort of thing a diamond heiress would wear—if she had unusual tastes, that is."

"Unusual tastes! Yes! That's it! I am not your everyday, run-of-the-mill diamond heiress. I have unusual tastes!" agreed Kit enthusiastically. "And then we can use some of the things we have collected on our travels, and if I look odd—which of course I shall—it will only be a sign of eccentricity. What is odd in ordinary people is mere eccentricity in an heiress, I am certain. Oh, what a relief! For a while there I thought we would never be able to pull this mad thing off. But now, if I am to be eccentric and unusual—well, that is so much easier. So, what else can we use?" She burrowed back into the trunk, while Maggie began to tidy things back into the wardrobe.

"What about the peacock shawl?" Kit drew out a large, very fine black Kashmiri shawl, upon which was embroidered two peacocks facing away from each other. Their embroidered feathers gleamed with iridescence in a thousand gleaming shades, almost as magnificent as the original birds. It was edged with a silken fringe, so long that it almost touched the ground. The insipid white gown could hardly be seen.

"And this!" She pulled out a length of shimmering

gold material, so fine and delicate that her skin glowed though the fine transparent weave.

"And the Maharani's headdress!" She placed an intricately wrought silver headdress over her hair. It settled close, hugging the shape of her head, a row of dainty glittering silver pendants adorning her brow.

Kit settled on her heels beside the trunk, a billowing tangle of exotic finery tumbled around her. "Oh, Maggie darling, what a good thing we brought all these bits and pieces with us. I thought only to keep them for a rainy day—to sell them to raise some cash, but they will be a godsend to us, now that I am a diamond heiress. A diamond heiress! Whatever was Papa thinking of?" She shook her head in rueful disbelief. "But if we use these as a basis, and have one or two more spencers and pelisses and perhaps a riding habit cut to a similar unusual design...I might, I just might actually look the part!"

"And how do ye think we are going to pay for these extra pelisses and habits and whatnot?" said Maggie grimly. "A fine heiress you will look if the dressmaker comes a-dunning us and ye can't pay."

"Oh, Maggie, my deah," said Kit, affecting a drawl very reminiscent of some of the society ladies she had met, "'tis terribly provincial of you even to consider it. One does not—positively not, my deah—bother ones head with tradesmen's bills. Your mantua maker should be grateful—positively grateful, my deah—that you consent to wear her offerings in such distinguished society."

Maggie glared. "Don't tell me ye're planning to diddle some hardworkin' woman out of her hard-earned—"

Kit giggled. "I knew you would be horrified, but indeed, that is how some of them speak. And of course we will pay the dressmaker. I remember, as well as you, how hard it is to earn a living as a seamstress. My thumb is still practically scarred from the number of times I pricked it with a needle."

"And what do ye think we will pay her with, Miss Optimism?"

Kit grinned cheekily. "Oh, we will be able to pay, Maggie dearest—do not fret yourself. By the time the dressmaker's bills come in, we will have plenty of money to pay her with."

Maggie eyed her narrowly. "Miss Kit! I thought ye'd given up playing those tricks!"

Kit instantly thought of a tiny gold phoenix with a glinting ruby eye. She squashed the guilty thought. "Oh ye of little faith," she said airily. "There will be no tricks involved—I promise you. But Aunt Rose goes to so many card parties and one thing I did learn from Papa was how to win at cards—and, no, I will not use his methods. I have no need of them. I have always been lucky at cards, you know that, Maggie."

"Aye," agreed Maggie gloomily. "And ye know what they say about that, don't ye? Lucky at cards, unlucky at love."

There was a small stir in Almack's when Kit and Miss Singleton arrived the next evening. Miss Rose Singleton was clad in one of her usual gowns, trailing a number of gauze scarves. However, Miss Catherine Singleton, who had only ever been seen dressed in white or the palest of pastels, was again wearing a white dress, but there her usual pattern ended.

Tonight she positively caught the eye in a very exotic jacket of dark red silk with the most intricate embroidery in black and gold. An unusual tasselled cap was perched jauntily on her short dark curls. She wore embroidered slippers which curled to a point and carried a reticule to match.

It was a most picturesque, not to say outlandish outfit. The ladies buzzed with speculation.

Miss Catherine Singleton appeared oblivious of the minor sensation she was causing on this, her first appearance at the hallowed Marriage Mart. She curtsied demurely to each person her aunt introduced her to and said very little, apart from the common politenesses. She prettily agreed to dance with whoever asked her. Apart from her bizarre costume, she behaved like any other young girl making her come-out.

The discussion of the diamond heiress's eccentric attire, as Kit had predicted, lasted a short while, then moved on to more fruitful topics…

"Did you hear about poor Lady Alcorne, Hettie?"

Kit was seated in the main room at Almack's, watching the dancing and eavesdropping a little dreamily on a conversation between three elderly ladies seated nearby. They had shredded the reputations of three of her acquaintances so far. Kit was finding their conversation quite entertaining.

"Oh, yes, the Alcorne diamonds! No wonder she is not here tonight. Poor creature—her husband is reputed to be furious."

Kit pricked up her ears.

"Kit dear, why are you not dancing?" Rose came up from behind her, looking vaguely concerned. "You don't want to be a wallflower, now do you?"

In fact, that was exactly what Kit wanted to be at the moment. What did it matter if she missed one dance? She glanced at Rose to tell her so, and stopped. Sweet concern for Kit's welfare was all Kit could see and her heart melted. She was so little accustomed to someone worrying about her happiness that she had no defence against it.

Had Rose been a wallflower in her youth? Was that the reason she had never married? Had she ever had an offer? It was a pity, for Rose would have made the sweetest of wives and a truly loving mother.

Kit grimaced faintly. "My new slippers pinch a little. Don't worry, Aunt, I will join the next set, after my poor toes have had a short rest."

"Oh, dear, your poor feet." Rose peered at the odd slippers and nodded understandingly. "By all means rest for a moment or two, but it will not do if people see you sitting too long when all the other girls are dancing." She nodded encouragingly at Kit and floated off, trailing gauzy draperies behind her.

Kit resumed her eavesdropping

"In the family for generations, and you know what men are like. They'll blame whoever is convenient. And I heard she had neglected to lock the diamonds away."

Generations? Kit wrinkled her brows.

"But, Maud, I was certain someone said it was a highwayman. The blackguard bailed her up on the way home from the Parsonses' ball."

"No, no, Pearl, dear. That wasn't it at all—a robber broke in to the house in the dead of night. I had it from my dresser, who is first cousin to Lady Alcorne's housekeeper. Lifted the whole set from the dressing table in the very room where Lady Alcorne was sleeping."

"Good God! She could have been murdered in her bed!" said Hettie, who was really Lady Hester Horton, Kit learned.

"Oh, indeed! Quite, quite shocking! The state of the world today! A person is not safe in her bed."

"No, indeed! And do you know what else?"

From the corner of her eyes Kit saw the ladies lean closer.

"They say he might have been a Chinaman!"

"No! Good Heavens!"

"A Chinaman, Maud! But how do they know? Did someone see him?"

"No, but they found a torn scrap of paper near the window the rascal climbed through—and it had Chinese writing on it!"

"Chinese! But was it not a Chinaman who stole the Pennington Black Pearls?"

"Yes, that's right, Hettie. The Devenish boy saw him."

Kit smiled to herself. The Devenish boy, indeed!

"This paper, Maud. What did it say?"

"Well, they called in some chappie from—"

"All alone, Miss Singleton? Not dancing for some reason?"

Kit started and glanced up. "Oh, Mr Devenish, how do you do?" she murmured, keeping her face blank of all expression. Drat! Apart from wishing to continue her eavesdropping, he was quite the last person she wished to encounter just now.

She hadn't expected to see him tonight. From all accounts Almack's was by no means his cup of tea. And yet, here he was, looming over her when she least expected it. And when she had no other choice but to invite him to be seated on the vacant chair next to hers. Common politeness dictated it. Drat the man. She had no wish to be subjected to more of his questions, and after their encounter in the park, she was sure he would have more.

If he'd recognised her, that is.

She looked him over, feeling almost exasperated. How did he do it? He was the most plainly dressed man in the place, as if he could not be bothered with fashionable nonsense. He wore no rings, no fobs, no seals, no quizzing glass—not even a tie-pin, a small part of her noted guiltily.

His coat was dark and plain, though subtly well cut across those wonderful shoulders. He was dressed, most correctly for Almack's, in knee breeches and his cravat was simple, though elegantly arranged. Every other man in the room had gone to more trouble to dress for the occasion than he.

He should have looked like a plain black crow. And yet he looked magnificent.

His hair was newly barbered: cut short and brushed sternly back with water. It seemed he disdained pomade. Kit was glad; she disliked the smell of pomade. And clearly he preferred neatness, rather than style. She wondered whether he realised that enough small rebellious locks had survived the barber and the brushing to spring up, giving a faint impression of the Windswept Style.

A tiny smile quivered inside her. So that was why he had his hair cut so brutally short. It would not do for the world to know the stern Mr Devenish could grow a headful of curls any damsel would envy.

"Another danth? Yeth, yeth, of courth. Are you enjoying—?"

"Odd, that," he interrupted brusquely. His cold grey eyes bore into her, a faint, disturbingly mocking light in them.

She looked at him inquiringly.

"My sister-in-law, Lady Norwood, is of the opinion that you lisp only when you are nervous. Are you nervous?"

Kit did not know what to say. She gave what she hoped sounded like a nervous, schoolgirlish titter as a way of avoiding a reply. It sounded to her ears more like the whinny of a sick horse. "Oh, look," she said, "there's my friend Mith Lutenth. I mutht—"

"You didn't lisp at all in the park this morning."

Kit froze. "Park?" she said vaguely, twirling a dusky curl in the most inane way she could think of.

"After you'd been attacked by those footpads, I would have thought that if nerves had been in question, you'd have been lisping your head off then."

"Footpadth? Good Heaventh! But I really don't know what—"

"Doing it much too brown, Miss Singleton. I am not venturing a bow at random, you know. I saw your face when you hit me." Hugo smiled sardonically and raised his wrist. "And I bear your brand."

To Kit's horror a faint, livid mark was still visible. "Oh, no, I am so terribly sorry, I didn't—"

She caught herself up just in time. She could not admit to being out at dawn, unchaperoned. "I mean, you are mistaken about whoever you saw. It was not I. I slept until ten o'clock this morning, after the late night I'd had." She bit her lip and looked up at him remorsefully. "I don't know who did this to you, but I am very sorry you were hurt."

He snorted. "It would take more than a cut from a vixen to hurt me."

She flushed and, without thinking, reached out and took his wrist, cupping it between two soft hands. She peered at the thin red mark. "It looks rather red and angry. Did you put any salve on it?" Her finger lightly traced a line just below the actual mark.

A silent shiver went through Mr Devenish at her touch. He stared down at her, watching the soft, slender finger stroke gently back and forth across his skin. It was mesmerising.

He glanced at her face, his brows drawn darkly together in unwilling suspicion. Her head was bent, the tassel of her cap falling forward. Her pale nape was curved and delicate, her dark curls wisping gently around it. Was this another one of her tricks? He wanted to pull his hand back away from her soft touch. He was unable to move, transfixed by her touch. He could feel his heart beating within his chest, pounding the blood though his body.

He inhaled deeply to clear his head and found himself inhaling the scent of her, the faint citrusy tang of something in her hair, the warm aroma of—he inhaled again—was it vanilla and rosewater coming from her body? Whatever it was, her scent was ravishing. He loathed the way so many females drenched their bodies with strong-smelling perfume. Not Miss Catherine Singleton. A faint hint of roses, and yes—he leaned forward imperceptibly and breathed deeply again—he was sure it was vanilla. Roses and vanilla.

She had removed her outlandish red jacket and he found his eyes drawn to the scooped neck of her gown, to the fine creamy skin. His gaze sharpened and he felt a tiny spurt of triumph as he noted several tiny faint freckles, which she had dusted with rice powder to disguise. She might try to hide them from the world, but she would not hide them from him.

Mr Devenish felt a sharp of jolt of surprise as he caught himself on that possessive note. Good lord! What was he thinking of? She was a mystery to be investigated, that was all, and on his young nephew's behalf. He was here on business, no more. It was what he was good at.

If he wished to be rid of the constant drain of his

nephew and sister-in-law on his time and purse, he'd best make certain that any heiress Norwood snapped up would be rich enough to bolster the family fortunes sufficiently. It was not merely his nephew's interests he was pursuing here, it was his own. Once Thomas was safely buckled to a fortune, his uncle would be free.

And this was the heiress Thomas had chosen; this creature of rose and vanilla, who parried his questions with artless simplicity and went out to ride at dawn.

An heiress with a lisp that came and went. A diamond heiress who never wore diamonds. A sheltered young innocent, chaperoned at all times—except when she was fighting off footpads alone at dawn. A girl who claimed to have beaten off robbers in Jaipur when she was fourteen. Who may well have stolen his tie-pin under the eyes of hundreds of London's finest. She looked barely seventeen now. But he'd wager Sultan she was a good deal older than she looked.

"How old are you?" he snapped.

She blinked and looked up at him in surprise. And beneath his sharp gaze her eyes turned from the clear depths of blue innocence, to glowing sapphires, glittering with mischief.

Mr Devenish frowned. He had never been drawn to sapphires. Untrustworthy stones. But he was drawn to her eyes, even when they weren't innocent and clear, but sparkling opaquely as they were now.

"I thought that was a question a gentleman never asked a lady," she murmured, releasing his hand.

He caught hers in his, refusing to break the contact. "Yes, but I am not a gentleman. Ask anyone. How old are you?"

Her eyes twinkled as she pretended to think for a moment. "I'm as old as my eyes, and a little bit older than my teeth. And you, sir?"

"I'm thirty-two," he said bluntly. And old enough to know he shouldn't be holding hands with a chit only just out in a place where anyone might walk by and see them. But he didn't let go of her hands. His thumbs moved back and forth across her skin.

Her hands were not as soft as those of most ladies of his acquaintance. There were faint callouses, and not just from riding. If he didn't know better, he would have suspected she'd had to do menial work at some time. Interesting that. He would have to find out why. Another mystery to unravel.

"Thirty-two," she said admiringly, quite as if he'd declared himself ninety-two. "That's quite old, isn't it? I suppose your children are almost grown by now." Her eyes danced, and he recalled her offer of a rusk the night before.

"I don't have any children," he said brusquely.

"I'm sorry," she said with quick remorse. "It was a thoughtless comment."

Confound the wench! She was a minx and a

baggage and a mystery! One minute the lisping innocent, the next a cool-voiced little Amazon wielding a whip in her own defence. And now, this soft-eyed, soft-voiced woman, with the not-quite-soft-enough hands.

"I don't have any children because I have never been married."

"Oh." She appeared to consider the matter. "So you have sworn off marriage." She nodded understandingly. "Many men do not care for marriage, I know." She smiled at him and he caught a glimmer of mischief again. "They prefer their, er, male friendships."

Definitely this chit was no naïve schoolgirl!

Innocent, but not naïve. The unselfconscious way she had taken the hand she'd marked had convinced him that she was inexperienced in the ways of the flesh. Guilt, rather than flirtation, had been behind that action. She had touched him more like a repentant child than a woman bent on seduction. So an innocent, but a worldly one, for all that.

"But I *do* enjoy the company of women," he assured her grimly.

She nodded artlessly. "Oh yes, many of the—er, many unmarried men do so, I know."

The minx was deliberately teasing him! She could not truly believe he was a man-milliner, surely! But he couldn't help but retort sharply, "I'll have you know I have enjoyed a number of liaisons with women. *Intimate* liaisons."

She turned her head away, suddenly the shy schoolgirl. "I do not believe you should be speaking of such matters to me."

He was aware of the truth of that. Good God! What on earth was he about, discussing his mistresses with a gently reared young virgin! And a relative stranger, to boot! Quite disgraceful of him. He felt his face reddening.

"Er…" he began awkwardly.

"Oh, it is quite all right—Papa was a little too free with his tongue, too," she surprised him by saying. "I expect you will continue to be so, as well. It is difficult, I know, for gentlemen to change their habits after a certain age."

"After a certain age—" he began wrathfully, but before he could bring her to a proper understanding of his youthful vigour, she had tugged her hand free and was waving to some other young thing.

"Oh, there is my friend Miss Lutens and I must speak to her most particularly about something. I beg you will excuse me, Mr Devenish, but I truly must go. It was very pleasant speaking to you, and…" she paused in her rush, and her voice lowered "…I am truly very sorry about what, er, what happened to your hand. Goodbye." And she curtsied and hurried off to join a gaggle of young women in white.

He watched her move gracefully across the room, baffled, annoyed and fascinated, despite himself. He still knew almost nothing about her. Oh, he was coming to know her in small ways...

She had three or four tiny freckles just below the hollow in her throat. And that she tried to hide them.

She sat a horse like the huntress Diana and faced unexpected danger bravely and boldly.

She could apologise with a liquid softness in her eyes that caused him to see another Miss Singleton hiding behind the mischievous girl with the quick and clever tongue whose not-quite-soft little hands held him even as she tied him in knots with her nonsense.

But who the deuce she was, where she had come from, where she had spent her childhood, and where the devil that diamond mine was? About those questions he was no more informed than when he had first clapped eyes on the chit!

Less! The more he knew of Miss Singleton, the less he understood about her.

Mr Devenish did not care to play the ignoramus any longer.

He strode to the card room and scanned its occupants quickly. Aha! Sir George Bancroft! Old Bancroft had been an intimate of his father. He was reputed to be "a very downy fellow, old Bancroft". If anyone recalled anything about Miss Singleton's father, it would be Bancroft.

* * *

"Oh, Miss Singleton, I am so very glad you are here tonight. Sir Bartlemy is being very...attentive!"

Kit frowned. "And did you try to hint him away as I suggested?" She glanced at her young friend's distressed face. "Yes, I can see you have. Impervious, is he? Horrid old Octopus! Did you bring your hatpin?"

Miss Lutens giggled. "Yes, but I am much too embarrassed to use it."

Kit nodded. "Yes, I can see that it is a little more stuffy here than I had realised. Still, merely because we are keeping the hatpin in reserve, does not mean we cannot act in some less drastic fashion."

Miss Lutens sighed. "I feel so much braver when you are here."

Kit glanced around. "I would very much like to teach Sir Octopus a lesson, and at the same time demonstrate my technique to you, but I cannot do it here. Aunt Rose has dinned into me a thousand times that I must behave perfectly. Almack's seems to be her holy of holies, and I cannot think she would like it if I sent Sir Bartlemy to the rightabout on my very first appearance here."

Miss Lutens looked horrified. "Oh, no," she agreed hastily. "It is of the utmost importance that we appear in our best light at Almack's. We could not do anything untoward—it would ruin our chances."

Kit repressed a smile. Rose Singleton was not the only one who'd been dinning advice into young heads.

"Yes, so we will remain together tonight and defeat Sir Bartlemy temporarily by our bosom-bowish refusal to be parted. Is your dance card filled?" She peered at it. "Yes, well done. I have two here which I had promised to Lord Norwood and if we just scratch out this—" she scratched out Sir Bartlemy's name from Miss Lutens's card and inserted Lord Norwood's, then wrote Sir Bartlemy's name on her own "—now we can all be comfortable. There! Now the Octopus has no excuse to be bothering you tonight." She handed back the dance card to Miss Lutens.

Miss Lutens regarded the dance card with wide, shocked eyes. "But, are you allowed to change the cards like that? I thought—"

"A lady has the privilege of changing her mind, does she not?"

"I suppose so, but will not Lord Norwood mind?"

Kit laughed. "Now, how could Lord Norwood possibly object to dancing with a sweet, graceful creature like yourself?"

Miss Lutens blushed. "Oh, no, please do not say so. But I thought you had an understan—"

"No, no. That is just a silly rumour. And besides, Lord Norwood does not have enough adventure in his life—he will very much enjoy playing the gallant knight, rescuing a damsel from a monstrous octopus. And, speak of the devil, here is Lord Norwood come in good time for the next dance. Sir

Bartlemy will not be far behind, if I'm not mistaken. Lord Norwood—" She beckoned him to hasten to her side.

Lord Norwood, flamboyantly dressed in a tight bottle-green coat, pale yellow pantaloons and highly starched shirt points of extravagant height, lengthened his stride slightly. He reached her and bowed meticulously over her hand. "Miss Singleton."

"Lord Norwood, there is no time to explain, for I can see him coming now, but Miss Lutens and I have exchanged your name on our dance cards."

"Exchanged my name—" Lord Norwood looked outraged.

"Oh, please do not take offence. It is quite urgent that you play knight to her damsel. Miss Lutens has been very much distressed by Sir Bartlemy's style of gallantry," she said meaningfully, fixing Lord Norwood with a clear determined look.

For the first time Lord Norwood turned to look at Miss Lutens. Her wide hazel eyes regarded him anxiously, showing both her innocence and her distress. She bit her soft pink lips worriedly. Lord Norwood blinked, and stared.

Kit hurried on, "I am better able to deal with such things than Libby here, so if you will just escort her on to the dance floor—" She gave him a little push. "Go *on* my lord. Sir Bartlemy is coming!"

Miss Lutens gave a little jump, cast a hunted look

over her shoulder and shivered, which galvanised Lord Norwood into masterful action. He ushered Miss Lutens on to the dance floor with a protective air, bending over her in a solicitous manner, saying something in a low voice. Miss Lutens smiled up at him, tremulously.

Kit watched them go, a speculative light in her eye. She smiled, then turned to greet Sir Bartlemy.

"Oh, Sir Bartlemy, you are looking for Miss Lutens, I know, but I'm afraid we have been very naughty, Miss Lutens and I," she began. "I did so much wish to dance with you and so I persuaded Miss Lutens to switch partners with me. Are you very angry?" She smiled winsomely.

Sir Bartlemy looked a trifle put out for a second, then his gaze ran over her in an overly familiar manner that set her teeth on edge. He bowed and smiled in a self-satisfied manner.

"Not at all. Miss…Singleton, isn't it? I do recall your dear aunt introducing us." He smiled again. "I would be only too delighted to partner you in this dance." He took her arm in a hot moist grip, pulling her close to his plump, scented, none-too-clean person. His eyes delved into the neckline of her dress.

Kit tried not to grit her teeth. She allowed herself to be escorted onto the dance floor, thanking goodness Miss Lutens was not yet approved for the waltz. A country dance would be bad enough with

Sir Bartlemy for a partner. No wonder Miss Lutens found it so difficult to deal with him.

"You're a naughty little puss, aren't you, to trick Sir Bartlemy like that, but I forgive you." He leered and ran his hand up her arm, just brushing against the side of her breast.

She calmly slapped it away. "Keep your roving hands to yourself, Sir Bartlemy."

He chuckled and moved a little closer. "Sorry, my dear, forgive an old man's short-sightedness." His hand returned.

Kit slapped it away, hard, and much less discreetly.

He chuckled again. "Prudish little vixen, aren't you? But as sweet as honey. I like a spirited filly." His hand squeezed her arm suggestively.

Instantly all Kit's good intentions of behaving perfectly at Almack's flew out of the window. No wonder Miss Lutens had had so much trouble. This man was in dire need of a lesson! She allowed herself to be led towards a set that was just forming and glanced around the room, wondering where Mr Devenish had gone to. He was nowhere to be seen. Good, she didn't want him to witness what she was going to do next.

Mr Devenish wended his way between the crowded card tables and the rooms which were set aside for those who preferred cards to dancing. He was making slow progress across the room. Common politeness forced him to stop at almost every table, greeting this person or that, parrying avid questions and broad hints about the cause of his unexpected appearance at Almack's. His good humour was rapidly decreasing.

"No, no, Lady Enmore, just here to speak to Sir George over there."

The devil take it! Every old tabby in creation seemed to be here, eying him in that speculative, knowing way that old ladies had developed into an art form.

"No, Mrs Bunnet, I have no intentions—yes, it probably has been ten years. A matter of business, you know. Yes, I have seen my cousin. I believe she is dancing."

"How do you do, Mrs Peake? No, I haven't been here for a long time. No, no." Falsely hearty laughter. "The Marriage Mart? Good God, no! And how is Mr Peake? Oh, I'm sorry. I didn't know. Please accept my condolences." He gritted his teeth into a sympathetic grimace and pressed onwards, feeling stifled by the heat and the clash of perfumes and the stench of elderly curiosity.

It was his own fault. He hadn't been seen in the hallowed rooms of Almack's since he was a young sprig who didn't know any better. It had been a good ten years or more. No wonder a buzz sprang up at every table after he passed. The whole world imagined he had come, at last, in search of a wife.

Finally he reached Sir George Bancroft.

"If it isn't young Devenish!" exclaimed the old man, as Hugo bowed. "Sit down, young feller, sit down. Will you have a glass of something?"

"No, thank you, sir, I just—"

"Quite right! You know what I've been reduced to?" The old man glared at him, his bushy white eyebrows twitching in indignation. "Orgeat! Orgeat—would you believe it!" He glared at the glass at his elbow. "Frightful swill! But that's Almack's for you. Nothing decent to quench a fellow's thirst and only chicken stakes at the tables, but there! It makes the ladies happy if I escort them on the odd occasion... But *orgeat*!" He shook his head.

Mr Devenish turned and saw Lady Bancroft and her unmarried daughter bowing and smiling across the room at him. He bowed in return, but ventured no closer. The Bancrofts' daughter was a devout woman of grim aspect and saintly utterances, and though he'd known her all his life, he was damned if he was going to speak to her under the eyes of the tabbies and have them all in a frenzy of speculation over it. He was not going to talk to any unmarried woman unless he could not possibly avoid it.

He drew Sir George aside where they could talk with relative privacy.

"Sir, what can you tell me about Miss Catherine Singleton's father?"

"Singleton? What's that? I don't know any Catherine Singleton. You mean Rose Singleton. Fine girl, Rose. You thinking of making her an offer? Bit long in the tooth for you, I'd have thought, but a devilish fine girl, all the same. Pity she never married."

Mr Devenish gritted his teeth. Was marriage-mindedness a disease everyone at Almack's had? "No sir. I am speaking of Rose's niece, Miss Catherine Singleton."

The old man stared at him from under beetling brows. "Niece? Never knew Rose had a niece! Never heard aught about a niece before today." He frowned, looking rather puzzled. "How can Rose have a niece? Her only brother died years ago."

Now it was Mr Devenish's turn to look puzzled. "Died years ago, you say? How many?"

The old man shrugged. "Must be more than a score of years now, but I can't be sure. Forced to leave England, don'tcha know. All hushed up, o' course, but that was the nub of it. Died soon after, in Italy or some such place."

"Are you sure, sir?"

Sir George Bancroft shrugged. "Well, that's what we heard. Some feller from the Embassy wrote to Singleton's father, had him buried out there. Of course, all this was before that scoundrel Napoleon got his hands on the place. I suppose he could have had a daughter out there…but…" He shook his head doubtfully. "It was a long time ago but I remember it well—Singletons are related to me, don'tcha know. I'd have heard if there had been a daughter—on the right side of the blanket, that is. Family wouldn't have bothered with a by-blow—sent a bit of money perhaps, but that's all. No, Rose hasn't got any niece I've heard of."

Hugo didn't know what to think. He was sure Miss Singleton was older than she appeared, but doubted very much that she was close to twenty years old. And if this tale was true, she had to be at least twenty-one or so to be Singleton's legitimate daughter.

A half-Italian by-blow raised in obscurity? He could not imagine it. There was touch of quality about her that was impossible to fabricate. And she could not have been brought up in Italy: her English was too pure for that. Besides, he doubted very much if a lady like Rose Singleton would have the temerity to introduce her bastard niece to society. It just didn't make sense.

"Rose's brother, sir, what was he like?"

Sir George Bancroft stared down his nose for a long moment and sighed. "Charmin' likable sort of chap, Jimmy Singleton. Tragic, when he died, you know. Cut down in the prime o' life! Ah, well, that's life for you, eh, Devenish. Never what you expect, is it? Now, must get back to the game. Delightful chat." He stumped away back to his card game, leaving Mr Devenish frowning.

If James Singleton died more than twenty years ago, then why had his daughter implied he'd died recently? And if he'd died in Italy, what was her connection with New South Wales?

Chapter Five

Kit was enjoying herself. The Sir Roger de Coverley was one of her favourite dances. She caught Miss Lutens watching her, from the next set. Kit winked. "Watch this," she mouthed silently, and turned back to her partner.

Sir Bartlemy Bowles oozed oily satisfaction at the thought of a pretty young girl being so taken with his manly charms that she would forsake her own handsome young partner. He smirked as he pranced forward and back, taking advantage of the movement of the dance to peer down the front of Kit's dress. It was by no means a fashionably low decolletage, but Sir Bartlemy's hot gaze made Kit wish to tug her neckline up to her chin.

Kit smiled artlessly back at Sir Bartlemy. He had addressed every word exclusively to her bosom. The trait was not an endearing one. He had leered, ogled, squeezed, stroked and whispered nasty, suggestive comments in her ear under the guise of sophistication. His breath was bad, his clothes reeked of body odour and perfume and he danced with mincing perfection.

Kit, demurely correct, skipped lightly forward and took his sweaty hand for the *chassez* movement.

"Ouch!" Sir Bartlemy winced as her foot accidentally collided with his shin.

"Oops, sorry, Sir Bartlemy," Kit murmured and skipped back.

Sir Bartlemy pranced back into place, a little less lightly, then frisked forward to take her hand again for the chain, keeping a wary eye on her feet.

"Oof!" Kit's closed fist encountered his cheekbone. Hard.

"Oh, dear. Sorry, Sir Bartlemy, I wasn't watching," Kit murmured. "This is such a complicated dance, is it not?" She twirled daintily around and skipped back.

Miss Lutens was watching, her eyes wide with mingled horror and delight. Kit grinned and swung into the next movement.

"Bloody H—ouch!" Sir Bartlemy cursed as one diminutive slippered foot stamped surprisingly heavily on his instep.

"Oh, dear, how clumsy of me," cooed Kit prettily. "Poor Sir Bartlemy, being partnered with such a Clumsy Clara."

Sir Bartlemy gritted his teeth in a smile, muttered

something gallant and hopped back into place, favouring his left foot.

It was their turn to twirl down the line. "Oof!" gasped Sir Bartlemy. Her foot had accidentally smashed against his ankle bone.

"Ouch!" She'd missed her step and crashed heavily onto his other instep.

"What a difficult dance it is. Oh, Sir Bartlemy, you poor thing! I'm not terribly good at this, am I?" called Kit apologetically, as she floated lightly and gracefully into the next movement.

"Yeouw!" A hard little heel had accidentally ground down on to masculine toes.

"Ouch—damn—er!" An ankle bone received a second sharp blow.

"Oh, dear! Poor Sir Bartlemy!" she wailed each time in pretty concern, and danced enthusiastically on. The Sir Roger de Coverley was, after all, one of Kit's favourite dances.

At last the dance finished. Kit felt exhilarated, quite ready for her next turn on the floor. She glanced at her dance card as Sir Bartlemy escorted her off the floor. Oh, yes. The supper dance, a waltz with the Watchdog. She looked around, only to find him watching her, a slight frown on his face.

Sir Bartlemy led her up to Mr Devenish, limping heavily. He bowed. "Thank you, Miss Singleton, for a most... memorable dance," he said. He turned to

Mr Devenish and handed her over with every evidence of relief, adding, "I believe you're her next vict—er, lucky partner." He winced as he touched his cheekbone, which was still red under the powder.

Mr Devenish bowed slightly.

"Mind your feet, old man," Sir Bartlemy whispered as he passed. "Pretty little gal, but devilish clumsy. Looks graceful enough, but damme, kick on her like a mule." And he hobbled off in the direction of the exit. Sir Bartlemy had apparently decided on an early night.

Mr Devenish stared after him, a thoughtful look on his face, then turned to Kit. "How very interesting. I seem to recall you are particularly light on your feet." His brow arched in a silent question.

Kit had no intention of enlightening him. "I am well enough in a dance which I have been taught, but that one was new to me, so I am afraid I may have been a trifle clumsy."

"Indeed? So you are skilled in the waltz, a new dance that is all the rage, yet have never danced a traditional dance like the Sir Roger de Coverley before?" he said smoothly. "How very odd. I quite thought it was a favourite with all the ladies."

Kit had no answer for that.

He regarded her sceptically. "Yes, I thought so," he murmured. "I do not suppose your extraordinary clumsiness had anything to do with Sir Bartlemy's reputed tendency for, er, shall we say, excessive familiarity." His statement ended on a faint upward inflection.

Kit said nothing. She glanced vaguely around the room, trying to look like a brainless ninny, hoping for some distraction to draw his attention away from her. The Watchdog was all too perceptive for her liking.

She cursed herself for her impulsiveness. She could not regret her punishment of Sir Bartlemy, but it should most certainly have been kept for a less conspicuous occasion. Heavens, it wasn't as if she had never had to put up with unpleasant male attention before. It was vital to her plans that she stay as inconspicuous as possible. She groaned inwardly.

She became aware of what Mr Devenish was saying in a rather irritated and gruff voice.

"And there was no need to jeopardise your comeout in such an outrageous fashion. Of course you have no male relatives, but that doesn't mean others cannot act on your behalf, curse it! That little worm won't bother you again. I will see to it."

He was offering to protect her from the likes of Sir Bartlemy, Kit realised. The thought hit her with a rush of warmth. What a nice Watchdog!

She'd never had anyone offer to protect her before. Apart from Maggie, that is, and that was not quite the same.

What would it be like to have a watchdog of her

own, acting as her protector, her shield? A watchdog to protect her from octopi like Sir Bartlemy. Someone to whom her welfare would be important; who would worry if she were hungry, or frightened, or in danger.

She recalled the way he had come to the rescue of an unknown female in the park, thundering down on the footpads on his magnificent black horse, a mysterious black knight appearing almost magically out of the morning mist. And the charmingly solicitous way he had enquired after her state of mind afterwards. He had even escorted her home—or would have if she had not been forced to escape him. All that protectiveness for an unknown female.

Kit did not need a watchdog, of course. She had survived the last twenty years quite well and had learned to deal with a vast range of unpleasant and even dangerous situations with very little help from anyone. So she did not *need* a watchdog…

But the thought of such protectiveness aimed at her was very appealing.

It could not be. She shook herself mentally. It was simply not possible. She had a job to do. She had made a promise to her father. And to herself. There was no place in her schemes for a watchdog.

Kit shook her head decisively. "No, I thank you," she said, smiling at him warmly, so as not to hurt his feelings. "I am very well able to deal with the likes of Sir Bartlemy. And besides, as well as punishing Sir Bartlemy, I was demonstrating to my friend Miss Lutens how she could—" Kit stopped, aghast, as his lips twitched in a sardonic glimmer. She had as good as confessed to Mr Devenish that her clumsiness had been deliberate.

Mr Devenish's lips twitched again. He was clearly enjoying her evident confusion. "There is no need to look so appalled," he murmured. "I would never have believed that you were capable of such accidental clumsiness. I have danced with you myself, do not forget, and found you exceptionally light and sure on your feet."

Kit mumbled her thanks.

"Yes," he added cynically, "I am much inclined to believe that every instance of clumsiness you have exhibited has been with an ulterior motive in mind."

Kit froze. His next words confirmed her sudden fear.

"That stumble at supper the other evening, for instance…"

His faint, mocking smile bored into her. Kit felt like a mouse encountering a cobra. She waited with bated breath for his next words.

Was he planning to denounce her as a thief here? At Almack's? Oh Lord, Rose Singleton would die at the disgrace. Up to now, the worst she'd feared was that Kit would do something as shocking as dance the waltz before she'd been approved to do so by one of the patronesses. That was the worst Rose could conceive of.

Kit closed her eyes briefly. Rose Singleton would rue the day when she succumbed to the blandishments of Kit's father. What a way to repay Rose for her kindness; her protégée being pilloried for theft. She opened her eyes again, prepared for the worst.

He picked up her dance card and scanned it briefly. "You are free for the next dance. Shall we?" And he held out his hand to her in a masterful fashion.

Breath left her body in a great whoosh of relief. He had not meant to denounce her at all! She had panicked over nothing.

She glanced up at him to read his expression. He stared down at her, his eyes, cold, shrewd, knowing and a trickle of ice stiffened her spine. He might be saying nothing, but his eyes told her the truth. He *knew* she'd stolen his tie-pin. He was holding it over her head.

Oh, he was a formidable watchdog, all right. She'd just forgotten whose watchdog he was. Not hers. He was protecting others from her. He was protecting Thomas, his nephew, Lord Norwood.

Kit made three resolutions at that moment. The first was that she would have to turn Thomas's interest away from her. And very soon. Secondly, she needed to be far more wary of Mr Devenish in future—he was far too perceptive—dangerously so, in her case.

Her third resolution was that she really should not ever dance with him again. Most particularly not the waltz. That was even more dangerous. She had learned at the Parsons's ball that whirling around the room in his arms had a very definite weakening effect on her common sense.

Even when not dancing, he had the power to weaken her defences; his offer to protect her from the importunities of Sir Bartlemy had completely undermined her natural wariness and look what had happened—he'd led her straight into a trap!

No, she could not possibly dance with him again.

She stared at his outstretched hand. It was strong and unfashionably tanned, not at all the hand of a gentleman. She shouldn't touch it, not if she had any common sense left. But how to refuse him, when she had no acceptable polite reason? And when her foolish female brain was telling her one more little dance wouldn't hurt. Foolish female mouse brain. Dance with the big handsome cobra, go on…

The opening strains of the music for the next dance began. As she heard it, common sense returned in a rush. A beatific smile spread across her face. The mouse had won.

"I am most terribly sorry, Mr Devenish," she cooed, "but as yet, I have not been approved by any of the patronesses to dance the waltz at Almack's. And I would not dream of disobeying my aunt's strict advice in this matter. I must, reluctantly, refuse you."

Mr Devenish frowned, bowed curtly, and walked away.

Kit watched him passing through the crowd with a mixture of triumph, relief and regret. She could not afford any more encounters with Mr Devenish. He was by far too knowing.

...every instance of clumsiness you have exhibited has been with an ulterior motive in mind...that stumble at supper the other evening, for instance.

So if he knew, then why not denounce her? That, quicker than anything, would solve the problem of his nephew's interest in Kit.

No, he could not possibly know it. How could he? In his world, ladies did not steal gentlemen's tie-pins at supper. Her guilty conscience had led her to see more significance in his words than there actually was.

If he truly thought her a thief, Kit would even now be residing in Bridewell Prison, instead of very properly sitting out a waltz at Almack's. Perhaps he might suspect...but that was all.

If Kit was to succeed in her plan, she had to ensure no one, no one at all showed more than a passing interest in the activities of Miss Catherine Singleton. Mr Devenish was interested in Catherine Singleton for one reason only—Thomas. Therefore, to be free of Mr Devenish's unwanted interest, Catherine

Singleton would have to get rid of Thomas. Immediately.

Kit had few qualms about it. Thomas was no more enamoured of her than the next woman. If it was love Thomas felt for Kit, it was what Maggie called cupboard love—love of Kit's supposed diamond mine.

Yes, she would give Thomas, Lord Norwood, his *congé* immediately—tonight, if at all possible.

And then Mr Devenish would leave Miss Catherine Singleton alone.

Kit, the determined daughter with a great deal of common sense and the plan to retrieve the family honour, knew it was the only possible solution.

It was the other Kit, the foolish female mouse-brained one, who wistfully wished it could be otherwise...

Kit glanced around the room. Aha, there was Thomas, standing leaning up against a pillar, chatting to—good Heavens! He was chatting to Libby Lutens and another young lady. How very interesting. Clearly he was still protecting Miss Lutens from the attentions of the Octopus. Perhaps watchdoggery ran in the family.

Kit watched approvingly. Up to now, she had not been at all impressed with Lord Norwood; he had stuck her as a dull and rather feckless young man. This protectiveness of Miss Lutens showed her a new side of him. Possibly it was new to him, too. Whatever, she liked Thomas the better for it. It was almost a pity she had to spoil his night by giving him his *congé*.

But it had to be done.

She rose from her seat and began to cross the floor.

"Miss Singleton." It was a warm, feminine voice with a decided air of command. Kit turned. She recognised that voice.

"Lady Cowper." She curtsied to the lady, one of the formidable Lady Patronesses of Almack's.

"It has come to my attention, Miss Singleton, that you are lacking a partner for this dance," said Lady Cowper. "May I present Mr Devenish as a desirable partner? I can recommend him; he dances the waltz exceptionally well." She smiled at Mr Devenish in an almost roguish fashion. He smiled and bowed to her. Kit gritted her teeth.

"Shall we, Miss Singleton?" He held out his hand to her, a faintly mocking smile on his lips.

Kit, aware of Lady Cowper's eyes upon her, curtsied demurely and laid her hand on his proffered arm. She darted him a smile of saccharine sweetness. "I hope I shall not dithappoint you with my clumthiness, Mr Devenish," she lisped pointedly. He was quite aware she had no wish to dance with him again. No serious wish, at any rate.

"Oh, I do not fear any return of that old problem," said Mr Devenish, escorting her on to the dance floor. "After all," he murmured in her ear, "continuing vouchers for Almack's will depend on your ability to rid Lady Cowper of the impression that you are cow-footed in the extreme. You would not wish to distress your aunt by being refused, now would you?"

Kit jerked back and stared up at him in surprise.

"Your performance in the Sir Roger de Coverley did not go unremarked," he remarked dulcetly. "If you wish to accompany your aunt to these occasions in the future, you will ensure that no doubt remains in Lady Cowper's mind of your lightness and grace on the dance floor. She was by no means inclined to approve you to waltz, but I managed to convince her to give you a second chance."

"You managed to convin—"

Kit was given no opportunity to finish her sentence, for in one masterful swish, he swept her out into the twirling throng on the dance floor and she was lost.

She hoped she was giving a demonstration of lightness and grace, but she had no idea; all she was aware of was the music and the man in whose arms she floated.

At the end of the dance, it was all she could do to remember to thank him for the dance. She suspected she had just continued to stare at him for some moments after the music had finished and they had stopped dancing. Finally she recalled herself, and she managed to mumble some sort of a thank-you-for-the-dance-sir.

He stood, staring down at her, a smug look of satisfaction in his eyes. He was aware of her state of…of *floatiness*—drat the man—and was enjoying it. He knew the effect waltzing had on her.

She must never dance the waltz again—it should never have been allowed. Lady Cowper did not know what she was doing…or maybe she did.

Kit sourly recalled the look in Lady Cowper's eyes when she referred to his exceptional abilities on the dance floor. Hah! She knew, all right! The waltz truly did undermine morals—especially when danced with a big black Watchdog.

Kit resolved never to dance with him again.

Suddenly all her resolutions of a few moments before came rushing back. She'd already resolved not to dance with him and look what had happened!

She had to get rid of Thomas, immediately. Then she would be safe.

"Thank you for the dance, Mr Devenish," she said again, and headed immediately to where young Lord Norwood was handing an ice to Miss Lutens.

"Thomas, I must speak with you, immediately."

Mr Devenish watched as his nephew escorted Miss Singleton to a less crowded part of the room. He noted the alacrity with which Thomas abandoned the pretty Miss Lutens to follow Miss Catherine Singleton. He scowled as Miss Singleton sat down on a bench and patted the seat beside her invitingly. He glared as Thomas sat down close beside her. He ground his teeth as she laid a hand on Thomas's arm and began to murmur softly in Thomas's ear.

Confound the wench! She'd floated in his arms, all soft-eyed and a little bit dazed from the waltzing. And then she'd wrenched herself away from him and headed across the room, like an arrow, straight to Thomas.

Blast Thomas! If he wasn't such a worthless fribble, he'd have no need of an heiress!

Blast society for frowning on a gentleman earning an honest living in trade! If it wasn't for that, he could teach Thomas how to be independent, not to need an heiress. But Thomas would not risk social disapproval merely for the freedom to marry for love; he had heard his uncle disparaged for his vulgar connections too often to risk the same himself.

Hugo flung one last jaundiced glance at the couple in close conversation on the other side of the room, then raised his hand to call for a drink. He lowered it again in annoyance. And blast Almack's and its ridiculous rules on refreshments! He needed something much stronger to drink than orgeat!

On that bracing note, Hugo left.

Kit was feeling a little nervous. It was one thing to tell herself that she didn't like Lord Norwood very much; it was another to tell him so, directly. And she was going to have to be very direct; so far none of the hints she had been giving him so delicately had taken root in Lord Norwood's handsome head. She was going to have to be blunt. But she did not wish to wound him.

She told herself crossly that he was not seriously interested in her; that he had merely been going through the motions of courtship in obedience to his mother's behest.

But he had spoken pretty words to her and though she did not believe he meant them, she may have been wrong.

Kit disliked the hypocrisy she'd found in England where men, believing she had a fortune, pretended love. It was more honest in India or China, she decided, where everyone haggled openly over the dowry. At least then, no one was deceived.

It was better to be blunt, she decided.

"Lord Norwood, I think it would be better if we were no longer seen together," she said firmly. "People are starting to speculate, and as there is no possibility of us ever making a match, we should nip such conjecture in the bud. Do you not agree?"

"Hmm, yes, indeed," agreed Lord Norwood, his gaze fixed on something or someone out of Kit's view.

"I am sorry," Kit murmured.

"Ah, well."

"I did not intend to upset you. I didn't, did I?" persisted Kit.

"Hmm? What?" Thomas glanced down at her. "No, no, not at all," he said heartily and returned to his observation of the room.

Kit felt a little annoyed. "Then that is all I have to say." She stood up to take her leave.

He jumped up, startled. "Oh, is that our dance? Righto." And he tucked her hand under his arm and led her towards the dance floor.

"Thomas!" she hissed.

He turned, puzzled.

"I am *not* going to dance with you!"

"You aren't?"

"No. We shall not be seen together any more, do you understand?"

He blinked.

"There is no possibility of you and me, er, of any…"

He looked puzzled.

"No possibility of a match between us," Kit said brutally.

"Oh. No possibility. You are certain, then?"

Kit nodded firmly. "Absolutely certain. I am very sorry for it, and I have no wish to wound you, but I feel it is best to be honest."

He nodded. "Yes, honest. Righto, then." He made as if to go.

Kit hesitated. She laid a hand on his arm to detain

him and whispered, "If it's any consolation, I don't have a fortune, you know."

"Oh? no? Pity, that." His eyes were fixed on something across the other side of the room. A face-saving tactic? Kit wondered.

"No, I have no fortune, no money at all."

"Ahh." He nodded vaguely, still staring across the room.

Kit glared at him. He wasn't listening to a word she said. "Yes, I am a penniless, nameless adventuress, come to deceive you all. I thought you ought to know."

Thomas glanced back at her and smiled down at her in a vague fashion. "Well, that's all right, then. I'll take my leave now, if you don't mind." And he bowed and hastened away, making a bee-line for Miss Lutens.

Kit watched, half-amused and half-annoyed. After all her anxiety about hurting his feelings, the clothhead obviously had no feelings to hurt. Not for her, at any rate.

Oh, well, she'd achieved her aim. With Thomas out of the picture, his Uncle Watchdog no longer had any reason to investigate Miss Catherine Singleton. He would probably start interrogating Miss Lutens instead.

Excellent. She wouldn't ever have to speak with Mr Devenish again. Nor would she ever again be forced to waltz with him. Very good. She was really pleased about that. In fact, she was utterly delighted.

It was just that for some unaccountable reason, she had suddenly developed the vilest headache. The odious ratafia, she was sure. She shouldn't have drunk any. It didn't agree with her. It didn't agree with her at all.

Oily grey water slapped languidly against the piles of the wharves and hulls of the ships riding at anchor. A lone gull wheeled and screamed into the leaden sky.

A fresh, faintly damp wind blew across the river, carrying a whiff of the stench of the hulks moored rotting on the river, filled with convicts awaiting transportation. The stench of misery and hopelessness.

That smell was overlaid with others, closer by, more immediate: hot tar; the smoke of a fire burning rubbish in a brazier, and a pot of cabbage soup bubbling atop it; the acrid smell of the Thames, river weed, rotting fish and the pervasive stink of human ordure; the faint tang of exotic spices from a nearby trading ship.

Hugo narrowed his eyes and inhaled, letting the mix of odours sink into him. It was deeply familiar.

With one sniff, he was transported back twenty years or more, being tossed aboard as a shaking ten-year-old, a small bundle of clothing wedged under his arm. A boy from Shropshire, who'd never so much as set foot on a boat, let alone seen the sea.

The servant deputised to deliver him to the ship's

master had been a kindly enough fellow, had patted him on the shoulder, awkwardly, saying, "T'will be reet enough, young master. You'll be back soon enough, I'll warrant, all growed and strong, looking like a proper sailor laddie."

And then the boy Hugo had been taken below, into a place that croaked and groaned like a living thing. A place that was dark, and which heaved and shifted under his feet. A place which stank, of the sea and turpentine and men who didn't bathe from one year to the next. Aye, he'd never forgotten that smell. Nor the creak of wood, the rhythmic slap of waves.

Hugo strode on, stepping over ropes and avoiding puddles of fish guts with automatic dexterity. This place had no fears for him now. He was no longer a ten-year-old boy. He was in control of his own life now.

The docks swarmed with life in some places, and were deserted in others. Beggars, skulking miscreants, cripples, watching the seamen aboard the ships with bitter, envious eyes. From the corner of his eye he caught a quick movement, the whisk of a rat slipping from crevice to crevice. Hugo repressed a shudder. He was unafraid of most things, but a rat was one creature he detested, with an intensity he had never been able to overcome. He still bore scars of the rat bites he had received as a boy.

He reached a large warehouse and entered it, nodding familiarly to the man guarding the entrance.

He ascended a flight of stairs and entered an office at the top.

A large burly man rose to greet him.

"Mr Devenish, sir, and grand it is to see you. Sit ye down, sit ye down! Why did you not send for me, sir, you know I would have—"

Hugo took the hand that was offered to him and shook it warmly. "Patchett. I'm still a seaman, you know. I like to feel the deck of a ship beneath my feet and get a breath of the sea in my lungs from time to time." He grinned. "Not that this air can be called sea air, mind."

The older man laughed. "No indeed, sir. Filthy stuff, I'll warrant."

Hugo interrupted him. "Not so much of this 'sir' nonsense, if you please. That's all very well when were in some sort of business meeting with others, but this is just you and me, Patchett. I may be the owner of the shipping line now, but I'll not forget that I was once a shivering cabin boy and you were the mate who protected me from that sadistic devil who was captain then."

Captain Patchett waved his hand. "Ah, belay that, laddie. Ye don't need to thank me—ye more than made up for any good turn I did ye. Now, what is it that ye want with me? If it's about that last shipment—"

Hugo raised his hand. "No, no. No problems there.

I am more than satisfied with the business side of things. No, this is…personal."

Captain Patchett's beetling grey eyebrows rose. "Is it indeed, laddie? Then take a seat and you can tell me what you want of me. Can I pour you a drop of something to keep out the cold?" He reached for a bottle of rum and, without waiting for Hugo's response, poured out two beakers of rum and handed one to Hugo.

"To health and fair voyages."

Hugo drank.

Captain Patchett leaned forwards. "Now, laddie, what's the problem?"

"It's about a woman—"

Captain Patchett's meaty fist smote the desk in front of him in triumph. "A woman is it, indeed! And about time, laddie! I've been waiting for the day ye told me ye'd finally decided to wed, and—"

Hugo cut in, coolly. "This woman is my nephew's intended, not my own."

"Oh." Captain Patchett subsided with a disappointed sigh. "Yer nephew. Very well then, tell me what ye need."

"She is a woman of some mystery."

Captain Patchett sniffed and poured them each another tot of rum. "All women are, laddie. All women are."

"She has arrived in England, from some foreign shore—"

"Ah, a foreigner."

"No, an Englishwoman. With her maid, I assume. Young, quite pretty, dark haired, creamy ski—"

"The maid?"

"No, the woman. The maidservant is a woman in her middle thirties, comely enough, but nothing out of the ordinary. The young woman is unquestionably a lady, and a little out of the common way. There is…" Hugo paused, considering how best to describe Miss Singleton "…a, a, oh, I don't know how to put it, but there is something about her that puts her above the common run of young ladies."

Captain Patchett eyed him shrewdly. "Your nephew's intended, you say."

Hugo nodded. "Precisely. She is reputed to be an heiress—"

Captain Patchett raised his eyebrows.

"—but of what, I'm not so certain. The rumour says diamonds, but…"

The old seaman frowned. "If there's brass, it can be traced, laddie. You can't keep a fortune a secret for too long."

Hugo nodded. "I know, but I'm not so very certain that there is a fortune."

"A fortune hunter, begad! After the title, is she?"

Hugo shook his head slowly. "Possibly. I'm told all women covet titles. But to my mind, she shows little encouragement to Thomas. Of course, she could be playing hard-to-get." He shook his head. "To tell the truth, I'm not at all certain what she's after. If she is indeed an heiress, then it all makes sense, but if she isn't, I don't understand what game she's playing."

"Why shouldn't she be an heiress?"

"No reason that I know of, except it's all too much based on rumour for my liking. And the girl herself denies it quite openly…" his eyes narrowed "…only in such a way that you're never quite sure whether she means it or not. I don't know what to make of her—damned if I've ever met such a girl in my life! But my instincts tell me she's playing some deep game."

Captain Patchett nodded wisely. "Ah, well, those instincts of yours have made us both rich, laddie. I'd have to say, if your instincts tell ye to check up on the lass, you listen to 'em."

But Hugo wasn't listening. "She's infuriating! One minute she's pretending she lisps, the next it's as if she never has lisped in her life and why would you ever imagine such a thing! She can ride like a young Amazon, and has the coolest head in a crisis. And she dances like thistledown with me, and yet I've seen her half cripple an old man with her clumsiness on the dance floor."

Captain Patchett sat back in his chair, grinning broadly. "Well, well, well. Ahh, laddie, I never thought I'd see that day."

Hugo eyed that grin. It had a distinctly annoying quality. "What do you mean by that? I don't see what is so amusing!"

Captain Patchett chuckled. "No, I dare say you don't." He hastily framed his face in a more serious expression. "So, this clumsy young Amazon is your nephew's intended, you say."

Hugo nodded, frowning. "Boy and his mother are determined to marry him to a fortune, and solve all their difficulties. If she does own a diamond mine, then they'll both be out of my hair for good. Which will be a relief to me, I can say."

Captain Patchett nodded. "Yes, laddie. Then you'll be free, won't you?"

Hugo nodded. "Yes, I'll be free." He did not add that he was as sure as could be that the diamond mine was a fraud and that the girl herself was not who she claimed to be. Nor did he intend to mention that he was quite convinced his nephew's intended was an accomplished pickpocket. And that far from this whole wretched business leading to himself being free, he was getting more and more entangled in the whole sorry mess. No, there was certainly no need to explain that. He had a feeling that he'd said too much as it was.

"Very well," said the captain, "what information have you on this girl? Give us her name and an approximate date of arrival, for a start. I'll put out the word and we should be able to find out when she arrived in England and on which ship. Any idea where she hailed from?"

Hugo shook his head. "She is very evasive on the subject, which only adds to my suspicion, but there are some who say she came from New South Wales."

The grizzled old seaman pursed his lips. "No good ever came out of New South Wales, I'll warrant! But there's no shortage of men who've come from there. There's a vessel in just yesterday. They'll have fresh news. Any heiress—in fact, any pretty young girl— will be news in that benighted hole. If they've seen her, they'll talk of her, count on it."

"And she mentioned India once. Jaipur."

The old man made a note. "That's more like. India is the place for fortunes and diamonds."

"And I've seen her wear an embroidered jacket and silver jewellery of the sort that I'm sure is only found in the Spanish colonies of America," added Hugo gloomily. "Of course, she could have purchased them from a trader, or been sent them as a gift…"

Captain Patchett refilled his beaker. "I begin to see the extent of the problem, laddie. She could have come from anywhere, could she not?"

"She could."

"Ah, well, if she arrived on a ship—and she must have—we'll find her eventually, mark my words. The seafront is a place where people hear much and talk little—unless it's to the right people. And laddie, I'm one of the right people. I'll find out about yer girl for you."

"My nephew's girl," Hugo corrected him.

Captain Patchett grinned. "To be sure, yer nephew's girl."

"What do you mean, you have agreed you will not suit?" snapped Lady Norwood. "Have you taken leave of your senses, Thomas?"

Thomas shrugged. "Well, she says she does not care for m—"

"What on earth does it matter whether the girl cares for you or not? Of *course* she doesn't care for you, but that doesn't matter a snap!" She snapped her long, elegant fingers and glared in frustration at her son. "Does not care for you, indeed! Pray, what has *that* to do with anything? We are not discussing some vulgar middle-class emotional muddle here, we are talking about something far more important— marriage! I did not care for your father above half, but did that stop me from wedding him? No! Of course not. And this girl is an *heiress*!"

Thomas pulled a face. "But she says she does not care for me."

Amelia sighed gustily and flung her reticule down on a side table. "Well, there you are, then! That is your cue, you foolish boy! Since the chit is obviously mired in nonsensical missish notions of love, you must *make* her care for you, chuckle-head! Woo her, Thomas! Charm her, flatter her, coax and listen and agree with her, and before long she will care for you—enough to agree to wed you, at least—and *that* is what is important here!"

Thomas hunched a shoulder, looking mulish. "To tell you the truth, I had as leifer not wed—"

His mother snorted. "And who will pay our—your debts, pray?"

Thomas reddened. "Er…"

"Oh, wonderful! 'Er' indeed." Amelia tittered furiously. "Well, 'er' will butter no parsnips, my son, and 'er' will no doubt be a marvellous comfort to you when we are all dragged off in chains to debtors prison, and 'er' will—" She broke off as her butler opened the door to announce a visitor. "Oh, Hugo—about time! I sent for you hours ago! What has kept you this age? Will you talk some sense into this foolish son of mine! I cannot believe the folly he has committed! I have been unable to reason with him and refuse to utter another word on the matter! I wash my hands of him!" She flounced over to the fireplace and stood there glaring at the two men.

"Good afternoon, Amelia, Thomas." Hugo strolled into the room, nodded to his glowering sister-in-law and her sulky-faced son, and seated himself easily on a *chaise-longue*, quite as if he was unaware of the atmosphere in the room. Crossing one long leg over the other, he leaned back and said, "Well, Thomas, you had better tell me what it is that has so upset your mother?"

Thomas scowled. "It is not as if it is my fault. I cannot help what others think."

"Hah! If you would only show some resolution—" began Amelia furiously.

Hugo held up his hand. "Did you not say you would not utter another word on the matter, Amelia?"

"Oh, but—"

Hugo glanced coolly across at her and she subsided with a squeak of annoyance.

"Thomas?"

Thomas gave a great gusty sigh and said in a rush, "Miss Singleton has informed me that she does not care for me and that she wished me to stop paying her attention. She says it was causing people to talk. But, Mama—"

Hugo's eyebrows had risen. "She said that, did she? How very, very interesting."

There was a short silence.

"Well, is that all you can say about the matter?" said Amelia waspishly. "'How very, *very* interesting?' Oh, what a great help that is, to be sure! Men! Such useless creatures!"

Hugo glanced at her, faint amusement evident. "Oh, some of us have our uses, I seem to recollect.

But as to Thomas's break with Miss Singleton, I congratulate you, Thomas."

Thomas gaped.

His mother spluttered with indignation. "Congratulate? You congratulate him? And what of his loss of the diamond mine, pray tell? Do you congratulate him for whistling a fortune in diamonds down the wind? Oh! How is Thomas ever to prosper if he does not marry the girl? Heiresses do not grow on trees, you know, Hugo!"

"No, they do not. Nor do diamond mines grow in New South Wales, I am very sure of that. Of if they did, you may be very sure there would have been a great public outcry long before this."

"What are you saying? The mine is a hoax?"

Hugo nodded. "I believe so."

"With what evidence?"

"None but my own common sense."

"Hah!" exclaimed Amelia scornfully. "And yet half of London apparently does not have the same common sense."

Hugo inclined his head. "Apparently not. Half of London chooses to believe in whispered reports of a diamond mine in a convict settlement—with no evidence whatsoever."

"Hmph!" Amelia flounced back to her seat.

"I have been investigating the girl's background, and not only have my sources never heard of diamonds in New South Wales, but I can discover no record of any Miss Singleton arriving in the country."

"Well, what is that to us? I am sure that any number of people enter and leave this country without others knowing about it."

Hugo made a steeple out of his fingers. "Generally they are the sort of people who have something to hide."

Amelia digested that.

"But if Miss Singleton had anything to hide," said Thomas, "why would she enter society in the way she has?"

"Why indeed?" said Hugo. "That is what I intend to find out."

"But if the girl has given Thomas his *congé*, then why bother investigating her any further—unless you mean Thomas to renew his suit?" Amelia sat forward eagerly. "That is it, isn't it? You mean Thomas to court the girl after all. There is a fortune! There must be! You have found out something, haven't you, Hugo?"

Hugo shrugged. "It is a matter of complete indifference to me who Thomas courts."

Thomas sat up. "Do you mean that?"

Hugo eyed his nephew thoughtfully. "A man must choose his wife for himself. It has naught to do with anyone else."

Thomas turned to his mother triumphantly. "You see, Mama!"

But his mother was watching Hugo with eyes narrowed in suspicion. "You want those diamonds for yourself! It's plain as the nose on your face!"

Hugo rolled his eyes. "Do not be ridiculous, Amelia. I told you, there are no—"

"It's my belief you plan to marry the girl yourself!" continued Amelia, with growing fury. "How very typical! It's your wretched cit blood! You cannot bear to see anyone in this family except yourself get a fortune! You would even cut your own nephew out for it!"

Hugo glared at her. "Oh, don't be so stupid! If that girl owns a diamond mine, I'll eat my hat! There is no question of cutting Thomas out."

"But—"

"You know I have no interest in marriage."

"Then why are you so interested in the girl? It is not like you to show such uncommon interest in young ladies of the *ton*!"

Hugo stiffened and replied coldly, "I am merely interested in the puzzle the girl presents. I do not like to be hoodwinked, that is all."

"Pah!" snorted Amelia inelegantly. "I do not believe a word of it!"

Chapter Six

"Miss Kit?"

"Hmm? Yes, Maggie?" Kit was busy fashioning a new reticule to match a green double-silk pelisse decorated with an exotic design in black and silver beads. She planned to make a matching reticule and hat from black satin, embroidered with green ribbon, black beads and silver thread.

"There's been people asking questions."

Kit glanced up, then put down her sewing. "People? What people?"

Maggie's brow furrowed. "I don't rightly know. Men, mostly. Askin' some of the others below stairs questions about you and me."

"Men? What sort of questions?"

Maggie shook her head grimly. "About when we arrived in London, how, and where we lived before that."

Kit looked worried. "I don't like the sound of that. Who can find such stuff of interest?"

Maggie snorted. "One fellow even had the cheek to accost me the other day! Came up beside me as I was walking to the market. Me! I'm a decent woman and so I told him. I don't talk to strange men and I don't gossip with no one, let alone a nosy great jackanapes!" She tossed her head indignantly at the memory.

Kit watched the gesture and smiled to herself. "Was he handsome, this jackanapes?"

Maggie sniffed.

Kit's lips twitched. He was handsome. "Big fellow, was he?" Maggie had ever an eye for a big man, respectable to the core though she was.

Maggie sniffed again. "Big clumsy ox. Nearly tipped my shopping out! Tried to carry me basket! As if I was the feeble sort. Or feeble-minded. These Londoners—no more trustworthy than those scoundrels in India."

Oho, thought Kit. The man who had accosted Maggie on her way to the market had apparently been allowed to escort her home again, if he'd attempted to carry her full basket. How very interesting. Maggie was so strait-laced, she'd never encouraged a man before—not even several very respectable Englishmen they'd met abroad. On the other hand, she'd never seen Maggie in England before. Perhaps her rigid standards had relaxed a little in her home environment.

"Offering to carry your basket? He sounds like a gentlemanly fellow to me."

Maggie sniffed for the third time. "Gentlemanly, my foot! All he wanted was to pump me for information about you, Miss Kit. Oh, he wasn't as obvious as some of those others, but it was 'Oh, Miss Bone, are you newly come to London?' and 'Oh, do I detect a hint of an accent in your voice, Miss Bone, some fascinating, exotic country no doubt?'" She snorted. "I soon put him right!" Fascinatin' exotic accent, indeed! Nothing but good honest Yorkshire in my voice, and so I told him—the cheek!"

Kit giggled.

Maggie glared at her. "It is not funny, Miss Kit. He was well out of order, speaking to a respectable woman without a proper introduction. The jackanapes! And, what's more…" she added awfully "…he had the cheek to ask me when my half-day was!"

"And did you tell him?" Kit enquired mischievously.

Maggie bridled, tossed her head and did not deign to reply. She gave Kit a withering look of great dignity and stalked from the room.

The manner of her exit set up wild speculation in Kit's mind. Clearly her intensely proper maid had not directly informed her inquisitive swain of her half-day, but her heightened colour and something in the stiffness of her carriage made Kit suspect that when Maggie's half-day came, Maggie would not be too surprised if the big clumsy jackanapes would be waiting at the kitchen door.

Perhaps, for the first time in her life, starchy, proper, middle-aged Maggie Bone had acquired a beau. Kit certainly hoped so. Maggie had given up so much for Kit's sake; she should not miss out on the chance of love, too.

Kit returned to her sewing. Despite her delight in this new development in Maggie's life, the thought that people were questioning the servants about her could only be unsettling. She wondered who was behind it, for someone most certainly was. Maggie was no fool. And poor people did not generally go to extreme lengths to satisfy curiosity about strangers unless they were paid to.

And though she racked her brains to think of who might be investigating her, she could not come up with any obvious suspect. It could not be Mr Hugo Devenish. He had no reason to be making any further enquiries about her; she had broken all connection with his nephew. So who could it be?

Kit felt very uneasy. It was one thing to know who was pursuing you; it was another to have an unknown adversary. Or possibly several.

This task her father had set was becoming increasingly fraught with difficulties. She thought of the six compartments in the false bottom of the camphor wood trunk which sat upstairs in the bottom of her wardrobe. Two compartments were filled already; the two smallest ones, to be sure, but still…

If all went to plan, the third small compartment would be filled tonight—she'd done all the groundwork for it—and then she would be halfway there. Halfway to freedom.

The last three compartments were much larger and consequently more difficult to fill, but she refused to dwell on that. One thing at a time.

Mr Devenish stood in the shadows, cursing himself silently. It was but a short distance from the clubs in St James to his home. He had no business being in this neighbourhood at all.

It was not a good sign, he told himself. He was not a green youth in the throes of his first calf-love. It was pathetic for a grown man to behave like this. He'd not stood mooning outside a woman's house since...well, and that had been a long time ago and it had ended in his complete and utter humiliation.

His back itched as if his very skin could remember. It probably could, he thought. One did not easily forget a public horsewhipping.

He'd been twenty-two, a romantic youth, just returned to his homeland after a dozen years of virtual exile. And while he'd known quite a lot about barmaids and dockside whores and sailors' wives, he'd never met a true English lady.

He'd come home, with money in his pocket for the first time ever—the ship he'd bought with his mother's legacy had come in with a rich cargo. And though his so-called family hadn't welcomed him, others of the *ton* certainly had no trouble accepting the legitimate offspring of a mill-owner's daughter and an English lord. Not when he had money in his pocket.

Hugo sighed mentally over his younger self. What a fool he'd been. He'd been prepared for cruelty, corruption and vice. He'd seen and experienced it in almost every port in the world. He'd been educated in a rough, hard, ruthless, school—the life of a seaman. And he'd survived, as tough and hard and ruthless as the rest of the world he'd lived in since he was ten. Hugo Devenish was no pigeon to be plucked, no victim for whore, pickpocket or cutthroat.

But all his hard-won defences had dropped at the sight of a true English lady. A respectable English married lady. She had effortlessly peeled away the calloused outer layer and found the needy boy within, the boy who yearned for a gentle touch, who'd been snatched from his home unprepared and still wanted to believe in love. That poor stupid boy had had no defense against gentility and tenderness and kind words.

Ahh, but she'd been a beauty, so refined and delicate and sweet. He'd never felt anything as soft as her hands, as her skin, so pale, so smooth, so fine. She was everything he'd never known—clean, pure, precious, vulnerable. And he'd fallen for her tales of her husband's cruelty, and had conceived a desperate, hopeless plan to rescue her.

What a gullible fool he had been! The older Hugo recalled his youthful self with a sense of incredulity and scorn.

It had been a game, of course. She'd played it often. The tender refinement concealed the soul of a harpy—she'd led him by the nose into her dainty trap and then the enraged husband had burst in on them with his grooms, and they'd held him down and horsewhipped him, out in the street, in full view of his wife and the world.

And she'd laughed and taunted him. And when it was all over, the husband had carried her up to bed, laughing, while Hugo was left out in the street, to crawl away as best he could, bleeding. With his soul more thoroughly flayed than his skin ever could be.

It was the last time he'd had anything to do with so-called respectable women of the *ton*.

Until now.

The situation was in no sense similar, he thought, staring at the Singleton house. He was not mooning after a woman of the *ton*. He was investigating one. There was a great deal of difference.

He'd spent the evening visiting several clubs, ostensibly to play a few hands of cards, and take a drink or two in convivial masculine company. In reality, his intention had been to gather as much information, by dint of discreet, apparently casual questioning, about the elusive and mysterious brother of Miss Rose Singleton, who may or may not, according to various conflicting stories, have been the father of Miss Catherine Singleton.

He had learned much. And nothing. The stories conflicted too greatly. James Singleton had died in Italy around twenty-two years ago. No, he'd gone adventuring, "somewhere out east".

Few seemed to care, one way or the other. It became clear to him, as the night progressed, that the only people likely to know the full facts about James Singleton, would be the very people who were so unforthcoming about it—his so-called daughter and his sister.

He'd spoken to several of Singleton's friends, so far. At one time, they'd been an inseparable group. Then one had gone abroad—to the Indies—at much the same time as Singleton. Possibly those who thought Singleton had gone east had mixed the two up. The remaining six were in England, but had little to do with each other. He'd spoken to three so far— Pickford, Pennington and Brackbourne—without having learned a single useful fact. Each man, though perfectly affable in general, had been curiously reticent on the subject of James Singleton.

Hugo was increasingly intrigued. Not to mention frustrated.

And now, here he was, on his way from Pall Mall, to his home in Berkeley Square, and somehow he had ended up outside a certain house in Dorset Street—having passed his own house to get there! It was the brandy, of course. Quite an inferior sort.

He stood and stared up at the dark façade of the house. The bedrooms would be at the back, he supposed. It was quite ridiculous to imagine he would learn anything by simply standing in the street and staring at the house. The Misses Singleton would be well abed at this hour. It wanted but an hour or so until dawn.

It was a quiet, still night. In the distance he could hear the faint rumble of wheels on cobblestones, the calling of a watchman, the howling of a dog. A horse clip-clopped down a nearby street and disappeared into the alleyway which ran along the back of the Dorset street houses. And stopped.

Mr Devenish frowned. It sounded like the horse had pulled up behind the Singleton residence.

He walked around the corner and down the side, his footsteps becoming more stealthy as he reached the back lane. Cautiously he pressed his body against a wall and peered around the corner of the building, down the lane. He was just in time to see a familiar shape slip from the animal's back and toss the reins to a boy, waiting in the shadows. The man wore loose baggy pants and a long overtunic in a dark shade. A narrow braid hung down his back.

The Chinaman!

Without hesitation the Chinaman slipped though a door in the high wall which surrounded the house.

Hugo realised he was about to witness a burglary. And though the man had hurt no one so far in his criminal career—this time it was Miss Singleton who was in danger!

"Hey, you! Stop, thief!" he shouted and, brushing past the startled boy still holding the horse's reins, he burst through the side gate after the Chinaman.

He spotted him at once, still in the small courtyard, beside the back door. The man backed away, his face in shadow.

"You are trapped now, fellow," said Hugo. "Give yourself up."

The Chinaman did not respond.

"I don't want to hurt you, but I will if I must," said Hugo clearly, wondering whether the scoundrel understood English.

The man shifted slightly to the side, a wary, defensive move, and Hugo moved in response. A shaft of light hit him, and Hugo saw that like their previous encounter, his face was wrapped in some sort of scarf. He recalled that though the fellow was small and light, he'd proven confoundedly tricky.

Hugo moved forward, lightly, on the balls of his feet, fists at the ready, wondering whether the fellow had a knife. Most of the Chinese he'd known carried several. Hell! Why hadn't he taken his sword-stick tonight, or a pistol, or even his usual knife in the boot? That's what civilisation did—lulled you into a false sense of security!

"Come on, my bucko! We have a score to settle, you and I." Hugo moved lightly, readying his body for action, not taking his eye off his opponent. "I'm ready for you this time. It's not Queensberry rules here, you know. I'm no gentleman schooled at Jackson's—I learned to fight on the quays of Marseilles and the back streets of Tangiers." Ridiculous, Hugo thought, talking to a fellow who didn't seem to understand a word he said. The brandy.

Suddenly the Chinese moved forward in a rush, then darted sideways in a feint. Hugo dived forward to catch him, but the small man jumped back and then seemed to roll forward almost under Hugo's feet. The unexpected double manoeuvre nearly knocked him over, but he managed to keep his balance.

"No, don't!" the Chinese suddenly shouted in an odd, light voice.

Thud! The blow came from behind him—some sort of club or cudgel. It hit him hard on the side of the head, a glancing blow, and Hugo staggered under its impact. He lurched forward dizzily, cursing himself for forgetting the boy holding the reins of the horse.

Oddly, the Chinese didn't move. He just stood and

stared at Hugo in what Hugo almost thought might be concern.

Pretending worse dizziness than he felt, Hugo staggered forward and suddenly pounced, grabbing his arms and knocking the Chinese to the ground. Once again, he smelt the distinctive scent of sandalwood and incense.

"Aiee-ya!" That exclamation again. The man kicked back and caught Hugo hard on the ankles, knocking one foot from under him. The Chinaman rolled away and was just scrambling to his feet when Hugo leapt again.

"Aiee-ya!"

Hugo grabbed him by the neck. "I have you now, you scoundrel! Give up."

The man seemed to sag with defeat. He allowed Hugo to pull him slowly towards him, then suddenly he twisted and kicked out, hitting Hugo in the groin.

Hugo doubled over in instant agony and sank to the cobblestones. Waves of pain and nausea swamped him and Hugo gradually became aware of one thing. There was no sign of the Chinaman. He could hear a horse galloping away.

"The devil!" He groaned and tried to straighten his pain-racked body. His head ached from the brandy and the blow the boy had fetched with his cudgel. His entire lower body throbbed with agony. His ego was severely bruised also—to be felled by a boy and a very small man.

Hugo groaned again. He had to stand up before someone came from the house to investigate the noise. He had no desire to be caught in such an undignified position, bent double, crouched on the ground at the back of the house of a respectable spinster of the *ton*! He wanted to remove himself from the scene altogether.

He probably ought to inform the Misses Singleton that they'd been targets of the notorious Chinese Burglar, but if he did they would be asking questions. Embarrassing questions. They'd be worried about the state he was in. They might even try to minister to his injuries—some ladies did that, he understood.

And he was not going to explain how he'd been bested for the second time by a man half his size.

The blackguard had been chased off. He would not return tonight. Hugo would call on the Misses Singleton in the morning, and inform them of the danger. He would be more up to the task after a glass of the best French brandy, a bath and a good sleep.

"Have you seen Maggie?" asked Kit, poking her head into the kitchen. "I have rung for her several times and she has not answered."

"No, Miss Kit. I am sure I wouldn't know where Bone is," said the cook with formal coolness. Not all of the servants approved Kit's habit of calling Maggie by her first name. She also seemed slightly affronted at the intrusion of Kit into "downstairs" territory.

Kit had little patience with such pretension, but she hid her irritation. Maggie was her friend as well as her maid. Cook could have no idea of the circumstances in which she had Maggie had met and lived. They'd been of such an extreme nature, there was no place for formality and the division between servant and mistress. But it was the custom here for servants to be addressed by their surnames, and she was used to adapting, more or less, to odd customs.

"And what about you, Higgins?" she addressed the kitchen maid. "Do you know where my maid has gone?"

The kitchen maid glanced wildly at the outside door. "I dunno, miss. I, er, I think she popped out for a minute, to, um, fetch something. You want me to run and get her, miss?"

Kit noted the swift minatory scowl the maid received from the cook. The girl blushed and hung her head, avoiding the eyes of both. She knew something.

There was some mystery here.

"No," she said slowly. "I am sure Maggie will return when she has finished her errand. Will you please let her know I was looking for her and ask her to come upstairs at once?"

"Yes, miss."

Kit walked thoughtfully back upstairs. It was not like Maggie to go off without saying anything while Kit was in the house. It was not as if Kit kept her on the sort of close leash that most other servants were; Maggie was free to come and go as she pleased. Only, it was not like her to go out and not say a word. Particularly when she knew Kit had planned to finish the alteration of the gaucho jacket this morning. She was planning to wear it out this afternoon, and she needed Maggie to pin the hem at the back for her.

"Excuse me, Miss Kit." The butler, Porton, interrupted her thoughts. "Miss Singleton's compliments, miss, but would you please step down to the drawing room? The first of the morning visitors have started to arrive."

"Oh, yes, Porton. Of course. Is it that time already?" said Kit. The gaucho jacket would have to wait. She followed Porton downstairs to the drawing room, where two ladies had already arrived.

"Yes, Mr Devenish. The Misses Singleton are indeed at home to you. Please step this way."

Hugo followed the butler, taking in his surroundings as he did so. Not a wealthy home, but well enough. Furnished for comfort as much as style, but a little over-fussy for his taste. He had a seaman's dislike of clutter, and this house abounded in it—

little statuettes, china plates, amateurishly hand-painted, lace mats and embroidered cloths, little arrangements of dried grasses and flowers, vases, bottles, carvings, brassware, silver bibelots—scarcely a surface was bare.

The butler opened a door. "Mr Devenish."

Hugo entered and instantly regretted coming. At this early hour—for a so-called morning visit, that is—he had not expected to find anyone other than the Misses Singleton present, but in fact there were four other ladies as well. At the butler's announcement the room fell abruptly silent.

Hugo took a deep breath and greeted the ladies. Miss Singleton rose to greet him and made the necessary introductions. After a great deal of bowing and exchanging of greetings he was finally able to sit down, a little stiffly, feeling that he'd walked into a zoo—as the main exhibit.

One of the ladies, a matron clad in deepest purple, returned to finishing the tale she'd been telling when he arrived, and Hugo took the opportunity to inspect Miss Catherine Singleton in her home environment.

She was examining him with equal intensity, he realised with interest. Unaware of his observation, her eyes skimmed him from head to foot, almost anxiously, but then their eyes met. Her look of faint trepidation vanished instantly and was replaced by a bright inquiring glance, as if to ask him what he was thinking.

He responded with a bland look. She raised an eyebrow, turned pointedly to the speaker and fixed the bright interested gaze on her.

Hugo's lips twitched. He was coming to learn and appreciate some of her mannerisms. The gaze directed at the matronly lady was in fact a reprimand to himself, for daring to appear to imagine she might find anything about him of interest.

He set himself to wait until the other ladies had taken themselves off; he did not want to spread alarm unnecessarily.

It was more than half an hour before the last of the ladies made their departure, their obvious curiosity at Mr Devenish's visit having made them linger considerably longer than the usual morning visit. The moment the last lady left, he leaned forward.

"Now, Miss Singleton," he said, addressing Miss Rose, but including Miss Catherine Singleton in his glance, "I have some news which you may find disquieting."

The two ladies glanced curiously at each other. "Pray, do not keep us in suspense, Mr Devenish."

"I had…occasion to be passing this house last night." He ignored the way Miss Catherine raised her brows, a little pointedly, he thought. "And I noticed something suspicious occurring around the back."

"I see," said Miss Catherine affably. "You not only had…*occasion* to be outside our house, you had occasion to walk down our back alley too. How very odd. Is it not extremely dirty there? Can I ask why you were—"

"Hush, Kit," hissed Miss Rose Singleton.

Ahh, he thought. She was called Kit, not Catherine. It suited her much better. Kit.

"Go on, Mr Devenish," said Miss Rose encouragingly.

"To cut a long story short," he said with dignity, "I disturbed the blackguard known as the Chinese Burglar! He was about to break into your home."

Both ladies gasped in surprise.

"The Chinese Burglar! But how—?"

"Why did you not warn us? Did you summon the Watch?"

Hugo felt once again that his collar was a little too tight. "Er, no. I… There was a scuffle."

"Do you mean to say you vanquished him, Mr Devenish? How very brave you are, indeed!" said Kit admiringly.

"No. He…got away—ran off—rode off—on horseback, to be precise."

"Oh!" Kit Singleton sat back, disappointed. "You let him get away," she said reproachfully.

"Yes. Sorry."

Miss Rose Singleton was much more concerned.

"Oh, Mr Devenish, you could have been hurt, murdered! I believe those foreign criminals can be frightfully dangerous—"

"Unlike nice safe English criminals," interpolated Kit irrepressibly.

"Hush, Kit. You know what I mean. Mr Devenish could have been hurt."

Kit leaned forward, suddenly serious. "And were you hurt, sir?"

Mr Devenish hoped the sensation he was experiencing did not mean he was turning bright red. He was not going to explain to two maiden ladies just where the thief had managed to kick him to put him so effectively out of action.

"Not at all. A couple of scrapes and bruises, nothing at all."

Kit sat back. "I would have thought a man of your size could have vanquished a Chinaman," she said. "I believe them to be a small, slight people."

"He was very quick," said Mr Devenish stiffly.

"And how did you know it was the Chinese Burglar? Did you see his face?"

"No, I saw his long black pigtail."

"You saw his pigtail?"

"It bounced against his back as he ran away."

She sat very still for a moment, then suddenly smiled at him warmly. "Well, even so, it was very brave of you to tackle the fellow and I join my aunt in thanking you."

"Yes, yes, of course, but, Kit, you have not thought what this means," said Rose anxiously. "It means the burglar was after something in this house."

"My thoughts exactly," said Hugo.

There was a short silence.

"And he will be back!" exclaimed Rose. "Oh, Heavens! What shall we do?"

The door opened suddenly. "Mrs Groombridge," said the butler and ushered in another lady visitor.

Mrs Groombridge was big with news. No sooner had the polite greetings and pleasantries been disposed of than she launched into her story.

"Have you heard? He struck again last night! Who? The Chinese Burglar, of course! Colonel Grantley's house!"

After the initial outcry of surprise and amazement, it finally became clear: the Chinese Burglar had broken into the home of a gentleman called Colonel Grantley and stolen the famous Eyes of India.

"The Eyes of India?" asked Kit curiously. "What on earth are the Eyes of India?"

"Oh, my dear—of course, you are newly come to London, but they are very famous! They are jewels, my dear, the most fabulous emeralds—simply magnificent! I would give my eye teeth to own them— or I would have." She tittered. "There is a necklace, a tiara, one or perhaps two bracelets, earrings and several rings. Poor Colonel Grantley is devastated. And Mrs Grantley—inconsolable, poor dear."

"But how do they know it was the same burglar who robbed the other places?" asked Kit.

"Oh, my dear, haven't you heard? He left behind another sheet of paper, covered in that outlandish writing—all bird scratches, it looks to me. Quite pretty, but utterly incomprehensible."

"If you are not Chinese, that is," said Kit.

Mrs Groombridge looked at her hard as if suspecting mockery, but she could see none, so she decided to laugh instead.

"And does anyone know what the writing says?" asked Rose.

Mrs Groombridge nodded. "Quite meaningless, apparently. It is just pages of poetry or some such—torn from the same book."

"I did not know the Chinese had books," commented Kit. "I thought they only used scrolls."

Mrs Groombridge shrugged. "Well, I have no idea about that, but I can tell you, my husband has hired extra guards—we cannot be too careful, if there is a gang of foreign thieves about! I cannot imagine how the fellow got past the Watch! Disgraceful, that's what it is!"

They conversed a little more, but it was soon apparent that Mrs Groombridge knew very little more than the barest facts of the robbery.

She soon rose. "Oh, well, I must be off. So delightful to meet you, Mr Devenish, goodbye, dear Miss

Singleton and Miss Catherine. So many calls, so little time," and she bustled out.

The three inhabitants of the drawing room looked at each other in silence.

"Do you suppose," said Kit, "that having been foiled from his burglary here, he made off to Colonel Grantley's house?"

Mr Devenish looked thoughtful. "No," he said. "I don't."

"No," agreed Kit. "It is stretching credulity too far for him to be disturbed at a house which has few treasures and then just happen across a fabulous emerald set." She fixed him with a look. "Then what do you think he was doing here? It is a great mystery, do you not think so?"

"Yes," said Mr Devenish meditatively. "It is a mystery."

"Perhaps he was hiding the jewels. Or passing them to a confederate," suggested Rose.

"Oh, Aunt Rose, what a clever notion," agreed Kit instantly. "That's what it must have been. To think, our back alley used as a meeting place for a desperate gang of foreign thieves. How very exciting."

Just then three more ladies arrived and, feeling their inquisitive gazes boring into him, Hugo decided he could take no more of the company of respectable *ton*nish females. He left them speculating over the mystery of the Chinese Burglar.

* * *

"I have come to a decision," said Thomas, Lord Norwood. He cleared his throat awkwardly.

Hugo felt an odd tension steal into his body. He'd been feeling on edge ever since his butler had announced his nephew's visit. His nephew had never visited him before, not without his mother. Hugo raised an eyebrow in cold enquiry.

"I have—" Thomas broke off and ran his finger around his collar. "I have decided to take a bride."

"Indeed?" Hugo's voice was freezing. "I gather you have overcome all the dictates of common sense and finally proposed to the girl."

"Yes," croaked Thomas defiantly. "I am a man after all, and I make my own decisions. And that is why I have come to you—"

"And did she accept you?" Hugo forced his fingers to unclench as he waited for his nephew's answer.

Thomas blinked. "Of course she did. We are in love."

"In love!" Hugo's voice was scathing. "In love with her inheritance, more like!"

Thomas blinked. "But she has no inheritance."

"Yes, I told you so!"

"But how did you know? I have told nobody about it. Even my mother does not know."

Hugo frowned. "What the devil do you mean, even your mother doesn't know! She has been nagging you to this point for weeks!"

"But she hasn't. She wanted me to marry Miss Singleton."

Hugo felt a sudden lightness in the region of his heart. "And you are not marrying Miss Singleton?"

"No. It is Miss Lutens that I am now betrothed to. Miss Singleton introduced us. Only it is a secret."

Hugo blinked. He did not in the least care what his nephew did, as long as he didn't marry Miss Singleton. "A secret? Why?"

Thomas drew himself up with dignity. "I will not marry Libby—Miss Lutens—while I am encumbered by debt." He ran his finger around his tight collar again. "I have come to ask you if you would be so good as to teach me how to go on in business."

Hugo stared. "You don't care that you may be subjected to slurs about being in trade? You will, you know, and it can hurt."

Thomas shook his head firmly. "My wife and family's future security is more important than any remarks passed by small-minded people." He eyed Hugo warily. "So, Uncle, would you help me to learn how to care for my family?"

Hugo felt a sudden lump in his throat. He could not respond.

Thomas added, "If anyone can do it, you can. You saved our family from financial ruin before; will you not teach me how to prevent it ever happening again?"

Hugo held out his hand. "I will."

His nephew had become a man at last.

And Hugo was a member of a family.

Chapter Seven

"Mr Hugo Devenish."

The butler's announcement caused a flutter of interest among the various ladies gathered in Miss Rose Singleton's front morning room.

"Two visits in two mornings!" hissed one of the ladies.

"He is very rich, I believe," whispered another.

Kit almost giggled as Mr Devenish stared in hastily concealed alarm at the number of ladies in the room, all avidly staring at him; a collection of hungry hens eyeing a large, tasty grain of wheat.

He greeted each lady with correctness, if not ease of manner.

Kit smiled as he forced himself to make small talk. His cold, brusque manner should have been off-putting, but the ladies were not the least put off; they obviously regarded Mr Devenish as quite a catch and the more gruff and glacial his answers, the more effusively they tried to draw him out.

The gushing feminine responses disconcerted him, she noted. The man clearly had no idea of his own attractions. He was looking faintly hunted. It was rather endearing, Kit felt. This overheated morning room, filled with respectable femininity, was the first social situation in which she'd seen him where he wasn't all cold self-assurance.

Mr Devenish glanced across at her. "I actually came—besides wishing to pay my respects, of course—to ask Miss Catherine Singleton if she would do me the honour of accompanying me on a drive in the park," he said. "It is a beautiful day and quite mild. Miss Singleton?"

Absolutely not, thought Kit. She had no intention of being alone with him—even in public—again. He would be given no opportunity to question her again. She opened her mouth to refuse him prettily.

"Of course, Mr Devenish, she would be delighted," Rose Singleton responded. "It is a lovely day, and since I got rid of our antiquated landaulet, she has had little opportunity to go out for drives."

"Oh, but, Aunt, I am not dressed for driving," said Kit instantly.

Rose laughed. "Well, run upstairs, my dear, and change. Mr Devenish will not mind waiting, will you, sir?"

"Not at all," concurred Mr Devenish smoothly, a sardonic gleam in his eye the only indication that he was aware of Kit's reluctance.

"But, er, is it proper?" said Kit desperately.

A room full of ladies tittered.

"I imagine Mr Devenish has his groom with him, and a drive in an open carriage in the public eye is perfectly proper. But I meant you to take your maid with you, of course," explained Rose kindly. "Now, run along dear. Gentlemen do not like to be kept waiting."

Gritting her teeth in a smile, Kit ran along.

She rang for Maggie and began to strip off her muslin round gown. There was no sign of Maggie, so she rang again and, without waiting, started to change into a walking dress in blue with knots of red, black and white ribbon around the hem, cuffs and shoulders. It was a struggle to button the dress herself and she could not reach the last three.

Where on earth was Maggie? Her half-day off was not for several days yet. She was becoming almost unreliable. It was most unlike her.

"Oh, Miss Kit, sorry I'm late." Maggie rushed into the room, looking flushed.

"What kept you?" Kit asked.

Maggie busied herself with the buttons. "There, that's it, all finished. Going out, miss?" she asked, turning Kit around to inspect her.

Kit hastily explained that she and Maggie were going for a drive with Mr Devenish. Maggie's face fell.

"Me too?"

Kit frowned. "Yes. Do you not wish to go? I'm sorry, but I need you to chaperon me."

Maggie glanced at the door indecisively. "Oh, no, it's all right, Miss Kit, my dear," she said, making up her mind. "You need a chaperon and who better than me? I'll...I'll just fetch my coat." She hurried out.

Kit stared after her. Maggie was hurrying downstairs, not up the narrow servants' stair to where her room was. She was behaving almost...furtively. They would have to have a little talk after this drive.

A few minutes later Kit came downstairs, tucking a few stray curls under a blue Turkish cap, embroidered in black with a long silver tassel hanging from the crown. Maggie, looking smart in a grey coat and a plain grey bonnet, was waiting in the hallway, looking flushed again.

Mr Devenish was also waiting in the hall. His eyes ran over Kit and she felt a *frisson* of pleasure, feeling approval in his gaze, and knowing that she looked quite in vogue. Not that she wanted his approval, of course. Still, it was nice to know you looked all right. Especially when you fashioned some of your clothes yourself, with Maggie's assistance.

A smart-looking carriage awaited them in the street. A tall, wooden-faced man in grey and black livery stood by it.

Behind her, Maggie gasped and halted suddenly.

She muttered something and Kit glanced around enquiringly. "What is it? Forgotten something?"

Maggie shook her head grimly and thrust Kit forward, a black look on her face. Puzzled, Kit put out her hand to allow Mr Devenish to help her up the steps. Around the back, Mr Devenish's groom did the same for Maggie.

"Oof!"

Kit looked around.

Mr Devenish's groom was hunched over, gasping for breath like a fish. Maggie, looking like a militant, dignified queen, climbed into the back of the carriage without any assistance from the groom.

"Cheeky jackanapes!" she muttered. She caught Kit's eye and blushed. "Teach him to lie to a decent woman!" She cast a fulminating glare in the direction of the tall groom, whose face was suddenly wiped of all expression.

Kit's heart sank. Maggie's big handsome jackanapes—he must be Mr Devenish's groom. It all fell into place; the flushed and excited look on Maggie's face sometimes, her lateness, the odd times she slipped out. Poor Maggie had thought she'd been meeting her beau, but instead Mr Devenish had set his groom to spying on them.

Oh, there were times when she *hated* this masquerade!

Still, she supposed it was better for Maggie to

know his true purpose now than to discover the deception later.

She cast the groom a withering glance before she turned back in her seat. His expression was still wooden but his eyes were worried; at least he wasn't gloating.

Mr Devenish had observed the exchange. He leapt lightly up beside her, his eyes gleaming with amusement. "An independent creature, your maid." He took the reins in his hands. "She has a very handy left hook, I see."

Kit ignored him. She would very much have liked to box his own ears for setting his groom to spy on them in the first place, but she could not quarrel with him in such a public place.

As she watched, he unconsciously lifted a hand to feel the back of his head, gingerly.

Kit tried to ignore the pang of guilt.

"Let 'em go, Griffin," Mr Devenish said. The groom released the horses heads and then, to Kit's perturbation, climbed nimbly into the back, beside Maggie.

She heard Maggie sniff disparagingly and out of the corner of her eye, saw her move pointedly aside, gathering her skirts away from the groom's contaminating presence. Kit smiled to herself. Maggie was more than capable of dealing with the man. Kit need have no concern for that. It was almost in her to feel sorry for Griffin; he, presumably, had only done his master's bidding.

The horses moved off at a smart pace, tossing their heads a little and shying skittishly at passers-by and blowing leaves.

"They are a little fresh," explained Mr Devenish, "but do not be alarmed. They are very sweet goers."

"I am not in the least alarmed," said Kit coolly.

"Ah, no, you are an intrepid horsewoman, I had forgotten."

Kit bit her lip. He had never officially seen Kit Singleton ride, only a mysterious veiled lady.

"I would not say intrepid," she corrected him, "and since you have never seen me ride, I must only conclude that you say so to be polite. Please do not do so; Spanish coin has never interested me."

He glanced at her deliberately. "Does it not?"

Kit smiled brilliantly. She was not going to bandy words with him about counterfeits. "What a glorious day!" she gushed. "And how blue the sky is. I do not ever recall seeing the sky so blue in London before."

"Yes, and how very white are the clouds, do you not find," he responded affably. "So white they look freshly laundered."

"Yes." His ready response rather took the wind out of Kit's sails. She'd expected him to try and force the topic back to Spanish coin and counterfeits.

"Extremely fluffy. Such white and fluffy clouds I have very rarely seen in London, either." His lips twitched.

Kit glowered at him. She knew when she was being mocked.

"My maid, Maggie, has found the incessant rain a little wearying," she said after a moment.

"Does she now, and she a Yorkshire woman?"

"How do you know that?" Kit flashed accusingly.

He smiled slightly. "We chatted a little in the hall, earlier. Her accent is pure Yorkshire, for all that she has spent years abroad."

"Oh."

"India, was it not?"

Kit parried his question airily. "Oh, I do not know all of Maggie's history. Nor would I *dream* of prying. Some of us respect our servants' independence and privacy." It was as direct an attack on his setting his groom to spy on them as she could manage, given that she could not admit that there was anything unusual or mysterious about her or Maggie's background.

"But you yourself lived in India." It was not a question.

"Why do you say that?"

"So many of the exotic items of clothing you have become noted for are from India. And not generally available here, I think."

Kit shrugged. "I do not know what is available in the London shops. I am more familiar with Paris."

"So, that explains the elegance of your gowns," he

said at once. "And the decidedly up-to-the-moment air of fashion you have."

"Merci du compliment, monsieur," said Kit, cursing her unruly tongue. She should not have mentioned Paris. She wanted him to know nothing, nothing at all, about her background.

And why on earth was he still making his inquiries? she asked herself suddenly. She had sent Thomas away. So why was he still asking her questions? And taking her for drives. Had he not spoken to Thomas yet?

"How did you find the Channel crossing? It is often quite rough."

"Oh, that would not bother me," she said, neither confirming or denying that she had arrived in England via the Channel. "Luckily I am an excellent sailor; I never get seasick. Poor Maggie, however, suffers most vilely from it. How is your nephew, Lord Norwood? I have not seen him in an age, you know."

"He is well."

"Yes," Kit continued chattily. "I have not seen Lord Norwood in such a long time—I have been so busy, you understand, with other matters. He is a pleasant enough boy, but one cannot keep up with every chance acquaintance." There, Mr Watchdog, she thought, that should clarify your precious nephew's position in my life—a chance acquaintance.

They drove on in silence for a short time. He lifted

his hand to touch the back of his head again. She felt another twinge of guilt.

"Is your head very sore?" she said unguardedly.

"My head?" His gaze fixed her, piercing in its intensity. "Why do you ask?"

Recalling she was supposed to know nothing of his bout with the Chinese Burglar, Kit shrugged. "Oh, just that you have several times touched it." It sounded lame, even to her ears. He turned to look at her with a peculiarly intent gaze and, to her horror, she felt a guilty flush beginning.

"Oh," she cried, seeking another distraction. "Do watch out for that dog!"

"As the dog is chained to the lamp-post, I hardly think I am likely to run it over," said Mr Devenish drily.

Kit ignored the sarcasm. "Oh, I did not see the chain. 'Tis just that I am very fond of dogs." She felt her flush intensifying and hoped he would put it down to her error. Drat him! Men did not usually put her out of countenance so easily.

"That must have been difficult for you, growing up abroad. I believe in some Asian countries they are considered a tasty delicacy."

Kit knew that very well, having rescued several hapless creatures from a cruel fate, but his blunt words had provided her with the very opportunity she needed. "Oh, Mr Devenish, how could you ask such a frightful thing," she shrieked genteelly. "To eat dear little doggies! Oh! I feel ill at the thought!" She covered her face with a kerchief. "Horrid, simply horrid," she wailed from time to time, shuddering eloquently, waiting for her flush to die away and struggling, now, with the desire to giggle.

She peeped out at his face once, when his attention was taken with a carter trying to turn his wagon in too narrow a space, and decided he was not the least deceived by her ladylike distress. However, since it would hardly be gentlemanly of him to call her bluff, he had no recourse but to put up with it, as the compressed line of his lips confirmed. He glanced down at her, a penetrating dart of grey, and she hurriedly buried her laughing face in the handkerchief and uttered a small provocative moan of distress.

Mr Devenish's lips thinned even further, she noted. They were rather nice lips. Not that she was the slightest bit interested.

Before long they passed through the gates of Hyde Park and Kit abandoned her genteel horror over the horrid fate of foreign dogs, and sat up to see and be seen, for such was the purpose of driving in Hyde Park.

Hugo shot her a sideways look as she lowered the handkerchief from her face to reveal a pair of bright, interested, clear blue eyes. Not a sign of the distress she'd supposedly been labouring under for the last ten minutes. And with a very suspicious twinkle lurking there.

Women did not usually make fun of him. He was not used to it—but he discovered he quite enjoyed her teasing. His lips twitched at the neat way she'd parried his questions, keeping him well at bay with her faux horror.

To think he'd once thought this girl a simpleton, a dead bore. The little minx had played him like a fish. For a few seconds, he'd actually felt guilty about his brutal dog question. He'd hoped to surprise her into revealing some of her mysterious past, but she'd routed him. And was now laughing up her sleeve at him.

The saucy wench. She needed a good spanking and he itched to provide it. No, what he itched to do was…

No! Curse it! He was *not* thinking about kissing her!

Besides, he did not dally with respectable women of the *ton*. He had no interest in them at all. None!

Not that it would be possible out here in the open, anyway. Particularly with her maid and Griffin seated a few feet behind them.

There was a great deal of murmuring going on there, he suddenly realised. The maidservant was a comely woman, to be sure, but she was buttoned up to the chin and down to the wrists and ankles. Respectable to the eyebrows. She'd tossed her head and given Hugo and his groom the sort of look that women generally reserved for cockroaches and rats. Respectability outraged.

Her disdain had amused Hugo. Women of the servant

class generally looked at both himself and his tall, well-made groom with quite a different expression.

Griffin wasn't the talkative sort, either, yet the rumble of a deep voice coming from the back of the carriage sounded very much as if Griffin, at least, was conversing a great deal indeed. The maidservant, on the other hand, seemed to have some sort of a cold; all Hugo could hear from her was the occasional sniff and once or twice a scornful-sounding snort.

Griffin was wasting his time there.

Hugo allowed his horses to drop from a smart trot to a walk. There was less traffic than in the streets but it was almost as chaotic. The glorious weather had brought a great many people out, even though it was not yet the fashionable hour for promenading.

Miss Singleton had few acquaintances but she seemed as interested in the servant girls out walking with their beaux as in the members of the *ton*. He watched her covertly as she observed the strolling groups and the passing vehicles. Her unfettered enjoyment in the sights stirred something in him. She was full of mysteries and contradictions; unmistakably quality, yet so unpretentious. The paradox fascinated him.

"Your name is Catherine, yet I believe your family call you Kit."

"Yes," responded Kit unexpansively. She wasn't

going to explain any more. She had no idea how much he knew about the true James Singleton and whether or not he'd ever had a daughter. It was lucky that both Kathleen and Catherine could be called Kit for short.

"Yes, I've heard both males and females called Kit. Not that there is anything masculine about you, Miss Singleton," he added gallantly.

Kit kept a straight face. Little did he know.

A light racing curricle shot past, tooled by young bloods and going rather too fast for propriety or for safety. He watched her knuckles whiten as she gripped her reticule in anxiety for their safety. She relaxed as the curricle slowed and then stopped for the driver to greet a friend.

"Do you know one of those young men?" he asked curiously.

"No. But I was worried someone would be hurt. They were going much too fast, didn't you think?"

He shrugged. He was not concerned with strangers. But he found it interesting that she was.

Two ladies trotted past with a groom in attendance. The ladies chattered and laughed self-consciously, watching others watching them. One wore a smartly tailored riding habit, frogged *à la militaire*, with a starched stock. The other wore a sumptuous, pale green velvet habit. A lace jabot frothed down her long, elegant neck. Their hats Hugo privately considered ridiculous; one a mass of ostrich plumes, the other a silly little military-style shako covered with knots and ribbons.

He glanced at the young woman beside him, noting the almost hungry way she examined their outfits.

She ought to have any number of elegant riding habits and yet the one time he'd seen her riding she'd worn an old and faded plain blue outfit. An heiress who was a magnificent horsewoman yet wore a shabby old habit. Another mystery.

"What do you think of those horses?" he asked casually.

She grimaced. "Showy-looking slugs, for the most part, though that pretty little bay mare looks to be a sweet mover."

"If the velvet-clad potato sack on her back ever decided to go faster than a walk."

She laughed. "You are unkind. Not a potato sack, surely. She has a very elegant figure."

"And a most inelegant seat."

She laughed again. "Well, she looks very pretty, nevertheless, and not everyone has been lucky enough to grow up on horseback."

Her comments revealed an excellent knowledge of horses. He wondered where she'd lived, to have "grown up on horseback". He wished she would admit that it was she he'd encountered in the park that morning. Not that he had any doubt of it, but he did want her to admit it to him.

He didn't mind her having secrets, as long as she had no secrets from him. He caught himself up on the thought—Good Lord! What was he thinking? He forced the thought aside and willed himself to pay attention to what she was saying.

"There are some beautiful creatures here, but most of the ladies' mounts have no real spirit, by the look of them. The black one is a trifle sway-backed, don't you think? And I do not approve of people chopping poor horses' tails off—apart from looking undignified, it is not good for the animals."

"You prefer the tails to be left long, then," he murmured, his mind still wishing to explore the mystery of why her secrets disturbed him so much.

"Oh, look, is that not the Princess Esterhazy? The wife of the Austrian Ambassador—that small dark lady in the green walking dress. There, next to the lady with half an ostrich on her head—now that's another thing I much dislike—the excessive use of ostrich feathers. Don't you agree?"

Hugo glanced in the direction she was indicating. "No, it is not the Princess, though it does look a little like her. How old were you when you were taught to ride?"

"I forget. Where were you brought up, Mr Devenish?" she asked brightly. "We always seem to be talking about me, and I know so little about you."

She'd changed the subject again, the little minx.

And if he wasn't to appear boorish, he would have to respond to her question. "I spent the early years of my life in Shropshire," he said unexpansively.

She cocked her head at him in an interested manner. "The early years? Do you mean you moved somewhere else? Or do you mean you were sent to school at an early age? I must say, I think for the most part English boys are sent away to school far too young. Were you sent to school terribly young, Mr Devenish?"

"Not school—I was sent to sea."

"Sea? How very unusual—it is unusual, is it not? I have heard of few other gentlemen's sons sent to sea as youths."

"It is." He paused, as he was forced to make a wide detour around a cluster of people gathered around a carriage. "But as I have told you before, I am not the usual gentleman's son."

"Whatever do you mean? Do you mean your father was not a respectable person?" Though she spoke casually, she stared at him with an unusual degree of intensity, Hugo felt. Why would his father's respectability be of such interest to her?

"Not my father—my mother."

"Oh, and in what—no! I am so very sorry, Mr Devenish. I have been vulgarly intrusive. I should not have enquired into so personal a matter. Do you not think we shall have an early winter this year? Some of the trees are beginning to change colour already."

He smiled at her swift change of subject. "And how many winters have you spent in England? Would you know when the trees are supposed to change colour?"

She laughed. "Oh, ungallant, sir. Indeed, I never have seen an English autumn, but so many people have commented on the early onset of the changing colours that I thought it a safe remark to make. Well, then, tell me about Shropshire—I'm sure that is a perfectly unexceptionable topic of conversation."

He smiled. "Very well, then. Shropshire…let me see. It is one of the north-western Midland counties, close to the border with Wales. Its principal town is Shrewsbury, its principal activities are dairying, agriculture, with some forestry and mining."

She pulled a face. "Oh, sad stuff. I could as soon read a guidebook."

He sighed. "You are a very exacting task-mistress, Miss Singleton. Very well, it is a very pretty place, very green, with rolling hills and woodlands."

"Thank you, Mr Guidebook. It is all very interesting, of course." Her laughing eyes belied that. "What I really want to know about is your home, what you did as a boy, where your special places were, who you played with—that sort of thing. Not stuffy industries and such. I like to collect stories of other people's homes. I never had one, myself, you see, but I used to dream about the one I wished to have and make up stories to myself of how it would be, the furniture, the cosy rugs, a fire at night and a family gath—"

She broke off suddenly.

"You never had a home?"

She gave a hasty, brittle laugh. "Well, of course I did—everyone has a home, don't they?" she said, a little too emphatically, he thought. "I meant an English home. I used to make up stories about England—you know, as an exile does. Of course I had a home!"

He looked at down at her searchingly, but could not read her face. She was staring across the park at some children sailing a tiny boat on the pond. When she'd spoken of a home, there was a note in her voice that caught at his heart...

Had she never had a home of her own? He had no reason to suppose anything of the sort...except for that odd note in her voice...

He suddenly recollected his purpose in asking her for a drive—to learn more about her background. He had not anticipated this. He needed facts, not emotions and stories and nebulous things such as a tone of voice.

"Where was this home of yours?" he asked.

She laughed and shook her finger at him. "No, no! I asked you first. You must tell me of your childhood home and I will add it to my collection. And then, perhaps, I will tell you of mine."

"I cannot tell you very much of that. For most of the day I was under the strict supervision of a rather harsh, unimaginative tutor, who believed Latin and Greek were all a small boy needed to learn, and for the rest of the time, I was left very much to my own devices."

"But surely… What about your family?"

"My mother died when I was six."

"Oh, I'm sorry. Mine too." She laid a soft hand on his knee. "I know what that was like. Did you miss your mother terribly?"

"No," he said. "I never saw her much. She preferred London." Her touch was light, but he was terribly aware of it. He wanted to lay his hand over hers. He did not move. Such things were not done in public.

"Oh. Well, then, tell me about your brother, Lord Norwood's father. Were you very close? What games did you play together?"

Games? Hugo thought of the numerous occasions where his half-brother had thrashed him under the pretext of playing a game. He could not recall a time he had not been aware that his half-brother despised him. His father ascribed any vulnerability or weakness of the child Hugo as evidence, not of his tender years, but of his inferior breeding. His half-brother was a young thug, a bully and he soon discovered that their father was indifferent to anything he might do to the little boy twelve years his junior. He was the heir, the golden one.

"Oh, my half-brother was a good deal older than I, and we had not much to do with each other. He was not interested in the same things I was, so I kept fairly much to myself." Wherever possible.

Hugo was starting to feel uncomfortable, relating such things about his childhood. When spoken of in such bare terms, it sounded too much like a sentimental tragedy-tale for his liking. It was all in the past now, and nothing to be done. It was best to forget such things and get on with life. And her hand was still resting, oh so lightly, on his knee. Yes, the present was so much more pleasant than the past.

"In any case there is little further to be told, for my father died when I was nine, and my half-brother was killed in a hunting accident the following year, leaving a widow and infant son, and, soon afterwards, I left Shropshire."

"Oh, how sad. Where did you go?" She seemed suddenly aware of where her hand rested and snatched it back, looking faintly self-conscious. He pretended not to notice. His knee felt cold, now, where before her hand had warmed him.

He shrugged. "My father and half-brother had left things in a shocking financial mess, and so my sister-in-law returned to her father's home in Kent with her infant son."

"And you went with them, of course."

"No, that's when I was sent to sea."

She looked surprised. "I take it that was a family tradition."

"No."

"Did you want to go to sea?"

An image came to his mind of a ten-year-old boy, clutching a small bundle of belongings and shivering with fear and cold as his brother's servant walked away down the gangplank. "I wasn't consulted."

She frowned thoughtfully. "You were only ten, were you not? It must have been very frightening, to be sent so far from all that was familiar." She touched him again, softly on the arm. She was not aware she was doing it, he realised.

Hugo shrugged. "I became accustomed to it." He did not wish to think about those early terror-filled months; sleeping in the damp, dark hold with rats gnawing at his toes, the cruelties of the harsh captain, the early fears of being made to climb high in the rigging. He did not like to dwell on the past. It made him feel…he was not sure what, but he didn't like it. There was nothing he could do about the past. He preferred to dwell in the present. In the present, he was in control of his life. He glanced at the young woman beside him and his lips quirked. Control?

"I do not understand this habit English people have, of sending their children away to strangers when they are still so young. A little boy of ten still needs to be loved, even if he thinks he is old enough to be a man. I would never send a child of mine away," she said vehemently.

Her words sank deep into some hidden place deep inside him. He swallowed. His chest felt oddly heavy. He did not feel comfortable with such talk. It was too intimate.

"I have a house in Yorkshire now," he said quietly. "A new house; one I built myself."

"What is it like?"

"Quite plain, really. I have no taste for fussy embellishments and knick-knackery." He'd wanted a new house, one with no memories. A house for the future. It was a beautiful house, with spare, elegant lines and he was very proud of it. So why did it suddenly seem a little bleak and empty?

"Oh, what a shame! Nothing at all Egyptian? Not even one tiny crocodile-legged sofa?" she said, in mock sorrow. Her eyes twinkled and he knew at once she had similar taste to his, in that, at least.

He smiled. "You would like Yorkshire, I think. It is quite wild and yet beautiful. A man can feel free there, not closed in, like one feels at times in London. The moors are…a little like being at sea." But he was not here to talk of his home, he recalled. "So now, Miss Singleton, it is your turn to tell me of your home. Where did you live?"

She half-turned on her seat and faced him consideringly. "I think that is enough talk about the past for the moment," she said. "We are becoming a touch melancholy, and it is such a beautiful day. Oh, look, over there is Lady Norwood, your sister-in-law. Should you not stop and greet her?"

Hugo cursed under his breath. He looked in the direction she was indicating and groaned silently. Amelia was standing, staring at them with a peculiarly triumphant look of outrage. Catching him out in the act of stealing Thomas's heiress. And with the heiress's hand on his arm.

Hugo sighed. If they spoke to Amelia now, he could not vouch for her discretion: she had a hasty, impulsive temper. "Yes, I suppose I should stop and greet her, but I…I do not care to keep my horses standing in this fresh wind. Would you mind if we returned to Dorset Street?" A feeble excuse. She would never swallow it. They both knew the horse would take no damage standing a moment of two, even in a freezing wind. And today was a beautiful calm day with a slight pleasant breeze.

"Not at all," agreed Miss Singleton dulcetly. "I would hate to be the cause of injuring such beautiful steppers by keeping them out in such conditions." Her lips quivered, trying not to smile.

Hugo tried not to think about kissing them.

He ought to offer Miss Singleton some excuse for his impoliteness towards his sister-in-law, but he couldn't think, not with her sitting beside him, her eyes brimming with laughter and her lips quivering so temptingly.

He had to get away.

He needed to think. He was in danger of slipping under the spell of the smile in her eyes. And the one trembling on her lips.

His head was aching. He lifted a hand to touch it gingerly, to see whether the bump had gone down at all. She stared at his raised hand and he was suddenly aware of an odd, concerned, almost guilty look on her face.

She was chock-full of contradictions—a teasing minx one moment, a solicitous siren the next.

He didn't know what to believe. Or who: the wistful-voiced girl who yearned for a home, the indignant virago protective of children or the minx who made up stories and teased him.

He was supposed to be investigating her background. Not that there was any need, now that Thomas was wedding Miss Lutens. But he had been seized by a compulsion to know all about her. He finished what he started.

Once or twice something she'd said—or not said— had set off an alert inside him. But then her smile or her scent or a thoughtful look in her eyes had distracted him.

He had to go home and think about Miss Singleton, in an atmosphere of calm; to a place where he was not distracted by laughing blue eyes, warm lips and the faint perfume of rose and vanilla. He needed to concentrate on his investigations.

They swept past Amelia at a brisk trot, bowed politely and headed for the exit. She stood glaring indignantly after them.

"I don't like this, Miss Kit," said Maggie sombrely. "Surely it's gone far enough."

Kit continued changing her clothes. As she discarded each item, she folded it neatly and placed it on a large square of oiled silk which lay on the carpet. "I wish I'd never taken you into my confidence, that's what I wish."

Maggie made a disgusted noise. "Couldn't hardly avoid it, could you, not when I caught you at it." She sniffed disapprovingly. "If I'd know'd what you planned to do, missy…"

Kit tugged the top over her head, wrinkled her nose, then sneezed. "Pah, I hope that hot water is ready. I am in dire need of a bath."

"It is, and it's no use pretending ye didn't hear what I said. I don't approve, miss, and that's final." She turned and made to leave the room.

"Maggie." Kit put out her hand to stop her maid leaving. "This is what Papa trained me for, from the time I was a small girl."

Maggie sniffed disapprovingly.

"You know it is."

"Aye, I know, but knowin' and approvin' are two different matters. It's not right, Miss Kit, ye know it ain't."

Kit's brow furrowed. "Oh, please understand, Maggie. I made a promise. A deathbed promise."

Maggie rolled her eyes. "To a man who never kept a promise in his life!"

"But I am not Papa. I won't break a promise, not to anyone, let alone a dying man. And besides, he was my father. *Honour thy father and thy mother.*' Kit looked at her pleadingly. "What would you have me do?"

"I'd have ye do what's right!"

"But what *is* right?" said Kit softly. "On the one hand I must keep a sacred promise. A promise, what is more, to retrieve my father's—my family's honour."

"But to go and—"

"Yes, I know, but it is not *truly* wrong, Maggie. They stole what was rightfully my father's. Stole it from him wrongfully, out of jealousy and small-mindedness and spite. Men who conspired together and ruined his life. They turned him into the unhappy lonely vagabond he became. They forced him into exile. Don't you see? The flawed and bitter man you knew—it is all because of what they did to him, back then."

Maggie looked troubled, her face crumpled with anxiety. "I dunno, Miss Kit, I dunno. I'm just worried about ye, that's all."

Kit laid her cheek against Maggie's affectionately

and hugged the older woman. "Don't worry about me, Maggie dearest. I can look after myself."

Hugo Devenish lay in bed, trying to get to sleep. He had been trying to sleep for some time now, but his brain would not allow it. Over and over his tired sleepy mind tumbled the thoughts; fragments of the other mornings conversation, of things she had said during today's drive; impressions, wild thoughts, suppositions chased themselves round and round, giving him no peace.

A vision of her laughing blue eyes came to him. Beautiful eyes. Such mischief in them. And yet such sweet concern about his injured head.

Hugo sat up in bed and stared at the faint chink of moonlight coming in between the curtains.

She'd asked, "Is your head very sore?", not "Have you hurt your head?"

She'd known about his injury already. He recalled the odd flash of guilt he'd seen in her expression. Why on earth would she be feeling guilty about it?

Of course, she might have been watching from the window; after all, the encounter—he refused to call it a fight—had taken place at the back of her house.

But if she'd seen what happened, why had she not roused the household and come to his aid? It couldn't be fear—the way she'd coolly dealt with those footpads in the park showed she had courage enough for two. No, she wouldn't have cowered upstairs, watching two men fight. She'd have roused the household. She might even have come herself…especially if she'd seen him fall under a blow. She was clearly soft-hearted towards her fellow creatures; he'd noticed that during their drive.

It was all very perplexing.

What *had* the Chinaman wanted from the Singleton house? Diamonds? But she never wore anything of value—she was famous for it. And her aunt, Rose Singleton, would have little worth stealing: certainly no fabulous jewels, such had been stolen from Pennington, Alcorne and Grantley.

Pennington, Alcorne and Grantley.

Good God! Hugo clutched his sheets in his fists. It was the first time he'd put the three names together in his head. Separately they meant little to him, but together…

He lit the lamp and consulted a small list by his bedside. Pennington, Alcorne and Grantley! Those three names made up almost half the list he had complied of the old friends of the late James Singleton! It could not be a coincidence!

He was right to have suspected some mystery buried in the past. Pennington, Alcorne, Grantley, Marsden, Brackbourne and Pickford—and an unknown Donald Cranmore—all had been boon companions of the young James Singleton. And somehow, something frightful had happened and Donald Cranmore and James Singleton had left England never to return, and no one had ever spoken of it again. The others did not even socialise together now: that was why he had not immediately linked their names.

Only now, James Singleton's daughter had returned. And suddenly a mysterious Chinese burglar had appeared on the London scene. And three of James Singleton's erstwhile friends had been robbed of their greatest treasures.

There had to be a connection. It could not be a co-incidence. There was no doubt at all in his mind; Miss Catherine Singleton was somehow in league with the Chinese burglar. Perhaps she even employed him.

And if Pennington, Alcorne and Grantley had been robbed, then the strongest likelihood was that the next to follow would be Marsden, Brackbourne or Pickford.

Hugo cursed himself. He should have realised the whole much sooner. Good Lord, had he not suspected the wench of stealing his phoenix tie-pin on that very first night?

His suspicions had seemed utterly ludicrous then, the product of an unhinged imagination—sweet young innocents of the *ton* did not steal people's tie-pins. But now…

A sweet young not-so-innocent, who was not only

a pickpocket, but in league with the notorious Chinese Burglar...

It was still very difficult to reconcile what seemed to be logical, with the girl he had come to know. The lisping minx, the mischievous baggage who parried his questions with such gaiety, the sweet-faced girl who had taught Sir Bartlemy Bowles a lesson in manners—not many had noticed that, but he had. And then there was the cool young Amazon who'd beaten off footpads...

A thought occurred to him. Was that incident in the park a coincidence, or a falling out of thieves, perhaps? Neither of her two attackers were Chinese, he was sure of that: they were both far too big.

Hugo groaned and ran his hand through his already dishevelled hair. Was there no end to these plaguey questions?

And if his suspicions were correct, what the devil was he going to do about them—turn her over to Bow Street? See her hanged, or transported? Sent back to New South Wales, the site of the nonsensical diamond mine—in chains?

Never!

Oh, God! What was he to *do*?

He lay back in bed, tortured by the possibilities. Then a thought occurred to him and his lips curled in sudden wry amusement. He'd sworn he'd never again become enamoured of a so-called respectable lady of the *ton*. He thought he'd broken his own rule but it looked like he hadn't. If his speculations were correct, his lady was certainly not respectable. Virtuous, he thought, but not respectable. What a paradox! If he wasn't so furious, he'd laugh.

Chapter Eight

There was a slight stir in several quarters when Mr Hugo Devenish made his entrance at Uppington-Smythe ball a week later.

"Good grief! It's Devenish," whispered Maud, Lady Gosper to her neighbour. "I thought he was on the barest of civil terms with the Uppington-Smythes. What the deuce is he doin' at their ball, Hettie?"

"I believe the attraction is the Singleton gel—the new one, not poor Rose, of course," responded Lady Hester Horton.

"Oh, yes. He's pursuing her quite openly. He was at Almack's last Wednesday night again; he hasn't missed a week since the gel arrived in Town," said the Honourable Pearl Hamnet.

"Well, he certainly dances attendance on her on every occasion, but as to whether the gel is encouraging his pretensions, that's another matter," said Hettie.

Lady Gosper looked at her and scoffed. "Gel don't

want for sense, does she? Full o' juice, that Devenish boy—not like the rest of his family. O' course she'll be encouraging him, Hettie."

Hettie shrugged. "I had it from Rose that the gel's been devilish fidgety about the way he's been following her around. Can't seem to attend any occasion— rout party, soirée, even the theatre, but what Hugo Devenish will turn up. And besides, you forget, Maud—she has no need of a fortune—she's an heiress herself."

The three elderly ladies critically observed Mr Devenish pass through the crowd, bowing, smiling coolly and exchanging a few words with each acquaintance he met. Without appearing to have made a bee-line, however, he was, in the space of a few minutes, bowing over the hand of the elder Miss Singleton, before bowing to her niece.

"Boy's got good manners, even if he has got cit blood in him."

Hettie shook her head. "Makin' a complete cake of himself, Pearl."

Maud made an irritated gesture. "Rose needs to take a firmer hand with that gel—gettin' fidgety indeed! The Devenish boy is a good match for that chit, cit blood or no cit blood! In my day a gel would marry whoever she was told to and that was the end of it. Whistlin' a good match down the wind, indeed!" The old lady snorted. "Even if she is an heiress!"

Pearl leaned forward conspiratorially. "My husband tells me they're laying bets on it at White's."

Maud made a rude noise. "Pah! Of course they are—that doesn't mean anything. Men will bet on anything. Nothin' better to do with their lives, poor, simple creatures!"

On the other side of the room another hasty colloquy was taking place.

"Thomas, I told you! See, he is here again—pursuing her in the most blatant possible fashion! It's an absolute disgrace. I told you not to believe him—she must be an heiress, else why would your uncle be pursuing her so shamelessly!"

Thomas shifted uncomfortably and glanced around. "Hush, Mama. People will hear you."

"I do not care who hears me!" snapped Amelia, lowering her voice, nevertheless. She continued in a loud whisper, "Now go at once and be nice to that girl, Thomas. Heaven knows she must be feeling neglected—you have scarcely spoken to her in days and days."

Thomas sighed. "Very well, Mama, but not just now. I am promised to dance with another young lady."

Amelia stamped her foot in annoyance. "Oh, must you forever be playing protector to that little nobody! I am certain Sir Bartlemy is nowhere near as bad as you have painted him. Look! There he is dancing with the Langley chit, who looks perfectly happy."

They both turned to watch the dancers, who were engaged in a lively Scottish reel. Sure enough, there was Sir Bartlemy mincing smilingly up to his partner, the youthful Miss Langley, his hand out-stretched. Miss Langley held out her hand to take his, but she unaccountably missed his groping fingers and her small fist collided with Sir Bartlemy's cheekbone.

Amelia frowned. "Clumsy chit. Her mother needs to find her a new dancing master."

There was a smothered sound from Thomas.

"I must go, Mama, I am promised in the next dance."

Amelia sniffed. "Gallantry never paid any debts, my son."

Thomas drew himself up with dignity. "I never expected it would, Mama. I will pay my own debts."

His mother looked shocked for a moment, then rolled her eyes dismissively, but a frown marred her smooth forehead as she watched her son walk away from her.

Mr Hugo Devenish was well aware of the stir, the gossip and the speculation that attended his arrival at the Uppington-Smythe ball. He was becoming used to it now. He did not like it, but he could appear indifferent to it. It was in a good cause, after all. He had commenced the hunt.

"Miss Singleton." He bowed over both her hand and turned to her niece.

"Oh! Mr Devenish! What a coincidence," gushed Kit in amazed accents. "Fancy finding you here!"

He inclined his head, acknowledging her irony. She looked beautiful, he thought. Tonight she was dressed in the usual long white gown worn by most of the young ladies in their first season, but hers was topped with an outlandish jacket, heavily embroidered with exotic scenes of elephants and temples, all in the most violent colours, and glittering with what appeared to be a hundred tiny mirrors scattered across it. She wore a small square tasselled cap over her dusky curls, similarly embroidered and glittering with tiny mirrors.

Bizarre indeed, and yet her air of unconcern, of complete confidence, made it appear stylish in the extreme. He glanced around the room and noted several ladies wearing small, square, tasselled, embroidered caps.

Kit widened her eyes in a show of mock surprise. "Yes. I had absolutely *no* idea you might come. Of course I also had *no* idea you would go to Almack's last week, nor to Lady Barr's ball. On the other hand, it was no surprise at all when you also happened to be visiting the Tower of London when I was there—naturally you would visit it frequently, and also inspecting Lord Elgin's marbles—I understand they are quite fragile, so naturally one must keep an eye on them in case they crumble to dust suddenly. And as for running into you at both the Pantheon Bazaar and Hatchard's Bookshop and—well, gentlemen do frequent silk merchants and read books, I know. But this ball? I am stunned."

He bowed again, apparently oblivious of her sarcasm. "Yes, it has all been most delightfully co-incidental, has it not?"

He winced inwardly as two ladies near enough to overhear their conversation nodded meaningfully at each other. He hardened his heart.

He was convinced she was up to no good. He was certain she was in league with the Chinese Burglar. A law-abiding citizen would inform the authorities. Hugo had always believed in the law. Without law there was only chaos.

But he could no more hand Kit Singleton over to the law than cut off his own hand.

That being so, he'd decided to follow her so closely that one of two things would happen; either he would trap her in a meeting with the Chinese burglar, and then take some sort of action to sever their connection forever, or he would prevent her from being able to make an assignation with the scoundrel, which would have a similar effect.

And if his suspicions were wrong, if they were merely the product of a disordered imagination, of too much brandy and too many late nights, then all he had done was...

Hugo swallowed. All he had done was set the *ton* by its ears and raise everyone's expectations that he was about to make her an offer. Of marriage.

If she was innocent, then Miss Singleton's expectations would be raised also.

Hugo straightened his spine. He couldn't afford to worry about that. Falsely raised expectations did not compare with the threat of the gallows or transportation.

So he'd followed her to each social occasion she attended. He'd attended more balls than he'd ever been to in his life and had even discovered what a Venetian Breakfast was like: not to his taste. But on a number of occasions he actually arrived before her, thanks to information received from his groom, Griffin. She could not, in all accuracy, accuse him of following her.

"So, would you care to dance, Miss Singleton?" he said blandly.

Kit felt like slapping his amused knowing face. She scowled. He'd been haunting her all over town in the most ridiculous and frustrating fashion and she was most certainly not going to encourage him by dancing with him. She opened her mouth to refuse him.

"Yes, of course, Mr Devenish. She would be delighted," said Rose Singleton in a soft, determined voice. "Give him your card, Kit dear."

Kit dear handed it over with a look that was calculated to slay.

Mr Devenish looked imperviously satisfied.

"Not the walt—"

Too late. Mr Devenish, having scribbled his name in two places, smugly handed back her card. Kit glanced at it and gritted her teeth. Of course—first the supper dance and then the waltz. Perfect! Her plan for the evening was quite, quite ruined! She'd been certain he would not come tonight; he was well known to be on very cool terms with the Uppington-Smythes, which was why she'd wanted to come.

If he wasn't there to dog her every footsteps, she would be free to get on with her plan. It had all been falling into place so neatly…until Mr Watchdog Devenish stuck his long pointed nose in where it wasn't wanted.

Not that his nose was really long and pointed, she thought irrelevantly. It was a solid sort of nose, longish and aquiline, but not at all pointy. Rather a nice nose, in fact.

Or it would be if he kept it out of her business!

The dance before supper was a cotillion. There were not many opportunities for conversation, but Kit was determined to have it out with him, somehow.

"Why are you following me?" she said quietly.

Hugo looked down at her, his face grave, concerned, implacable. "I seem to have appointed myself your guardian angel," he said lightly.

"But I don't need a guardian angel. Aunt Rose looks after me perfectly well."

He twirled her lightly around and she sighed and allowed herself to be spun, knowing herself to be wax in his sure, strong hands, and yet wishing it were not so.

"Perhaps the sort of guardianship I am performing is one which your aunt is incapable of."

She craned her head back a little so she could look him full in the face. "What do you mean, incapable of? She is a very good guardian! And besides, I am nearly of age—I need no watchdog!"

His face looked a little weary. "Well, there, we must disagree. I think you do not realise what danger you court."

Kit's pulse leapt at his words. He could not mean… He surely did not believe… She glanced up at his stern, harsh-featured face again and those oddly cold, grey eyes met her gaze.

He did mean it.

They danced on in silence for a few minutes. Kit's thoughts were racing wildly. He could not possibly know. There was no way he could. He was just being…bossy.

"Actually, I do not feel much like going in to supper," Kit said as the dance drew to a close. "Thank you for the dance, sir. However, I find I am not at all hungry. But please, if you wish to dine alone, feel free."

He smiled faintly. "I would not dream of deserting you. As your partner for the supper dance, my honour as a gentleman is at stake."

"Oh, very well." Kit almost stamped her way towards the supper room. Was there no shaking this wretched man?

She sat and watched him fill plates for two people. "In case you change your mind," he said blandly.

Kit gritted her teeth at his presumption, but she was in fact quite hungry so, making a show of reluctance, she allowed herself to be tempted. He had selected a variety of food that was exactly to her taste. Although she had only two crab patties; he had served himself three, or was it four? She watched them disappear swiftly. He reached out and served himself another two, then hesitated and took one more, a little sheepishly. Her bad mood slipped away. It was very difficult to remain angry long with a man who had such an obvious weakness for crab patties. She nibbled on her own and felt strangely at peace.

After they had both cleaned their plates in a most unfashionable manner, he said, "Miss Singleton, would you care for an ice?"

She looked up at him. The man was not the only one with a weakness for certain dishes. "Yes, please." She sighed. "I am very fond of ice-cream."

Mr Devenish signalled a waiter, who returned in a short time and placed a dish of smooth, creamy ice-cream in front of her. Kit thanked him and began to eat, while he sipped meditatively from a glass of wine. She was aware of his occasional gaze, warm upon her skin, as she ate.

She was just enjoying her third mouthful of the cold, delicious confection when he leaned towards her and said quietly in her ear, "It is time the Chinese Burglar disappeared from your life. He endangers your life and your freedom."

Kit spluttered in surprise. The ice-cream went down her throat, the wrong way. She began to cough.

Solicitously he patted her back. "Can I fetch you some water?"

She nodded her head, eyes streaming, glad for the reason to send him away.

He returned with the water. She drank several mouthfuls down, playing for time.

"Are you all right?"

"Yes, yes," she gasped, scrabbling for composure.

"I believe my question shocked you." His eyes bored into her.

She shook her head. "Shocked me? No, no," she said. "I merely choked, er, on…on a bone."

His brow rose and he nodded in grave sympathy. "A common difficulty with ice-cream, I find—the bones."

Some mistakes you walked away from. Kit finished her water, slowly.

Mr Devenish watched her a moment, but said nothing. The ghost of a satisfied smile played about his lips.

Kit tried to make a recovery. "So, you think I am in danger, that that Chinese criminal is planning to steal something of mine or my aunt's. I suppose since you discovered him near my aunt's house that time, he might be—"

"I mean nothing of the sort. I think you understand me very well."

"But—"

He stood up. "If you have finished your ice, Miss Singleton, perhaps we may return to the ballroom."

Frustrated, wishing to rid his suspicious mind of any notion of any connection between herself and any burglar, Chinese or otherwise, Kit stood, aware of the impossibility of a public argument in a crowded supper room.

She was still determined to argue it out with him; she had to disabuse his mind of any notion that she had any connection with the recent spate of burglaries. His name was down for another dance; she would insist they sit it out and talk, like civilised beings.

The band struck up the last waltz for the evening. He arrived just seconds before the music started. She glanced up at him, disdainfully. He looked very fine and reserved and elegant in his formal clothes. He said not a word, but the very faintest of smiles curved his lips and his hard grey eyes demanded impossible things of her.

She was *not* going to dance with him. She already knew it was folly to dance with him, let alone a waltz. Much better to sit and talk.

He held out a masterful hand. It was a nice hand, square, long-fingered, a little battered.

Spinelessly, Kit allowed herself to be led onto the dance floor. He drew her into his arms, those strong, sure, arms and she closed her eyes and allowed herself to be swept away by the music and the magic and the man. It was the stuff of dreams…

His big warm hand cupped her at the waist, his touch burning through the fine soft fabric of her gown. His other hand gripped her hand firmly, possessively. He twirled her around the dance floor with an ease which had a touch of arrogance in it; it felt as if she were floating. There was no need to watch her steps; she was in the hands of a master. She needed only to give herself up to the rhythm of the music and the expertise of her partner.

She could smell the faint tang of the soap he used, the fresh scent of newly washed linen, pressed with a hot iron. He seemed to give no thought to the steps of the dance; his eyes clung to hers, drawing her to him, with the inevitability of a whirlpool.

The music shimmered and seduced. The man was all she was aware of and Kit gave herself up to the dream, floating and twirling in a magical daze.

For it was only a dream.

It could be, for Kit, nothing more.

Maggie was waiting up for her. "Well? How did it go?"

Kit noted her maidservant's heavy eyes. "I told you not to wait up for me, Maggie. I can perfectly well undress myself and put all my things away—you know that—so why did you wait up for me?"

"You know why," was the grim reply.

"Well, nothing happened, and I'm going straight to bed tonight, so you may sleep easy." It was not quite a lie. Bad enough Maggie had guessed Kit's plans; she didn't want her implicated any further.

Maggie looked her over, and said shrewdly, "Something has put you all end upon beam!"

Kit hoped she wasn't blushing. After that wonderful, magical waltz, she'd drifted home, only vaguely attending to Rose's chatter. She'd been in a blissful haze, conjuring up impossible, wonderful daydreams in which somehow, everything was different, and she could stay in England, and be courted like a normal girl…

Then they'd reached Dorset Street and as they'd climbed out of their sedan chairs, she'd noticed Mr Devenish's groom, Griffin, lurking in the shadows. Reality had crashed down all around her in all its nasty gritty irreconcilable contradictions.

She was still being spied on.

She'd stepped out of the sedan chair and mounted the steps to Rose Singleton's house, leaving her dreams in the gutter.

"That wretched man as good as admitted he's been following me. He spouts nonsense about a guardian angel, but I have another word for it—spy!" She did not mention the connection he had somehow made between herself and the Chinese Burglar. Maggie worried too much as it was.

Maggie made a non-committal noise and busied herself tidying away the clothes Kit was discarding.

"As if I need a guardian angel! I—who have been looking after myself perfectly adequately for years! Have you ever heard anything so outrageous! What business am I of his, I ask you? Even Papa never questioned my activities and he at least had the right!"

"Mebbe so, but I've always said your pa should have protected you a lot better than he did."

Kit pursed her lips. It was an old argument and one she knew from experience she could never win. Maggie had never approved of her father and nothing would ever change that. Perhaps Papa had been a bit lax in some areas—all right, she knew he had been— but that didn't mean she had to accept a perfect stranger foisting his presence on her! "But this Mr Devenish—he's not even a relative!"

She glanced at her maid as she said so, and surprised a look on her face which shocked her. "Maggie! You cannot mean you approve of him hounding me in this fashion!"

"Hounding!" snorted Maggie. "I wouldn't call it hounding. Does he nag at you constantly, telling you what to do and what not to do?"

"No, but—"

"Does he persecute you and interrupt what you are doing?"

"No," conceded Kit grumpily, "but—"

"So, he just happens to be where you are, and minds his own business like a gentleman is supposed to." Maggie curled her lip. "Doesn't sound like anyone's being hounded to me! And if keeping a friendly eye on you, and making sure you get home safe and sound is what you call hounding, well, all I can say is, good for him!"

Outraged by this betrayal in her own home, Kit snapped, "Why, what would you call it when wherever I go, there I find him or else that wretched groom underfoot! He was down in the street, outside, just now—the groom, I mean! How *dare* he send his man to spy on me!"

Kit stared at her maid, awaiting her response. Maggie looked oddly self-conscious, she realised.

"Well, Maggie? Isn't it outrageous?"

Maggie avoided her eyes, bustling around the room, tidying with a vengeance. The busy activity could have accounted for her maid's heightened colour, but suddenly another thought, completely unrelated to their discussion, leapt into Kit's mind.

"Yes, if Mr Devenish cannot follow me, he sends that big groom of his—what's his name—oh, you know, Maggie. Ruffin? Griffith?"

"Griffin," mumbled Maggie, polishing the bedroom looking-glass with quite unnecessary vigour.

"Oh, yes, Griffin, I recall now. He was the spy you mentioned the other day, wasn't he?"

Maggie scrubbed furiously at the pure surface of the mirror.

"The handsome one," added Kit provocatively. "The big, clumsy jackanapes."

By this time, Maggie's cheeks were pure, brilliant rose.

"Have you spoken with him since?"

Maggie mumbled something that might have been an affirmative.

"Often?"

"Hmmph!" Maggie straightened the bed covers violently. "Can't help it if he comes around, can I?" Her face was almost glowing with embarrassment, Kit noted gleefully.

"I do believe you have a *tendre* for Mr Devenish's coachman, Maggie dear."

"His groom, you mean." Then, realising what she had said, Maggie blushed even more furiously. "A *tendre* for the groom? What nonsense! Nothing of the sort. I'm a respectable woman, Miss Kit, and—"

"Oh my, oh my, Maggie dear," Kit crooned.

Maggie snapped the top sheet into a crisp fold. "No, not a bit of it. Downright foolishness to think of such a—"

She bent and snatched up a pair of Kit's stockings. Would you look at these hose, Miss Kit! I declare they look as if you've danced through a prickle bush in them! Ruined, utterly ruined!" She hurled the stockings furiously into the mending basket.

"Mr Griffin, indeed! Of all the ridiculous—!" She folded a petticoat of Kit's with unnecessary vigor, slapped it into a drawer and banged the drawer shut with some finality. "And besides, he's much too young for me."

"I wouldn't have said he was particularly young at all," said Kit pensively. "I'm sure Mr Devenish mentioned that Griffin was a stableboy on his father's Shropshire estate when Mr Devenish was a child…and as Mr Devenish is turned thirty-two, I believe, Griffin would have to be about ten years older, which would make him forty, or thereabouts. That doesn't seem too young to me. Nor too old. In fact…"

Maggie's blush faded a little. She snorted. "No, and well it might not. Forty! He doesn't look it!" She snorted again. "Men! There's no justice in the world! Once past a certain age, they only seem to improve in looks…"

She paused, a pair of Kit's slippers in her hands and stared at nothing for a moment or two, her eyes softening. To Kit's fascination, Maggie suddenly blushed a bright rosy red, all over again. She hastily bustled over to the wardrobe, hiding her face from Kit's inquisitive view. "What nonsense! 'Tis of no interest to me how many years Mr Griffin has. I'm an old woman Miss Kit—"

"Old woman indeed!" retorted Kit. "Don't try to gammon me, Maggie darling, for you've told me a hundred times or more—" she mimicked Maggie's accent "I was barely twenty-six when I set off for darkest India, to look after that poor, ill-fated Kirkshaw family and with not an idea in the world that even before I'd left English soil, they was all dead and perished of the yellow fever, and me all on me own in a heathen land." Kit resumed her normal voice. "And that was when I was thirteen, and I am twenty now. Which means, Maggie Bone, that you are thirty-three, and as Mr Griffin is—"

"Bite your tongue girl," snapped Maggie scandalised. "Thirty-three is old enough for a woman to give up thinkin' about…things. And besides, I've never been wed before and t'would be ridiculous for me to be thinking of taking such a step at my time of life."

She shook out a travelling cloak with a snap. "Not to mention indecent!" She blushed again and hurriedly rummaged though the wardrobe again.

Kit fought to keep a straight face. So that was the way of things, was it? She could barely recall the last time Maggie had a serious suitor, and then she had given the hapless fellow short shrift. There had been no blushing then. Nor any oft-repeated denials of interest. Maggie had simply sent the poor man off with a flea in his ear for his presumption and discouraged, he'd left.

Now, unless Kit was mightily mistaken, her maid was smitten.

Kit resolved to take more notice of Griffin. He was clearly a man to be reckoned with. In the seven years of adventuring, she had almost never seen Maggie Bone flustered. And now, the mere thought of the tall, silent, burly groom had done it.

Maggie's revealing words—*"Not to mention indecent!"* echoed in Kit's mind. She hid a smile. Oh, yes. Her dear, staid, practical, stuffy Maggie was indeed smitten, if she had allowed herself even to think of the activities of the marriage bed.

"Goodnight, Maggie darling." Kit kissed Maggie warmly on the cheek, an extra loving kiss for the blunt, selfless woman who'd shown Kit more love than anyone in her life. "Sweet dreams of a handsome man," she whispered and watched the rose flood her maid's cheeks again.

"Oh, get on with you, girl," said Maggie gruffly. "You get to sleep now, do."

Kit snuggled down in her high bed, relishing the feel of the cool, clean linen sheets. Maggie would have her Griffin, she vowed. Kit would make it happen. Love ought not to be ignored, not when it was there, on your doorstep, being offered.

A dark, sombre face appeared in her mind. A firm, unsmiling mouth, and cold grey eyes...only they weren't looking at her coldly, not at all...

Kit turned over and thumped her pillow into a more comfortable shape. It was Maggie she was supposed to be thinking of, Maggie and Griffin. Not...anyone else.

In any case, after this was all over, she was going to live in Italy. She didn't have a choice. She couldn't stay in England even if she wanted to.

She did want to...

But it was not possible, so there was no point even considering anything else. Not that he—no! She was not considering impossibilities. He was just some bossy, infuriating man who'd decided to follow her about and interfere in her life because he had nothing better to do.

English gentlemen never did have enough to do,

she decided. It was not a good feature of this culture. And once she'd gone to Italy he'd forget all about her, and find some other girl to follow about and annoy, only she'd be some good, well-brought-up, proper, virtuous English girl, not an unknown foreign adventuress, and she wouldn't be annoyed by him following her around. She'd probably enjoy being harried and protected by a big bossy brute; most girls would. Especially when they had nothing to hide…

And then he'd marry the well-brought-up proper English girl and take her to the lovely home he had built in Yorkshire and…and then he'd…he'd waltz with her…

She turned over again and thumped the pillow. She did need to get some sleep; she was so tired her eyes were weeping.

And she had a big day ahead of her tomorrow.

A slight shadowy figure moved in the darkness, stepping cat-footed across the slate tiles roofing the Brackbourne family mansion. The illicit visitor peered over the edge of the roof, looking down to the ground, four stories below. A long black pigtail dangled from beneath a small black cap.

A very thin, very light, strong rope coiled over the edge, dropping noiselessly down to a couple of feet above one of the second-storey balconies. The intruder checked the rope, then slipped cautiously over the edge, winding one foot around the rope like a circus performer, then sliding down it to land lightly on slippered feet.

The balcony, with its carved stone balustrade and marble paving, framed a very handsome pair of French windows which opened on to the balcony from the master's sitting room. The intruder tried the handle, then pulled out a bundle of oddly-shaped metal sticks, which clinked faintly. First one, then another was inserted carefully into the lock of the doors; there was a soft clear click, and the lock was undone. Two catch-fasteners then caused a slight delay while they were negotiated and then the windows opened and the intruder stepped inside.

The room was very dark, but the intruder did not pause to allow her eyes to adjust to the gloom. She hurried over to the door which led out on to the landing and silently turned the key. She had no wish to be disturbed.

The room was richly furnished; lined with books and beautiful objects. The outline of two small paintings glowed against the silk-hung surface of the wall, their gold-leafed frames gleaming softly. The paintings were a pair, quite small—about eighteen inches square, but exquisitely done.

The subject of both was a naked woman; in one she was surrounded by cherubim, innocent and laughing. In the other painting, there was a tree and a serpent, the woman clasped an apple, the cherubim were half-grown boys and the things they were about to do did not look at all innocent.

Kit smiled. She had done her homework well. These were what she had come for; the Bronzino paintings. There was a deep square compartment waiting for them at the bottom of her camphor wood chest at home.

She removed the loose black Chinese tunic she was wearing and slipped a kind of harness off her back. She laid it on a large mahogany table. Carefully she lifted down one painting, laid first a sheet of silk, then a soft, thick piece of felt over it. She wrapped the whole painting in oilcloth and laid it on the harness. She did the same with the second painting, then fastened up the harness and swung it back onto her back, buckling the straps carefully. Then she dropped the tunic back over her head, hiding the harness completely.

She pulled a crumpled piece of paper from her pocket and let it drop untidily on the floor, then she slipped back to the French windows and onto the balcony. Grinning to herself, she closed and locked the French windows and the catch-fasteners too—there was no point in advertising how easy they had been to open. Let Lord Brackbourne be baffled by the mystery when he realised he'd lost the Bronzino paintings and had no idea how the thief had got in.

People always put locks and bolts all over their

ground-floor windows and doors, and also the next floor up, but after that—well, for some reason they almost never expected burglars to be able to fly like birds. Or climb like monkeys.

Swiftly she climbed back up the rope, coiling it around first one foot, then the other, rising to the roof rapidly and silently, with little apparent effort. It was a technique she'd been taught when she was eight. It was second nature to her now. In seconds she was on the roof. She coiled the rope up, wrapping it around her waist under the tunic, then padded silently towards the back of the house, where there were lower outbuildings attached to the main house. Here, a high wall, embedded with vicious-looking iron spikes, led from the kitchen area to the street.

Lightly and carefully, Kit stepped between the spikes; her small, narrow feet were a definite advantage here. She came at last to the dark street and waited, listening, until she was certain nobody was around. Then she took a deep breath and carefully dropped down the ten or twelve feet on to the cobblestones. This was the most dangerous part of the whole operation—the cobblestones were uneven and it was only too easy to land crooked and twist an ankle—but she landed without mishap and vanished into the shadows.

Moments later a horse trotted out of a dark street.

On its back rode a gentleman wearing a greatcoat and curly-brimmed beaver hat. Whistling softly, the gentleman trotted off into the night.

In the darkness the Watch could be heard, "Four o'clock and all's well."

Outside a back gate of a Dorset Street house, a boy waited, fidgeting in the shadows. Finally he heard the sound of hooves on stone. He whistled softly and a gentleman in a greatcoat and curly brimmed beaver hat whistled back to him. The gentleman dismounted, tossed the boy the reins of the horse, then followed it with a shining gold guinea. The boy mounted the horse and rode away smiling, clutching his precious gold coin.

The gentleman slipped in the garden gate, unlocked the kitchen door and slipped inside and hurried silently upstairs. There, safely in her bedroom, she carefully removed first the great coat, then the Chinese tunic, then the harness. She opened her camphor wood chest, lifted out its contents and the false base, then laid the Bronzino paintings carefully in the compartment which awaited them.

Kit then stripped off the clothing belonging to the Chinese burglar, folded and wrapped it carefully in oiled silk, and hid it in the false bottom of the chest. She then replaced the contents of the chest and closed the lid.

There was a large can of water sitting beside the

still-glowing fire in her bedroom. It was an agreeable luxury, a fire in her bedroom, and she didn't often ask for it, but on these nights it was vital.

She poured the warm water into a large basin, picked up a sponge, soaped it with her special rose soap and began to wash her naked body from head to toe. She had to remove every trace of the sandalwood and incense scent with which she'd impregnated the Chinese Burglar's clothing.

The sense of smell was a powerful aid to memory and perception. Your smell could identify you to others; another lesson she'd learned as a child. If you wanted people to think you were Turkish or Portuguese or French, you used perfumes associated in people's minds with Turkey, Portugal or France. If you wanted to be thought Chinese, you used Chinese incense.

Had Kit been disturbed in the act, as she had by Mr Devenish, even if he hadn't seen the pigtail or the clothing, he would have smelled her in the dark and assumed the culprit was a foreigner. People questioned their eyes and their ears, but they weren't conscious enough of their sense of smell, so they let it influence them, more strongly than it should.

The Chinese Burglar was a fellow who stank of joss sticks and foreign incense. Kit Singleton was a young lady who smelled delicately of rose petals. There could be no connection between the two. Kit scrubbed until her skin was pink.

Chapter Nine

The lights in the Royal Opera House dimmed and the heavy plush velvet curtains drew slowly back. The stage was lit by bright lights. Kit leaned forward, fascinated. She and Aunt Rose had been invited to attend the opera in a small party arranged by an elderly friend of Rose's, Lady Hester Horton, and the performance was about to commence.

The orchestra began. A stout man in tights and an old-fashioned doublet strutted to the front of the stage and began to sing.

Kit's Italian was a little rusty, but she was able to pick up most of the words—he was singing about love, of course… Interspersed with the passionate Italian, other fragments of dialogue wafted to Kit's ears.

"Another robbery last night…becoming an epidemic! None of us safe in our beds any more."

The tenor sang on, his voice tragic with passion and unrequited love.

"I blame the Watchmen—drunk as wheelbarrows, no doubt."

The tenor strode about the stage, singing, watched secretly by his love…

Kit was seated at the front of the box. Lady Hester, knowing she had never been to the opera before, had seated her there, adjuring her to, "Sit up and make sure everyone sees that lovely blue thing, my dear. Oh and make sure you notice who else is here, tonight—here, take these glasses. Got to see and be seen, my dear, see and be seen."

Meanwhile Lady Hester and her cronies, Lady Gosper, and the Honourable Pearl Hamnet, retired to the back of the box, where the noise of the music would not disturb them so much. Kit leaned back in her chair and eavesdropped unashamedly.

"What did the devils filch, Hettie?"

"Haven't you heard, my dear? Brackbourne's precious Bronzinos."

"What's a bronzino?"

"A little statuette, Pearl, made of bronze, obviously," explained Lady Gosper kindly.

Kit stifled a giggle.

"No, no, Maud, they are paintings—a little risqué, I have heard—painted by a sixteenth-century painter, Bronzino—an Italian chappie."

"What?"

"Bronzino—an Italian painter. Dead now, of course."

The music swelled, the tenor poured his passionate heart out at full voice and Maud had a little trouble hearing.

"What, who's dead? Can't hear with all that dratted caterwaulin' goin' on," shouted Maud. "What happened to the fellow with the bronze statues?"

"Bronzino—it's his name, dear," Hettie shouted back, just as the tenor finished. Her words echoed through the auditorium.

A ripple of laughter ran through in the audience.

Maud, relieved that the music had stopped for a moment, responded in disgust, "Oh, an Italian, I see. Big on art, the Italians. Went to Italy once—paintings and statues all over the place! Amazin'!" She cast a glance of misgiving at the tenor on stage. "I suppose he's Italian too."

"Yes, dear. He's very good, isn't he?" said Pearl. "Don't you agree?"

Maud pursed her lips and listened as he started the next song. "His tights are too dratted tight, that's what I think!"

Giggling, Kit returned to the marvellous spectacle that was the opera. The music was beautiful, the costumes magnificent. She felt wonderful; relaxed and at peace with the world.

Four compartments filled; only two to go.

The operatic heroine's maidservant was disguising her mistress as a boy. Kit watched critically; it was not at all convincing, but the poor creature was in desperate straits. Kit hoped the hero was blind.

There was a slight disturbance at the rear of the box. Another person had arrived, late. It was very fashionable to arrive late, apparently. Many of the boxes were only now filling up and yet the opera was well advanced. It was a waste, Kit thought. And a nuisance, for the new arrivals were quite unworried about disturbing people with their noise and chatter. Kit was entranced with the music and she wished people would be quiet. But it seemed the last thing people came to the opera for was the music. It was simply the fashionable place to be seen and the highlight of the event was the interval between acts, when everyone would visit each other's boxes.

"Miss Singleton, you seem pale," said a deep voice beside her.

Kit turned indignantly to shush him. "I am not in the least bit pale," she hissed. "Good evening, Mr Devenish." She turned back to the stage.

"She is looking quite ill," he stated. "It is the stuffiness in here. I think I should take her outside for a breath of air. Miss Singleton, Lady Hester, what do you think?"

"Oh, indeed, yes. Take the gel outside," agreed Lady Hester instantly. "Can't have her faintin'."

Kit felt a firm, masculine hand on her forearm. Crossly, she shook it off. She wasn't the least bit ill and she wasn't going anywhere; she wanted to watch the opera.

He took her hand in a determined grip. "You are dizzy, perhaps. Let me help you to your feet, Miss Singleton."

Annoyed, Kit turned to him, equally determined he should do no such thing, but as she turned, she caught a glimpse of his expression. His eyes were glittering, his mouth tense and compressed. He was utterly furious. If she didn't go with him and listen to whatever he was clearly determined to say to her, he was clearly quite capable of having a loud quarrel with her right here, in public. And she didn't want that!

With bad grace she got to her feet and allowed him to lead her solicitously out of the box.

"I cannot think why you should—" she began.

He silenced her with a curt look. Wordlessly he gripped her arm and hurried her into a corridor, up a flight of stairs, down another corridor and into a small room where a faded *chaise-longue* and a small table were the only furnishings.

"Sit down," he said grimly.

Kit rolled her eyes and sat down. At least this quarrel would be in private, she thought.

He loomed over her. "Now, perhaps you would care to explain!"

Kit stared at him, outraged. "You burst into Lady Hester's box and drag me off in the middle of the most beautiful opera—I've never been to the opera before and I was enjoying it so much—under the most blatantly false pretext! And then you drag me, unchaperoned, down dusty corridors and up dark and narrow stairs to a room which is obviously designed for illicit assignations and then you demand that *I* explain?"

He was not the slightest bit abashed.

"I have done nothing wrong. You, on the other hand, have!"

She arched her eyebrows haughtily.

He shook his head. "Oh, do not give me that look of false innocence. I know what you are about! There is no point in denying what you got up to last night!"

She looked vaguely puzzled. "Last night? The Baden rout? It was a little dull, and I do believe I accidentally spilled some ratafia over Sir Bartlemy Bowles, but it was an accident, I assure you. You cannot be so very angry with me over an accident, surely."

"I am not talking about Sir Bartlemy!" he said through gritted teeth. "You may tip a gallon of ratafia over him, for all I care! No, what I meant was—"

"Really, what a splendid idea. I just might take you up on that generous offer," said Kit provocatively. "I'm sure when I explain to Sir Bartlemy that you gave me permission—"

"Will you be serious!"

Kit regarded him warily. "Since I do not know what you are talking about—"

"You know very well what I'm talking about!"

"But I do not!" she insisted. She was not going to admit a thing. He had not a shred of evidence, after all.

"The Brackbourne House robbery."

"Brackbourne House?" she said vaguely. "Oh, yes, I heard Lady Hester and her friends discussing it. What a dreadful thing. Lady Gosper blames drunken Watchmen."

He didn't rise to her bait. "You and I know differently, don't we?"

She arched her eyebrow again. "Do we?"

"I suppose you have them packed away in some secret location."

Kit gave him a puzzled look. "The Watchmen?"

He swore. "Do not play games with me!"

"Well, as I have not the slightest idea what you are so out of reason cross about, I cannot help it! I have no idea what you are talking about."

"You are responsible for the Brackbourne House robbery!"

She gave a great gasp of amazed surprise. "I? What on earth would give you the idea that I did the Brackbourne House robbery?"

She laughed incredulously and clapped a hand theatrically to her forehead. "Oh, yes, that's right, I did! It slipped my mind for a moment. I clambered up a drainpipe—or did I slip down the chimney? I forget which—and then ran off with Lord Brackbourne's bronze statues in my reticule!"

He made an impatient sound. "Oh, don't be ridiculous. You know perfectly well what was stolen. And I do not mean you did it yoursel—" He looked at her in sudden suspicion, an arrested look in his eyes. "You didn't, did you?"

She laughed.

"No, I…I suppose not…" He didn't look convinced. "At any rate, you organised it."

She gave him another look of amused disbelief.

"Or it was done at your instigation."

She gave another incredulous laugh. "Why on earth would I instigate such a thing?"

"Revenge on behalf of your father."

Kit forced herself not to react. He was most frightfully acute, the Watchdog.

"*Revenge?* Whatever for?" She was tired of doing incredulous laughter so she shook her head. "It sounds like you have been watching too many stage melodramas to me, Mr Devenish. Which reminds me, I would very much like to return to the opera if you have finished accusing me of breaking into people's houses and stealing their statues—"

"Paintings, blast it! You know perfectly well—"

"I thought my first visit to the opera would be

memorable, but I never could have imagined in what way! Imagine, hustled away from my chaperons on a pretext, dragged up shadowy corridors to a place of illicit encounters and accused of breaking and entering a lord's mansion and making off with his stat—" she caught his eye "—paintings, all for the sake of some thrillingly antiquated notion of revenge! You know, it's better than the opera, only it does not sound so pretty!"

He stepped forward. "No, it does not sound pretty at all, does it?"

She pouted. "You misunderstand me."

"I understand you very well, minx. I am not the slightest bit deceived by your airy act of innocence, so you need not waste your play-acting on me! Listen well. You endanger yourself and others and I will not stand for it, understand me?"

Kit sighed like a spoiled schoolgirl.

Infuriated, he grabbed her shoulders and shook her. "Listen, damn you! Don't you know what will happen if you are caught, you little fool? Do you wish to be hanged by your pretty neck? What have you done with the stuff? Give it to me—I'll make sure it is returned with no questions."

Kit's heart was pounding, but she managed to shrug coolly and say plaintively, "I still don't understand what you are talking about. What stuff?"

He shook her again. "Oh! You are infuriating!

What the devil do you think this will do to your aunt? Have you thought of that, miss, have you?"

Kit felt a surge of guilty irritation. How dare he raise the question which had plagued and worried her most! Rose might not be a true relative, but Kit was coming to care for her as if she were. "My aunt is no business of yours, Mr Devenish. Now please let me go. You are making me very uncomfortable!"

"You are lucky I do not strangle you!"

"Let go of me this instant!"

"I will, as soon as you admit to me what you have done!"

"I admit nothing! What I do or don't do is no business of yours!"

"It *is* my business!" He gave her a little shake and glared at her furiously. His long, strong fingers slipped from her shoulders and curled around her upper arms in an unbreakable grip. She could feel the heat of his angry flesh burning through the thin fabric of her sleeves. It felt like she would be forever branded with his mark.

She started to panic a little, feeling out of her depth. She'd had people—men—try to hold her against her will before, and she'd always been able to escape. She had many tricks up her sleeve, some of which Mr Devenish had experienced before, but she was oddly unwilling to use them. She twisted angrily, trying to pull away. "Let go of me, I said! I will not—"

"I'm not letting go of you until you tell me the truth!"

"The truth! The truth is you have dragged me here and you are holding me against my will."

"I will release you as soon as you admit what you have been doing." His voice deepened. "You can trust me, you know."

Even as she scoffed, a part of her wanted to tell him. It was a sacred promise to her papa. If he knew the whole story he would realise she was morally justified in what she had done.

But would he really understand?

No, he was a staid Englishman. The English revered property. What was that expression they had? Possession is nine-tenths of the law.

How would he understand? He would condemn her, as a criminal and a thief. He'd despise her. He'd look at her with contempt, as if she was as far beneath him as…as…

Better to leave him suspicious and steeped in uncertainty, than to confirm she was everything any decent English gentleman would despise.

Better his frustration and anger than his contempt any day.

"Let me g—" She tried to knock his hands away from her, but he was too strong. She bucked and twisted, raising her fists to hit at him. He caught them, imprisoning them in one big powerful hand, while the other one prevented her escaping. The struggle moved them backwards until finally she felt the wall behind her. He wasn't hurting her; he just refused to let her go. She'd never been held like this, imprisoned by the weight of a man's body. It panicked her a little and in desperation, she lifted a knee in an ignoble tactic.

He avoided it with a curse, and flattened her body and her legs against the wall, holding her motionless with the weight and power of his body. "Little vixen! So—"

He froze for a second and stared at her, shock suffusing his face and his body. They were so intimately pressed together, she could actually feel the shock pass through his body into hers.

"My God! That's not the first time you've done that, is it? We've tussled like this before. It was *you*, wasn't it? In that skirmish in the back yard of your aunt's house! Good God! A woman!"

She made a derisory noise, not terribly convincingly.

His eyes bored into her, stunned, outraged, incredulous. "Don't bother denying it. My body tells me the truth of it. *You* did those burglaries! The Chinese Burglar! It was you, all the time."

She muttered something indignant and avoided his eyes. His breath was warm on her skin.

She felt the knowledge pass through his body, felt the antagonism pass from him, and determination take its place. She was completely helpless, and oddly languid, now that he'd discovered the worst. It was not contempt she saw in his eyes. She was not quite sure what it was…

"Why the devil would you do such a thing? What frightful necessity would drive you to take such insane risks?"

She avoided his eyes, shrugging infinitesimally. She would admit nothing. He might "know", but he had no evidence; nothing that could hang her…yet.

"Did you hear me, Kit? Why would you do such a mad thing?"

It was not an accusation, but a question. His voice was low, intimate and the deep rumble of its timbre vibrated through her body. It almost sounded as if he cared. The faint caress in his tone almost undid her.

She had the overwhelming urge to simply tell him everything but if she did, she was sure she would end up bawling like a baby in his arms, and that would be such a feeble thing to do. She blinked the emotion determinedly away.

"I do not believe you have my permission to call me by my given name." It was a ridiculously missish thing to say, with her wrists still imprisoned over her head and his body pressing heavily against hers from knee to breast, but it was all she could think of.

"You haven't answered my question, Kit," he said softly again.

She turned her face away, but it was impossible not

to see him. He was so close his breath warmed her skin. "I have no intention of answering any of your ridiculous questions. I have no need to explain myself to you." Out of the corner of her eye she could see his jaw tense.

"There is *every* need, dammit! And I will have answers, none the less."

He must have shaved before he came to the opera. The clean tang of masculine cologne teased at her senses. "You are wasting time," she responded. "What I may do or not do is no concern of yours, Mr Devenish!"

"Curse it, girl, it is very much my concern!" She felt the anger rise in him again.

"Nonsense! There is no reason in the world why I should explain myself to you!" Again, she tried to pull her hands free. Again, her effort was in vain.

"There is every reason! And you *will* explain!"

"Why should I? I am not accountable to you! You are no relative of mine!" She bucked against him angrily but his body blocked hers.

"No, and I'm extremely glad of it!"

"Glad, is it? Hah! Not as glad as—"

He was already standing as close as a man could to a woman, body to body, chest to breast, skin touching, scents intermingling. He simply lowered his head and planted his mouth on hers, with firm, possessive deliberation.

It stopped her words, her breath, her heart.

His heart pounded against hers. Or was it her own heart? She couldn't tell.

He moved back.

She moved forward, staying with him.

He released her hands. Of their own accord, they twined around his neck and pulled him closer.

He fastened his arm around her waist and lifted her slightly, fitting her against him. They were like the twin Chinese symbols of *yin* and *yang*; her curves fitted into his. Her body flamed everywhere they touched.

Fire.

His lips urged hers to part. He tasted of passion and anger and need. The taste was addictive.

She had never been kissed like this in her life. It was as if a part of her that she never knew existed had suddenly leapt to life.

Abruptly he broke his hold on her and they parted, panting.

There was a long silence, broken only by the distant sound of the opera. And the sound of two people breathing raggedly, as if having run a mile.

"That is what makes it my business."

He looked furious, apologetic and triumphant at the same time.

Kit blinked dazedly at him, her senses still spinning, the imprint of his lips still on hers, the taste of him in her mouth, the scent of him clouding her mind. It took a moment for the sense of his words to penetrate her scrambled brain.

"Whatever you do is my business."

Wordlessly she shook her head. No.

His eyes blazed with intensity. "Oh, for the love of—! You must put a stop to this mad business. If it is the money, you need not worry about it. I have plenty of money."

She swallowed at the ragged huskiness of his voice and shook her head again.

He cupped her face. His hands were shaking. "I know I am not much of a catch, but I am very wealthy. It is an honourable offer I make you," he said with rough tenderness. "Marry me."

Tears swam in her eyes and she pulled herself away from his gentle hold. Blinking the tears away, she shook her head for the third time.

"I am sorry. I cannot."

"But surely—! You will hang, if they catch you!" He broke off, his face working. "If it is security you crave—"

Oh, yes, she craved security all right—how could she not?—she who'd never known a moment's security in her whole life.

But she craved love much more.

He'd offered her money and security. It wasn't love, but it was still a magnificent offer, more than she had a right to expect. What could she offer him?

An unknown name. A criminal past. A tarnished future.

Kit turned away from him, shaking. She fished blindly for a handkerchief. He handed her a folded square of fine white linen. "Here," he said gruffly.

Fighting for the light-hearted composure which had never deserted her before, Kit scrubbed the tears away and forced back the sobs which crowded her chest so painfully. She blew her nose, squared her shoulders in a determined fashion and turned back to face him.

"Thank you for your very kind offer, Mr Devenish," she said in a quavering voice which mocked her pathetic attempt at formality. "I cannot accept."

She walked to the door of the small room and turned the handle of the door. She hesitated, then turned back, smiling tremulously and biting her lip. "Indeed, I do thank you, but it cannot be. I am not for the likes of you. Please, in future, stay away."

Hugo Devenish watched the door close behind her.

I am not for the likes of you.

He ran his fingers through his neat hair, tousling it roughly with an unthinking hand and swore.

He had thought she belonged to him.

No one had ever belonged to him before. Not anyone. Not his mother. Not his father. Certainly never his half-brother. For a while, as a child, he'd thought his small baby nephew might belong to him.

He'd had planned to teach Thomas cricket and show him where to look for birds' nests, but that possibility had long disappeared.

But when Kit was in his arms she'd felt as if she belonged to him. It was—she was so right, so perfect…

He'd taken several women as lovers in his life but there had never been this sense of…completion. As if he'd come home. As if he had only just come alive now, in her company. It wasn't even lust, though he certainly had the most powerful case of lust he'd ever experienced before. It was more than lust… It was…

It was a dream.

He'd spent his life amassing wealth, and many fine things belonged to him. He had fine carriages, fine horses, a fleet of fine ships, a beautiful home and any amount of lovely things.

But he had nobody.

He had loyal employees, and a few friends, but that had all happened since he'd made his fortune, and he didn't trust that. Captain Patchett was his only reliable friend.

But this, this was different, this small girl with her laughing eyes and her mischievous tongue. Who dared to tease him and provoke him. Nobody ever teased him. He was too powerful these days for anyone to risk it. Even his own family mistrusted him, not to mention a good proportion of the rest of the world.

She was what he had missed, had craved unknowingly all these years. Not simply a woman, but this woman. This sweet, particular, bright, laughing sprite, with her mischievous lisp and her nonsense, her cool head and her mad, dangerous quest.

She belonged in his arms, in his life. He'd felt the truth of it in her kiss. His heart told him so. His body throbbed with the knowledge. As her body had throbbed in his arms.

But she'd refused him. Denied him again and again.

How could she, when her body had clung to his with such sweet passion? Her arms had wound around his neck with such loving fervour. Her mouth had met his like two halves of a magnificent whole, coming together for the first time. No uncertainty. No—

Yes, he thought tenderly. There had been uncertainty on her part, at first. He recalled her initial shock as he'd covered her mouth with his. She'd hesitated, as if trying to decide what she thought of his masculine invasion and how she would deal with it.

Of course there had been uncertainty. How could he have forgotten? He'd been so agonisingly aware of her response; part of him exulting in the delight of holding her, another part panicking lest she repudiated him.

He recalled the flame of elation when he felt her first tentative return of his embrace. And then suddenly, she was kissing him back with a clumsy enthusiasm and a wholehearted joy which had quite unravelled the last chains with which he'd protected his heart all these years.

But she'd said she didn't want him. *I am not for the likes of you.*

A girl dancing on a precipice, repudiating him.

Feeling as defeated as if he'd gone a dozen rounds with Mendoza, Hugo quietly left the opera house. It was a damp, miserable night, but the weather suited his mood and he decided to walk back to his house.

His footsteps echoed on the cold empty streets. He passed a dark alleyway and heard a faint, furtive shuffle. He would almost welcome footpads, he decided. A real fight was what he needed.

Dammit, why had she rejected him?

It was not as if she would receive any other offers. There was no diamond mine; if he was sure of anything, he was sure of that.

And he hadn't asked that she love him. Only that she marry him.

He recalled his own words, his first ever proposal of marriage. *If it is the money, you need not worry about it. I have plenty of money.*

He leaned against a nearby railing and groaned. What sensitivity! What finesse! Such fine heartfelt words of romance! *I am very wealthy... Marry me.*

He had as good as offered to buy her! Of course she'd turned him down—him and his money and his cursed tradesman's blood!

But he'd thought it might tempt her. After all, she'd risked her life for riches, over and over again! Pennington's Black Pearls, Alcorne's diamonds, Grantley's emeralds and now Brackbourne's Bronzinos.

Yet she would not marry him for the same.

Hugo almost groaned aloud again.

His fine new house, filled with all the beauty and elegance money could buy. Empty. A cold showroom of wealth. His life was just as empty, he realised. The house, the money—it hadn't been enough.

Kit had spoken of a home. Of love and family gathered around a fire. He wanted that. He wanted her. Wanted her to fill his life and his house, to fill it with laughter and mischief…and children.

He needed quite desperately for her to belong to him. She didn't have to love him—he wasn't asking that much; only that she be with him for the rest of their lives. To be with him, to let him protect her, to hold her at night, to sleep in his bed with him, to bear his children and love them. And teach them to laugh.

It had to be better than hanging for burglary! If only he could convince her of it.

Stubborn wench! He would find some way to protect her. She might repudiate him, but she could not prevent him from following his instincts.

His instinct was protect her, whether she wanted it or not.

She might not want his money, but he would use it and all the resources he had at his disposal in order to shield her from the worst consequences of her folly. He hurried home, where he sat at his library desk and began to pen a letter to Captain Patchett.

"Are you sure you want to go to this house party, Kit dear?" said Rose Singleton. "I think it would do you good, for you are, if you don't mind me saying so, looking a little peaky, and some exercise and fresh sea air will restore the roses to your cheeks. However, it must be admitted that most of the company will be a good deal older than you—I do not know whether there will be many young people at all—it is to be more or less a family and old friends' sort of gathering, not the sort of dashing social affair that you might have been expecting."

Kit smiled. "Oh, I don't mind. In fact, it would quite a pleasant change. But are you sure your friends are happy to have me stay as well?"

Rose laughed. "Oh, of course, yes. They will love you. Julia Marsden was a girlhood friend of mine—we attended the same seminary, you know, in Bath. And of course Sir William Marsden is a dear. He was an intimate of your dear papa's—though he was just Billy Marsden to us then—we grew up together, you know."

Kit nodded. "Yes, Aunt Rose. Papa did mention Sir William Marsden." *Indeed he did.*

"But if you are not inclined to go, you must say so. I do not mind at all staying in London."

"No, no," said Kit hurriedly. "You must not say so. I would love to attend a house party and to meet your's and Papa's old friends would suit me perfectly. You forget I have never visited an English country estate, and I am so looking forward to it."

"Of course, how very odd it seems, to be sure. Very well, if you are certain then, my love, I shall write to Julia and accept her invitation and we shall leave at the end of the week." Rose beamed with satisfaction. "You will like their home, I'm sure, my dear. It is quite lovely, with the most wonderful gardens and there is a beautiful lake where we can go boating, if the weather is fine. And the sea is not very far, either, of course."

Kit smiled at the middle-aged woman fondly. Rose was clearly very eager to go to the Marsdens' house party, yet had been quite willing to forgo her pleasure for Kit's sake. Never had anyone, except Maggie, considered Kit before herself. It was truly heartwarming, and Kit felt quite unworthy. She was, after all, using Rose, even if it was in a greater cause.

As for the house party, it was beautifully opportune. She'd been racking her brains for weeks as to how to gain access to the Marsden home. Now, with absolutely no scheming or planning on Kit's part, it had all fallen into place. The timing was perfect.

Now that the fourth compartment had been filled, it would be wise to be away from London for a time. Already people were speculating a great deal.

Her Chinese red herring—or should she say red carp?—was working splendidly, but she'd had too many close shaves as it was, and it would not be clever to push her luck, particularly with the Watchdog breathing down her neck at every turn. Better to let the excitement die down a little.

The house party would get her out of London and away from Mr Devenish and his all-too-suspicious mind. And his annoyingly acute brain. As well as his infuriating habit of turning up where he was least wanted. Not to mention those all-too-broad shoulders.

She sighed, thinking of those shoulders.

Yes, it was better to stay away. To take herself out of the paths of temptation.

Marry me. She closed her eyes. It was not possible, of course, but oh…the temptation…

Not so simple now, was it, the choice between a sacred promise concerning her father's honour and the offer of happiness…? Her father's dying words came back to her: *Women don't understand honour. Their minds are too cluttered with emotion.*

Her mind was certainly cluttered with emotion right now.

The house party would offer a welcome respite.

* * *

The hired post-chaise and four turned in off the road between two enormous stone-mounted gates, and down the long winding drive which led to the house. The Marsden family home, Woodsden Lodge, was a beautiful old Elizabethan house, set on a natural rise in the land, and surrounded by walled terraces. The house overlooked a deep, winding valley.

There was a fine open parkland to the east of the house, giving way to thick, verdant forests. To the west lay what Kit thought might be the kitchen gardens, surrounded by ancient grey stone walls. In the front was what looked like a wonderful rose walk, laid out in an ancient Elizabethan knot design.

"See that rose garden?" Rose said.

Kit nodded. "It looks lovely."

"It is Lady Marsden's pride and joy. Sir William gave it to her as a birthday gift one year. It is modelled on the very ancient one of her old home, but in the middle of the design, there is the most beautiful little pavilion, where you can sit and just smell the roses. Julia—Lady Marsden, that is—calls it her Romantic Rose Arbour." She laughed. "Sir William, of course, pooh-poohs the idea of any romance, and calls it the Folly of Love. He is deeply sentimental, you understand, and terrified lest anyone should discover it."

Kit laughed. How wonderful it would be if

someone—no one in particular, of course—ever built a romantic garden for her. It was the most romantic and lovely notion. Kit liked the sound of Sir William and Lady Marsden. She wished she didn't.

It would have been easier if Sir William beat his wife instead of making gardens for her.

The house itself looked very old to Kit's eyes. Built of the dark grey stone which was obviously the local building material, it was tall and square and could have seemed forbidding except for its multitudes of large square mullioned windows placed at regular intervals across the front.

Two servants ran out to greet them as the carriage pulled up in the paved courtyard which framed the front entrance. By the time the groom had put down the steps for them to descend the carriage, Sir William and Lady Marsden were coming down the steps from the porched entrance of the house to greet them.

"Oh, Rose, my dear," Lady Marsden said. "Oh, I am so pleased you came. I vow, I have not seen you for such an age—oh, I know we met briefly in Town, but that was just a moment or two—now you are here we can have as many long, comfortable cozes as we wish!"

The two ladies embraced affectionately. Kit stood back a little, smiling. It was clear that Rose and Lady Marsden were very good friends.

"And this is your little niece, eh, Miss Singleton?"

boomed Sir William, smiling kindly at Kit, who curtsied politely.

"Yes, this is my long-lost niece, Miss Catherine Singleton—but she prefers to be called Kit," added Rose.

"Well, then, Miss Kitty it is," agreed Sir William. "That'll clear up any confusion—this profusion of Miss Singletons. For the duration of this house party it shall be Miss Rose and Miss Kitty, eh? How's that?"

"That will be delightful, sir," agreed Kit, feeling a little surprised. There was no mistaking the genuine friendliness and kindness in Sir William's eyes. Yet he was one of the men on her father's list.

Sir William, like the rest of London society, had accepted the tale of the long-lost niece. If he really knew who her father was, he would never have invited her here, let alone been so friendly and welcoming.

He offered her an arm.

She took a deep breath and placed her hand on it. She had been braced a little for the possibility of some unpleasantness. This was the first one of her father's enemies who she had had to be on terms of everyday intimacy with, and the situation had been fraught with uncomfortable possibilities. But now…

She heaved a sigh of relief.

"Tired after your long journey, Miss Kitty, what?" enquired Sir William, patting her hand in a fatherly manner as he ushered her to the house.

"Oh, no, not at all. The roads are very good. I was just enjoying the air here," explained Kit. "So pure and cool and fresh. Delightful after the smoky air of London."

"Ah well, soon clear out your lungs o' that," chuckled Sir William. "Are you a young lady who likes to ride, p'rhaps?"

"Oh, yes, indeed I do."

"Good, then p'rhaps after a spot of somethin' to eat, you'd care to take a look at a few o' my nags. Dare say you'll find one or two are not so contemptible. Might be able to fit you up with a ride for tomorrow, what! If you care to, that is."

Kit beamed. "I'd be most delighted, Sir William. In fact, there is nothing I'd enjoy more."

They went into the house together, and as they went, Sir William pointed out little items he thought may be of interest to her. And she was interested. For all his bluff heartiness, he was a genial and kindly host who was going out of his way to make a young woman, a stranger to him and his family, feel very much at home. Kit found the whole thing a little disconcerting.

This friendly, seemingly kind-hearted man was one of the cold-blooded conspirators who had betrayed her father so many years ago.

"What do you say to a nursery supper tonight, Rose?" said Lady Marsden. "Most of our guests will arrive in a day or two, so Billy and I thought it would be nice to be simply *en famille* tonight with you and Kit."

Sir William joined in. "Thought we could have supper like we used to in the old days, Rosie, what? Join the girls up in the nursery, boiled eggs and toast soldiers, and crumpets and honey and fruit cake and cocoa." He looked a little self-conscious and added, "All bosh, of course, but it's the girls, y'see. Always feel a bit left out when there's a house party on." His gruff belittling of the nursery supper fooled no one. Sir William was a big softie when it came to his daughters, decided Kit. It was becoming quite impossible not to like him.

"No, like this, Miss Kitty-cat," laughed Nell, the oldest of Sir William and Lady Marsden's daughters. "You must hold the bread so, at an angle, and then it will toast easily."

"Ah, yes," said Kit, adjusting the angle of her toasting fork. "I see, it is really quite simple when you get the hang—oops!"

Everyone laughed as the nursery filled with the scent of burning toast. Sir William reached into the flames and snatched out the blackened chunk which had fallen off Kit's toasting fork. With much pantomime, he carried the burnt toast stealthily towards the window, hissed, "Don't tell Nanny," and flung it out into the night, to gales of girlish laughter.

"Aha! So that's what startled my horses when I arrived," said a deep voice from the doorway. "A missile of burnt toast. I suppose it is an improvement on boiling oil! But I thought I'd been invited."

There was a chorus of excited greeting from the little girls and Sir William. Rose and Lady Marsden joined in the hubbub, as Hugo Devenish was welcomed into the cosy little schoolroom.

"How do you do, Mr Devenish," murmured Kit, aware she was the only one not giving him a friendly welcome. But she couldn't. She was shocked to the marrow by his arrival. She'd thought him safely at a distance, in London. Clearly he'd been expected. But why had no one mentioned it?

"Come in and have a seat, Mr Devenish," said Lady Marsden warmly. "Your clothes are much too fine to ruin them as my husband does by sitting on the hearth rug with the children." She rolled her eyes in mock frustration at Sir William, who grinned back unrepentantly and winked at Mr Devenish.

"Dev, old fellow. Come here and show this girl how to hold a toasting fork," he said. "Wouldn't credit it— girl's been to India and all sorts of outlandish places but she's never toasted bread in front of a nursery fire before! Shockin' gap in her education! Rectify the matter myself, only I've discovered an appalling absence of marmalade. Can't have toast without marmalade, y'know. Off to see to the matter immediately."

"Oh no, it's quite all righ—" Kit began.

"I'd be delighted," interrupted Mr Devenish smoothly, as Sir William breezed out of the room, his youngest child, Molly, riding horsie on his back.

He sat down on the hearth rug, right next to Kit. In seconds little Sally, aged five, clambered over his long legs and plopped herself down in his lap. To Kit's astonishment, stern, unapproachable Mr Devenish didn't turn a hair. He simply seized a fork and bending his head to the little mop of golden curls, showed Kit and the child how to attach the bread securely to the fork.

Nell settled herself down with Kit, declaring she would show Miss Kitty-cat the way of it because there wasn't all that much bread left, and suddenly peace reigned in the nursery, as the important business of making toast took precedence over all.

Kit tried very hard to concentrate on following the commands of her toast instructress, but her eyes kept flickering sideways to the big dark man sitting on the hearth rug with the tow-headed moppet in his lap. His big hands were guiding the little ones, and he murmured encouragement in a low undertone. Sally scowled in grim concentration as she held the fork towards the fire, its weight unobtrusively supported by the man. After a moment or two, the little girl looked up at him.

"Now?"

"If you like." He nodded, and she carefully drew the fork back. They both inspected the toast and after a short consultation, solemnly pronounced it ready to be buttered. That was Lady Marsden's job, apparently. She buttered the toast lavishly, honey was applied and the toast was devoured by child and man alike, with gusto.

Kit watched the whole procedure, a lump in her throat. He sprawled, relaxed on the hearth rug, in his fine London clothes and his shiny Hessian boots, a small, decidedly sticky girl-child resting against his chest, sleepily licking honey from her fingers. He seemed not to mind at all, in fact he looked like a man who had been given a taste of Heaven for the evening.

Kit bit her lip. He looked so stern and severe and he'd been so gentle with the little one, it almost broke her heart to watch them.

He glanced over at her and smiled. He wasn't a man who smiled often. It made her want to weep again.

After that night at the opera, she'd resolved to keep him at a distance with the strictest, most rigid formality.

Formality was simply not possible; not when they were both sprawled on a hooked woollen rug in front of a crackling fire, the detritus of an impromptu picnic scattered around them and each with a sleepy child nestled against them. Or in his case, with a small tow-headed angel curled up in the crook of his arm, sound asleep against his heart.

Kit swallowed. Something seemed to be stuck in her throat.

"I think it is time we put these children to bed," said Lady Marsden softly. She stood and lifted Molly who was fast asleep, from her husband's arms. He in turn lifted the sleepy Nell from Kit's side and carried her through to the bedroom. Mr Devenish rose, Sally still asleep in his arms, and followed the Marsdens through to the children's bedroom.

He returned in a moment, stretching his arm. "Arm went to sleep," he grimaced slightly. "Little tyke weighs a ton."

Kit was not deceived. Like Sir William, Mr Devenish clearly loved children. And neither of them seemed to mind that they were only girl-children. It was an attitude Kit had never come across before. It wasn't because they were English, either. Her father was English and he'd been so bitter about her mother's failure to give him a son. He'd never forgiven Kit for being a girl.

Sir William seemed not to mind that his wife had given him three worthless girls. He didn't even seem to think they were worthless. Nor did Mr Devenish…

Kit wondered if Mr Devenish would be as sanguine if his own wife failed to provide him with an heir. Would he treat his own daughters with such tenderness?

She watched him standing before the fire, his back

to the room, his long strong legs braced in their black Hessian boots. She thought of the grave way he'd consulted with the little girl over the readiness of the toast. He hadn't acted like a man who thought little girls were a worthless nuisance.

His daughters would be lucky, she thought.

So would his wife…

Chapter Ten

"Kit, dear, you will be pleased to hear we are invited for luncheon to Gelliford House tomorrow." Rose smiled happily at Kit over the breakfast table.

"Oh, how nice," said Kit politely. "What is Gelliford House?"

"You have never heard of Gelliford House?" said Sir William, surprised.

Kit shook her head. "Should I?"

Rose looked at her, shocked. "But, Kit—Gelliford House!"

Kit smiled and shrugged ruefully. "Never heard of it. I suppose it is some frightfully grand mansion where Shakespeare lived, or Queen Bess or someone. You forget I did not grow up in England. I do not know all the famous places."

Rose exchanged a glance with Lady Marsden and then said quietly to Kit, "It is not famous in the least—only to our family. It was the house I was born in. All the Singletons were born there. Except you."

"Oh!" Kit realised she had blundered. Rose was supposed to be her aunt. She ought to know the name of her ancestral family home. "Sorry, Papa never mentioned the name of his home before. Is it far from here?"

"No, only a short drive. We shall leave after breakfast, and that will give us time to show you everything before luncheon," said Rose. "Our guests will not be arriving until at least four o'clock, and if we leave Gelliford at half past three, it will give us plenty of time to get home."

"We?"

"Oh, we are all invited," said Lady Marsden.

Kit's eyes went to Mr Devenish, who was addressing himself to a slice of ham. He glanced up, saw the question in her eyes and smiled faintly. "I have never been to Gelliford. It shall be most interesting to see your old family home. Did you spend your whole childhood there, Miss Rose?"

"Oh, yes, indeed, though it passed to a cousin when my father died. Papa was the second son, you know, so he was living there at his brother's grace. My cousin still lives there—I suppose if you called him Cousin George, it would be all right, Kit, dear."

Gelliford House was not as beautiful as the Marsdens' home of Woodsden Lodge, but it was much bigger. It was set in a deer park, with a drive leading up to it, lined with ancient oaks.

Cousin George proved to be a spindly, earnest man in his late fifties, with a very strong sense of his own worth and lineage. He greeted Kit a little stiffly, as if he was doing her a great favour in receiving her at all. Kit wondered what Rose had told him to make him accept her as a relative.

He turned to Rose. "Ah, Rose, I suppose that fellow found you, all right?"

Rose looked puzzled. "Fellow? What fellow, Cousin George?"

"Fellow came looking for you, couple of weeks back. Thought you lived here, for some reason. Sent him off to London."

"But who was he?"

Cousin George frowned, then shook his head. "Can't think of it for the moment. Thin dark fellow. Brown skin. Shouldn't be surprised if he was a foreigner. What have you to do with foreigners, eh, Rose?"

Rose looked bewildered. "I cannot imagine."

Kit felt anxious. She was the only connection with any foreigners. Was it some man who had known her father? Someone who had somehow made the connection with Kit Smith, vagabond adventuress and Miss Rose Singleton, respectable spinster of the *ton*?

"Forgotten his name, hang it," said Cousin George. "Never mind, it'll come back to me."

He showed them over the grounds first, then the rest of the house. The library was his pride and joy; he was something of a scholar, Kit surmised, and he would have lingered there all day, pulling out this volume or that to show them. However Rose was most anxious for them all to visit the portrait gallery before lunch.

"The paintings are the most interesting, I think," she said. "They date from the earliest times and the whole family is there."

"Yes," agreed Cousin George. "It is really a very comprehensive collection. Any student of physiognomy will find it a source of fascination to trace the development and inheritance of the family features. You, for instance, Cousin Kit, have your grandmother's eyes."

"Oh, really?" she said. "How astonishing." It was more than astonishing, since she was no relative at all to this family. And her father had remarked more than once that she had her mother's blue eyes.

"Yes, I thought so too. And the dresses and jewellery are very interesting too," added Rose. "It was the custom for the ladies—for everyone, really—to be painted in their finest dresses and jewels, displaying the family wealth, you know."

"Yes?" said Kit politely, not terribly interested in jewels or dresses.

She felt, rather than saw Mr Devenish give her a sharp look. She glanced across and found herself on the receiving end of a very stern minatory look. Why would he look at her in that way? she wondered. As if she was a naughty child about to do mischief. But she'd been on her best behaviour, a little bored perhaps, but no one could appear fascinated with Cousin George's tedious lectures.

Then it hit her in a flash and she wanted to giggle. He couldn't, surely, think she was planning to rob Gelliford House?

"These jewels, Aunt Rose, are they still in the family?" she asked innocently.

As Cousin George explained that some indeed were still in the family and in fact were stored in a secret vault in the house, Kit watched Mr Devenish out of the corner of her eye. She managed to keep a straight face as his frown grew blacker and blacker.

He did. He thought she was going to rob Gelliford House. What enchanting sport!

"Let us all go into the Great Hall," said Cousin George. "That is where the portrait gallery is situated."

Everybody moved forward, and Mr Devenish reached to take Kit's arm in what he no doubt thought of as protective custody, but she skipped sideways and attached herself to a surprised Cousin George.

With a Watchdog bristling a pace behind her, Kit sauntered towards the Great Hall, arm in arm with

Cousin George. "Tell me, Cousin George, these family jewels, are there any diamonds? I have a particular interest in diamonds, you see."

Behind her, she could feel Mr Devenish stiffen.

"And how much do you think these old family pieces would be worth today, Cousin George? As much as that, you think? Really?"

Mr Devenish came abreast of them and scowled blackly across at her. Kit smiled serenely back and returned to her questioning of Cousin George.

"I hope they are securely locked away. I don't suppose you'd care to show a long-lost cousin the secret vault, would you, dear Cousin George?"

She made sure that each question wafted to the ears of her glowering one-man audience, though she was fairly certain he could not hear her cousin's responses, uttered as they were in a dry and dusty voice. She fanned the flames of the Watchdog's suspicions all the way to the Great Hall.

Cousin George naturally began with the oldest paintings, many of which were rather gloomy and stiff, in Kit's opinion. She was very glad she wasn't related to these people—they were a dreary lot for the most part, she thought, though some of the women struck a chord in her.

Grim-faced men abounded, looking important, or self-con-sequential, or simply dull. She disliked the hunting scenes most, where a gentleman and his son or sons, bristling with weaponry, would be posed with hunting dogs at their feet, horses behind, and a variety of slaughtered beasts scattered around—hares, pheasants, perhaps a boar, sometimes even a stag.

Posed with the adults were stiff little children from every age, dressed as miniature adults and looking solemn and uncomfortable. Some of the little girls were in tightly laced corsets and looked as if they could barely move, poor little creatures.

The ladies certainly exhibited a variety of fashion, making Kit realise how transient a thing beauty was; in some periods, it seemed that the ladies needed high foreheads to be thought beautiful; some had their hairline plucked so high, it looked to Kit's eyes as if they were almost bald.

"Admiring the jewellery?" grated a deep voice behind her. "I am watching every move you make, don't forget."

Kit giggled. "Yes," she said in a melodramatic whisper. "I have winkled the secret of the hidden vault from poor, unsuspecting Cousin George and will be back here at dead of night to plunder the place and loot its ancient treasures. Then I will depart on my midnight steed."

"Oh," he said stiffly. He stared at her a moment, as if trying to decide whether she was truly teasing, or whether she was playing a double game and pretending to tease, to put him off the scent.

Kit winked cheekily.

The hard grey gaze softened slightly. "You are a baggage, miss," he said severely, but his lips twitched. Then his face hardened again. "You have no idea of the danger you court. But know I am watching you. You have clearly not taken to heart what I said to you the other night—"

Not taken to heart? How could she not have taken it to heart—his words were enshrined there forever. Kit would never forget him saying it, in that ragged, tender, gruff, matter-of-fact voice. *Marry me.*

"You will hang, if they catch you!"

Kit flushed. "Oh, that."

"Yes, that, miss! And I will not allow you to risk yourself any further. Your neck is too pretty to stretch."

She shrugged lightly and strolled towards the next painting. Of course she was worried about being caught. She was not stupid. She'd known from the start that the keeping of her promise to her father entailed the risk of her life. But she'd made the promise and the rest followed. And she had learned young that if you lived a life of risk and danger, with an axe poised to fall on your neck any moment, you had two choices: live in fear, or take each moment of joy as it came. She, like her father, had chosen the latter.

Hugo clenched his fists. He had rarely been so frustrated in all his adult life. He had become accustomed to ordering things—and people—how he liked them. It was his instinct to protect what was his. He protected his home, his belongings, his employees—even, in his own way, his less-than-appreciative relatives. But there was never anyone he wanted— no, *needed* to protect more than Miss Kit Singleton.

He'd never met anyone more in need of protection in his life.

He'd never met anyone so determined to court the most horrifying of dangers.

And all for a set of baubles. What could drive her so hard that she would continue to risk her life over and over, in such a daring, bold, mad masquerade?

Hugo clenched his fists harder and glared at a Singleton ancestor.

It was so unnecessary. He'd offered to buy her whatever baubles she wanted. She hadn't considered it for a moment, confound it! What good was money when it could not protect the people you lo—! He caught himself up on the thought.

The trouble was that Miss Kit Singleton was very emphatically not his. She had said so time and time again. He never thought he would ever offer marriage to a woman, and when he had she hadn't even considered it for a moment.

It was more than frustrating, it was…

She didn't want his money. She didn't want his protection. She didn't want his name. *I am not for the likes of you.*

She didn't have to marry him. She didn't have to have anything to do with him if she didn't want to—just as long as she let him make sure she was safe. And happy.

He needed most desperately to see her safe and happy. He would give anything, do anything to have it so.

But she had made it more than clear that there was nothing she needed or wanted from someone like Hugo Devenish.

It was a very bitter pill to swallow.

Cousin George presided over the viewing; to Kit's dismay, he appeared to have an exceedingly lengthy and rather dry lecture to accompany each painting. Discreetly, she detached herself from the group and drifted ahead. The so-called Great Hall was, in fact, a long, narrow room, a little dusty, rarely visited. Sun shone through high, narrow windows, setting golden motes of dust dancing in the air. Having departed the group somewhere in the reign of Henry VIII, Kit steadily worked her way towards the present day.

Behind her the drone of Cousin George's voice faded. Footsteps echoed on the oaken floor.

Kit wandered along the line of paintings, inspecting the portraits with polite interest. Who were these people? It was really quite interesting, comparing their dresses, their clothes, the heavy and elaborate wigs. She was interested to see the things they considered important—the possessions they had painted with them: the gold watch so carefully and lovingly rendered;

the jewels first displayed on a stiff, proud young bride; then, a hundred years later, the same jewels adorning her great-great-grandson's new young wife. And, as Cousin George had promised, there was some discernible continuity in the family features...

She saw the children first. A young boy, aged about eleven, and a girl, about five years younger, a King Charles spaniel at their feet. They boy looked a little like... Kit faltered. No, it was coincidence. All young children looked a little alike. It was the chubby face of childhood.

Nevertheless, she looked hard at the painting, taking in the facial features. The little girl had blue eyes and long golden ringlets, the boy's hair was darker and his eyes were that indistinguishable colour between brown and green. Kit was haunted by a feeling that she knew these children...

The golden ringlets could have become the wispy flyaway hair of the adult Rose Singleton, but if so...

She moved on to the next picture. It was the same two children, only grown up; she could see that at a glance. The girl was seventeen or eighteen, and so very lovely. Her hair was a richer gold, her eyes just as blue, her features delicate and fine. It was a youthful Rose, before she'd had the vibrancy of youth and high spirits drained from her. But it was the young man with Rose who drew all of Kit's attention. A young man who looked uncannily like…

Papa! He looked just like Papa. But…

It could not be.

She felt suddenly light-headed. In silence, as if quite alone in the room, she delicately touched one finger to the painted face of the young man. And then moved across to that of the young woman, the young Rose.

Papa and Rose? But how?

She moved back to the previous painting, her heart racing. The faces were chubbier, less finally formed, but the people were unmistakable. Papa and Rose.

Papa and Rose. Brother and sister in truth? It could not be.

Kit's mind reeled. She had assumed her imposture as Rose's long-lost niece was simply another of Papa's schemes, but if these pictures were genuine, and she could see no reason why they would not be…

But if that was the case… What if Rose was—her aunt?

Kit struggled to absorb the notion. The two paintings called into question everything she had ever believed about herself, everything her father had ever told her.

If she was not an impostor…

If Rose was *truly* her aunt…

She'd thought she was alone in the world—except for Maggie. If she was not…

Oh Lord, this changed everything!

"Kit, my love, do come here," called Rose. "This is your paternal grandmother, Matilda, the lady George mentioned. A particularly good portrait of her by Hogarth. See how alike your eyes are? What do you think, Mr Devenish? Are they not identical?"

Hugo glanced at Rose, then to Kit. To his surprise she didn't move. She stood in front of two paintings, staring as if transfixed, first at one, then the other.

"Kit, dear?" repeated Rose.

She didn't so much as blink. Whatever was in those pictures had completely and utterly gripped her attention, to the exclusion of all else, Hugo thought. He moved closer.

Good God! She'd turned as pale as paper. Her body was rigid and even as he watched, she started swaying on her feet. He leapt to her side and caught her under the elbow, just as her legs started to buckle beneath her.

He snatched her against him and swung her into his arms.

"Put me down," she muttered feebly, "I'm perfectly all right. Just—"

"You were about to faint!"

"Oh, pooh, nonsense," she grumbled, in a pale imitation of her usual lightheartedness.

He looked down at her and his arms tightened around her, holding her hard against his chest.

"Be quiet," he said softly. "You will accept nothing else from me. At least allow me this one small thing."

She must indeed be feeling faint, he thought wryly, for she subsided with uncharacteristic meekness and laid her head against him, in the hollow between his neck and his jaw. The weight of her hung heavy and right in his arms. Her tumbled curls tickled the skin of his neck. The scent of her clouded his senses... vanilla and rose...and essence of Kit. His brave, bold, mad little Kit. His woman in his arms...for one fleeting moment...

He longed to bring his cheek down to rest on her head, but Rose and the others had come running and were even now fluttering around with vinaigrettes and discussing burnt feathers.

"No, no, I am perfectly all right," Kit said, sneezing as a vinaigrette was thrust under her nose. "Oh, ptchaw! Take that vile thing away, please, Aun—" She broke off and stared at Rose as if for the first time. "Oh Lord, yes—Aunt Rose."

Rose thrust the tiny crystal bottle back under Kit's nose. She shuddered violently and drew back, turning her face away from the gathering, her face against his chest. "No more, I beg you, Aunt," she said in a muffled voice and then added in a whisper, "Get me out of here, Hugo."

It was the first time she'd asked him for anything, the first time she'd used his name.

A crust to a starving man, but who was going to quibble?

"I think she just needs a little fresh air. I shall take her outside and she'll be right as a trivet in no time," he said firmly and strode towards the door.

"Are you sure we shouldn't send for the doctor?" said Cousin George anxiously.

"No!" said Kit against his neck.

"No, no. She has not eaten anything this morning, and is just a little faint," said the man who'd watched her devour three slices of bacon and two pieces of toast at breakfast. "Fresh air is what she needs at the moment. If she does not recover in five or ten minutes, then we shall send for the doctor."

"But I don't need—" Kit began.

"Be quiet," he said to her softly. "You can argue the point as soon as you can stand on your feet and the colour has returned to your cheeks. Until then, you will do as I say."

She lifted a hand to her cheek. It was shaking.

"You're as pale as paper, you know. Now just be quiet and let me take you into the garden and you can tell me about what gave you such a shock in there."

Her eyes darted to his apprehensively. "How did you—?"

"Oh, don't be silly. I notice everything about you," he said simply. "Those two paintings looked ordinary enough to me, but something in them has knocked you all on end, hasn't it?"

He looked into her eyes. They were blue, troubled and betrayed. "Yes," she said.

Disdaining the suggestions of the others to take Kit up to her room, Hugo carried her outside into the sunshine. He refused to let her walk, and strode purposefully to the north-facing side of the house.

In a few moments they reached a herb garden, laid out in a huge cartwheel shape made of mellow red brick, worn and smooth with age, A carved stone seat and an ancient stone sundial stood in the centre of the wheel. He made his way to the centre and finally, reluctantly, placed his precious burden on the seat.

They sat, side by side in silence for a moment or two. He possessed himself of her hand, reluctant to break all contact with her. She seemed not to mind; in fact, she even allowed herself to lean a little against his shoulder. Her hands clutched his convulsively. She stared blankly in front of her, her eyes troubled and unhappy. Devastated.

The peace of the herb garden surrounded them. Many of the herbs were in bloom and the bees buzzed fatly from the purple spires of lavender to the small white flowers of the lemon balm. Thyme flowered at their feet, mingling with a drift of Sweet Alice, spreading around the base of the stone seat. Bruised thyme leaves sent up a clean, pungent fragrance. The perfume of the Sweet Alice teased their senses. Birds sang and chortled in the distance. The sun warmed the stone and the flowers lifted their faces towards it. A soft breeze danced in the dark curls of the girl by his side.

He was waiting for her to speak, but a part of him wished she never would. He would be happy if this moment could last forever.

His hand cradled hers, his thumb caressing the warm silky skin.

"It was my father in those paintings," she said at last.

He waited for her to explain. She said nothing more. Birds sang and chortled in the distance. Tiny butterflies fluttered back and forth across a clump of wallflowers.

"Yes?" he prompted.

"My actual, real father."

"Yes." Hugo was puzzled. "You mean in the Reynolds portraits?"

She shrugged against his shoulder. "I didn't look at who painted it—but the subject was Papa!" She turned to look at him and he was stunned by the distress in her eyes. He wanted to caress her face, but she held onto his hand, hard, refusing to release him. She didn't even know she was doing it, he realised. If he hadn't seen into her eyes, he would still have known she was upset by the restive way she gripped his hand.

"It was Papa!" she said again, as if still unable to believe it.

"Who did you expect to see?"

"I don't know—someone, anyone—just Rose's brother."

"But..." He trailed off. "You mean," he said slowly, "that until you saw those paintings, you thought that Rose's long-lost brother was someone else—not your father?"

She nodded her head, chewing on her lip in distress.

"You didn't know Rose was your aunt."

She shook her head miserably. "Not my real aunt." She leaned her head against his shoulder. "Oh God, what have I done? Why didn't he tell me?"

"You mean your father?"

She nodded again. "All my life, there was just Papa and me. And then, when I was thirteen, Maggie, my maid."

He frowned, opened his mouth, then closed it. There was something, some mystery there. But this was not the time to ask.

"Papa always said I had no other relatives in the world—only him—except perhaps some unknown cousin of Mama's, in Ireland."

Ireland. So that's where she got that colouring, he thought. Those blue, blue eyes, the creamy soft skin and the silky dark curls.

"But you came to Rose as her long-lost niece."

"I thought..." She blushed. "He did refer to her as my aunt, but..." She would not meet his eyes. "There were many women Papa told me to call 'Aunt'. They came and went, all through my childhood." She shrugged, shamefacedly. "I'd never heard of Rose. I thought…I thought…" Her hand tightened in his.

He put his arm around her shoulder and drew her even closer against him. "I understand."

She pulled away from him suddenly. "No, you don't! You know nothing, you understand nothing! You don't *know* what I've done!"

"I understand more than you think," he said.

She stared at him, her eyes troubled and bitter.

He proceeded to tell her all he had surmised, beginning from how he had begun to investigate her background when his nephew had expressed his intention of marrying an heiress—the new diamond heiress.

She groaned, drooping, her hands over her eyes in mortification. "I suppose you discovered that I was no such thing."

He nodded wryly. "Not so much discovered. There was no evidence either way, and you are a very difficult young lady to pin down. But I knew it, all the same."

Kit sat up suddenly and said slowly, "I thought it was just one of his schemes. It was so like Papa to make a scheme extra-elaborate by throwing in something like diamonds at the last minute… But if I really am Kit Singleton, if Rose really is my aunt, then, why…?"

"Perhaps he thought if you were thought to be rich, it would help you find a husband, though I myself would have thought—"

"No, I don't think he ever gave a thought to my marrying," she said absentmindedly. "He had another scheme for me."

Hugo waited for her to tell him, to admit, finally that she was the Chinese Burglar. He knew it, but he wanted to hear her say it. To him. Only to him.

Kit took a sudden breath. "You know, just as he was dying, Papa started to tell me he had written to Rose from New South Wales, but he died before he could tell me what it was about. Perhaps he had a different scheme in mind then and the two became confused..."

A bungler, as well as a selfish swine, thought Hugo angrily. What he wouldn't give for an hour alone with the callous knave who'd been Kit's father.

"Ouch!" Kit winced and tugged at her hand, and he realised he was clenching his fist over her hand.

"Sorry." He lifted her hand and kissed it gently. His long thumb caressed her skin tenderly.

"So what was this other scheme your father set you to do, if it was not to find a husband?"

She looked at him pensively, then took a deep, decisive breath. "No, there is no point. I have burdened you enough already with the troubles of my family."

"It is no burden. And I very much wish to know."

She glanced at the garden. "It is a lovely day, is it not? Shall we return to the others? The fresh air and the sunshine have quite restored me."

He ignored her attempt to change the subject. "The Chinese Burglar. I suppose he was your father's idea."

"No," she admitted ruefully after a moment. "The disguise was my idea. If you provide people with an obvious enigma, they often do not notice the true mystery."

"And this 'true mystery'—was it for money, or for some other reason?" he probed.

She smiled. "I said I was not going to burden you, and I will not." She rose. "I am feeling perfectly well now. Shall we return?"

Infuriating, stubborn little piece! Hugo did not move.

And yet, why was he not surprised that she would not confide the whole to him? He was furious at the whole situation, and immensely frustrated by her determined independence, but he could not find it in his heart to be angry with her. He admired independence. And loyalty.

If her story was to be believed—and he did believe it, despite all the other deceptions she had perpetrated—her father had lied to her all her life. What sort of a man did that? What sort of a man would send his only daughter into such a mad, desperate masquerade—*when there was no need for it?* Why have her pretend to be Rose's niece, when she was her niece in truth? And why, oh, why, set it about that she was a diamond heiress, when he must have known how easily such a huge fraud would be exposed?

And why had she committed those burglaries? She still hadn't explained that. Hugo was suddenly sure it was not about money.

"Pennington, Brackbourne, Alcorne, Grantley, Pickford, Cranmore and Marsden—all of these were once your father's boon companions."

She went suddenly very still.

"There was a mystery about the way in which your father left England. It was very sudden and very odd."

"Four of them—Pennington, Brackbourne, Alcorne and Grantley—have been robbed by the Chinese Burglar. Pickford and Marsden have been spared, so far." He noticed her flush and look away and was immediately alert. "And Cranmore seems to have left the country at the same time as your father—it was all hushed up."

"Cranmore?" She looked puzzled. "I have never heard of Cranmore."

It was a tacit admission she knew of the others in connection with her father. Hugo stood and took her arm.

"I have made enquiries. Something significant happened around twenty-two years ago, but none of the principals involved will talk about it. However, I think if we ask Sir William what happened, he would tell you. You have a right to know."

She hesitated. "You will not tell Sir William… everything? He is a magistrate, after all."

Did she still not trust him? He shook his head. "No."

Kit took a deep breath. "Very well then, I will ask Sir William to tell me his side of the story."

Hugo frowned. *His side of the story.* Interesting phrasing.

It was after supper when Kit and Hugo requested a private word with Sir William. The rest of the house-guests were involved in cards or gathered around the billiard table, so their presence was not missed. Sir William took them to the library.

"We were all young then, a trifle wild, as young men are. Mad about horses, up for any lark, drinkin' to excess every night and still able to get up with the birds to go huntin'—can't do that now, mind! Constitution won't stand it." He smiled reminiscently, then slowly the smile faded.

"It was the cards that was the trouble. Gamblin'. Jimmy Singleton…" He shook his head. "Became a fever with him. Had to win, all the time. More and more. Took to goin' to the hells—not places like White's and Brook's and Boodle's, where the rest of us went, but some of the, er, less savoury establishments. Not too fussy about the standards, if you know what I mean," he added, looking a little uncomfortable.

Kit nodded, biting her lip. She'd always believed

that aspect of her father had emerged after his exile from England, not before.

"Thing is, he got… Well, it was as if the cards were the only thing that was real to him." Sir William sighed and stared sadly into the fire. "Changed him, it did. Not the fellow we knew…"

"What caused him to leave England, sir?" prompted Hugo.

Sir William heaved another sigh. He got up and poured himself another brandy. "Another one, Devenish? No. Miss Kit, a sherry perhaps?"

They each declined. Sir William took a large swallow of brandy and took his glass to the fire. He stood with his back to the fire, glass in hand, staring meditatively at a hunting scene on the opposite wall.

"It was here, at this very house, in fact. M'parents were up in London; we young bloods were down for a week of huntin'—Johnny Pickford, Brackbourne, of course, Pennington, Alcorne—he didn't have the title then—Grantley, young Cranmore, and your father. And me, of course. Young Cranmore was getting married in a couple of weeks and we'd decided to have a bit of a bachelor party. All very much as normal—a bit o' high spirits, but no harm in it. Only we got to playin' cards and drinkin'."

He paced around the room, obviously ill at ease. "It all boiled down in the end to a battle between Cranmore and Singleton. Cranmore was younger

than us, and not too plump in the pocket but…
well…never mind that side of it."

Kit and Hugo exchanged a puzzled glance. Never
mind what side of it? But before they could ask, Sir
William was continuing.

"Singleton was obsessed. Relentless. Goaded
Cranmore into betting more and more, pourin' more
and more wine into him, and pushin' him into drinkin'
more than he could handle." He shrugged. "Nothin'
really wrong with that, o' course. Cranmore was his
own man, after all. Ought to know his own limits."

He shook his head. "Trouble was, Cranmore was
losin'. He was scrawlin' vowel after vowel, and
Singleton kept acceptin' them, even though the rest
of us tried to get 'em to stop."

There was a short silence, in which the only sound
in the room was the crackling of the fire and the
ticking of the grandfather clock in the corner. "It
was almost dawn, no light yet, but you could hear
that racket the birds make just before dawn, you
know? Well, just around then, they finished up.
Cranmore said in a queer, cracked voice, 'That's it.'
Nothin' else. Just, 'That's it.' His face was this
terrible grey colour—I'll never forget it.

"And your father…" Sir William looked at Kit.
"Your father started laughing. He'd won everything.
Cranmore was ruined. Lost everything—money,
horses, property—even his family home.

"I remember Cranmore saying, 'I won't be able to get married now,' and your father just shrugged and said, 'So be it,' and kept fiddlin' with the damned cards—excuse me, Miss Kit—with the dratted cards. So in the end, Cranmore left. Had to give him a horse m'self. Singleton wouldn't let him take his own horse, wouldn't even let him borrow it and return it later."

Kit closed her eyes in shame. She had seen her father winning before; he was not a gracious winner.

"So poor young Cranmore rode off to break the news to his widowed mother and younger sister—"

Kit winced.

"—and o' course Alcorne and Grantley went with him to make certain he didn't do anything foolish, if y'know what I mean. And the rest of us just sat there, shocked. One of our friends had just made another one destitute, and that wasn't the worst of—well, we won't go into that. But Singleton just kept fiddling with the cards, and I must admit I got so confounded angry with him, just sitting there, grinnin' and shufflin' the cursed pack, that I snatched them off him and tossed them into the fire."

There was a long heavy silence. "And that's when we saw it. Saw the pinholes in the pasteboard, with the fire shining through 'em. No mistakin' it—Brackbourne pulled a dozen or more of 'em out of the flames so we could be certain—the cards were marked. Singleton was a wretched cheat. Not only

that, he'd used marked cards to swindle his own s—
well, doesn't matter who. Man was a cheat."

Hugo went to the side table and poured himself and
Sir William a brandy. He poured a sherry for Kit
without asking. She accepted it with shaking hands,
thankfully.

It was no surprise to find her father cheated. He'd
done it often in the last few years. But she thought
all those things—the lying, the cheating, the bitter-
ness, the drinking and the dishonesty—were a result
of his unjust exile from English society.

It turned out that they were the reason for it.

Nothing he had told her was true. Nothing! He'd
told her she had no family left in the world, and yet
Rose, sweet gentle Rose, was her aunt.

He'd told her he'd been victimised, abused and
exiled because of a great injustice done to him. But
the great injustice he had suffered was to be caught
cheating at cards. And not simply cheating—deliberately bankrupting a young man who was a friend
of his, a young man about to get married.

Kit writhed with shame inside. This was her
father. Her blood.

In the greatest irony of all, he'd sent her out to risk
her liberty and perhaps her life, to redeem his honour.

His *honour*!

Sir William spoke again. "Well, as you can
imagine, we wanted to tell young Cranmore his

fortune was safe after all, so Johnny Pickford rode after the others to tell 'em the good news… Only what we didn't know, was Pickford took a toss twenty miles from Cranmore's home, and was took up for dead by some villager and laid unconscious for days, while the rest of us had no idea." Sir William paced back to the fire, and unconsciously lifted his coat tails to warm his backside.

"By the time he came around and a message was sent back to us, and we'd chased after Cranmore, it was too late. The damage was done!"

Kit sat forward. "You don't mean—?"

Sir William stared. "What?"

"He didn't shoot…" She couldn't finish the sentence.

"Oh, no, no, my dear, no need to look so distressed. Cranmore hadn't killed himself, no, no. But he'd left the country. Settled his mother and his sister with relatives first and then signed on as an ordinary seaman on the first ship leaving for the east. Lad was so deeply ashamed of his foolishness that he swore he wouldn't come back until he'd regained his fortune."

"What happened to him?" asked Kit.

Sir William shook his head sadly. "Never saw the poor fellow again."

"But didn't anybody write?" Kit was appalled.

Sir William shrugged. "Nobody knew where he went. Didn't know where to write. His mother died soon after the whole thing and the sister married a

Scotsman—went to live in Edinburgh or some such place. Never saw her again, either."

He looked at Kit sorrowfully. "Dratted unpleasant tale. Sorry it had to be me to tell you."

"What did you do with Singleton?" asked Hugo. He had a fair idea, but wanted to be sure.

"Well, we all decided, best thing to do for the family's sake, hush the whole thing up. Singleton's family knew, of course, but no one else. He agreed to go abroad in exchange for a regular sum to be paid to him."

The Pittance, thought Kit bitterly. Another mystery solved. How typical of Papa to belittle something he should have been grateful to get. He hadn't deserved such forbearance.

"And his father decided it would be best if he was thought to have perished while doing the Grand Tour. So after a few months, a report was sent from Italy that he had died. And that was that. Until a pretty young miss arrived and we find that a new bud has bloomed on the family tree of the Singletons," finished Sir William gallantly.

The big, bluff man's unexpected kindness took Kit by surprise. She had been prepared for his disapproval, for discomfort and embarrassment.

But this ponderous, gentle compliment from a man both she and her father had wronged flayed her guilt like no righteous attack could have. Tears flooded her eyes.

A bud? A bud from a diseased branch, she thought bitterly. They had both sprung from the branch of the family tree that should have been cut off and burned, long ago.

She could not pretend to herself that she was any different from her father; they were too alike. He had lied and cheated. He had deceived his friends and caused grief to his family. Kit had done the same— some of it unwittingly, to be sure, but there was no question—she was a liar and a thief.

She had a chest upstairs with five spaces filled to prove it.

Five spaces, not merely four.

She felt ill. She had already robbed Sir William of his chess set; his priceless carved ebony and ivory chess set, the royal pieces of which were studded with precious stones.

She said shakily, "How can you not hate me? I am my father's daughter." Her eyes widened as she thought of something else. "All this time, you knew me to be Papa's daughter, and yet you welcomed me into your home. How could you do that, after what he did?"

Sir William smiled kindly. "I've never been a believer in the sins of the father and all that rot. Your father did what he did. This all happened before you were born. No, my dear Miss Kitty-cat, I took you as you came. And don't forget, you might be Jimmy's daughter, but you're also Rose's niece." He leaned forward and patted her on the shoulder. "Don't take it so hard, dear girl. Every family has its share of bad apples. Blood does not bind you; you choose the person you become."

Kit felt her insides shrivel with shame. Yes, she had chosen, that was true. Chosen the same crooked path as her father. Blood did bind you. She stood up. "Thank you for telling me, Sir William," she said in a low voice. "I… I think I shall go to bed now. Could you convey my thanks and apologies to Lady Marsden? I know I should wish her goodnight, but…" Her face crumpled and she looked away.

Sir William and Mr Devenish stood. Kit couldn't bear to meet their eyes; she couldn't bear to see how they would look at her now. In particular, she couldn't bear to look at Mr Devenish. He, even more than Sir William, knew the dreadful things she had done. And now he knew she came by her dishonesty naturally—it was in her very blood. In a low, trembling voice she wished them goodnight and left the room, sick at heart at all she had learned.

She and her father were not worthy even to be in the same room as these fine people.

Chapter Eleven

"Mr Cranmore to see Sir William and Lady Marsden."

"Yes, sir, I shall enquire, if you would care to wait."

"Did he say M-Mr Cranmore?" faltered Rose in a very odd-sounding voice. There was a sudden tension in the room.

She and Kit had been sitting in the front drawing room, writing letters. Or at least Rose had been writing letters; Kit had been trying to decide whether it would hurt Rose more to learn the truth about Kit and her reasons for coming to England, or whether it would be kinder to leave Rose in ignorance. It was very difficult to decide whether ignorance was the preferable alternative, or if cowardice was influencing her decision.

Kit glanced at her aunt and jumped to her feet, instantly concerned. Rose was as white as a ghost, her eyes suddenly huge and haunted-looking. "Aunt Rose, are you not well?"

Rose ignored her; she just stared at the doorway. She was trembling, her beautiful hands clenching the fabric of her gown into a mass of crumples.

Kit didn't know what to do. She had never seen Rose as anything except quite composed, a little vague, but still, composed and perfectly relaxed in whatever environment she found herself.

"Can I get anything for you, Aunt Rose?" Kit said gently.

Rose sat in her chair as if frozen, staring towards the open door. One shaking hand disentangled itself from the fabric of her skirt, and went to her hair, patting it into place in a preoccupied manner.

Outside, they could hear Sir William's booming voice. "By Jove, it's Cranmore! Cranmore, old fellow! Good God! We all thought you were dead! Only sayin' so last night!"

There was an answering masculine murmur, but no words were distinguishable.

Sir William spoke again. "Rose? Yes, she is staying with us at the moment. How ever did you discover such a thing? Good God, but it's a shock to see you after all this time! Through here, old chap, she's just in here."

At his words Kit thought Aunt Rose was going to faint, but instead she gripped the arms of the chair with claw-like hands and sat up rigidly. She looked to Kit like a woman who was facing execution—she was utterly terrified.

The man outside was Cranmore, the man her father had cheated. Obviously he had returned after all these years and had come to hurt Rose in revenge for what Rose's brother had done to him.

Kit shot to the door. "You can't come in! I won't allow it!"

Over Sir William's shoulder she saw Mr Devenish descending the last of the stairs, heading towards her in his measured, leisurely way. He'd clearly heard what was happening. Kit felt a quick rush of warmth and relief. He'd support her. He wouldn't let this man touch her beloved Rose.

"Now, now, Kitty girl," said Sir William. "You mustn't—"

"I won't let him hurt her. He can't come in! It's not her, you want—it's me. I am the daughter!" insisted Kit fiercely, flinging wide her arms across the doorway to bar their entry. She glared at the newcomer, a man of medium height and wiry build, with a dark sallowness that told Kit he had lived many years in the east. His hair was grey, his skin lined and his blue eyes regarded her shrewdly.

"I've never seen my aunt like this," she said vehemently to Sir William. "She's frightened of him." She turned back to Cranmore. "I won't have her upset, do you hear me? I won't allow you to harm a hair on her head!" she added in a low, urgent voice. "I know what happened and I promise you, sir, I will make reparation for what my father did to you. Only please, leave Rose alone. She deserves only kindness—she knows nothing of this. If it is revenge you have come for, I am the one you want."

The man looked at her oddly for a long moment, then shook his head. "You're a fine girl," he said, "but you're wrong. Rose *is* the one I want."

"No! You cannot see her!" said Kit desperately. "Sir William, please show this man out!"

Sir William didn't move. Kit sent a look of appeal to Mr Devenish. He looked back at her with a grave unreadable expression. There was a faint knot between his brows, as if he was coming to some decision. He didn't move either.

Sir William clucked in a soothing manner and shook his head. "Allow me to introduce you, Cranmore. This young lioness is Miss Kit Singleton, Jimmy's daughter and Rose's niece. Kit, my dear, this good fellow is no murdering savage, but a very old friend of your aunt's, Mr Donald Cranmore."

"Delighted to meet you, Miss Singleton. Indeed, I have no plans to hurt your aunt. Quite to the contrary, in fact." Cranmore smiled at Kit with a look of astonishing kindness.

She refused to be charmed. "I know who you are. And if you come as a friend, then why is my aunt sitting in there trembling like a leaf at the sound of your voice?"

"Because she is a foolish creature, and had received a great shock," said Rose's gentle voice behind Kit. "It's quite all right, my dearest girl. It was simply that I thought him dead these many years. I was in shock—I still am, I believe—but indeed, you must not bar him from the sitting room." Rose took Kit's hand, lifted it away from the door jamb and kissed her on the cheek. "Such a brave little defender I have in you."

Kit flushed. She'd made a fool of herself, apparently. As for being a defender of her aunt, the compliment was unbearable; some defender she was, here on false pretences and having robbed her aunt's oldest friends. Ashamed, Kit dropped her hands and stepped out of the way.

"Donald? Is it really you?" said Rose hesitantly and wavered suddenly. "Oh, Heavens! I think my legs are going to collapse!"

There was a rush towards her, but it was the stranger, Mr Cranmore, who reached her first. To Kit's astonishment he swept her middle-aged aunt off her feet completely and into his arms, then walked with her—much too slowly, in Kit's opinion—towards the long, plush sofa beside the window.

Kit stared, outraged. Her aunt didn't seem the least bit affronted by this manhandling. In fact, blushing like a girl, she laid her head against Mr Cranmore's chest.

"Come along Miss Kitty," whispered Sir William. "Time for us all to leave."

Kit turned, astonished. Leave her fainting aunt, unchaperoned and unattended, in the arms of a complete stranger?

"Come on, Kit." Mr Devenish wrapped a warm hand around hers. His thumb caressed her skin gently. "They need to be left alone."

"But…"

He drew her gently but firmly out of the room and allowed Sir William to shut the sitting-room door behind them.

Sir William looked from Mr Devenish, to Kit then back again. "You'll explain?"

She felt, rather than saw, Mr Devenish nod.

"But…" She glanced back at the room, uncertainly.

"Come." His hand was warm and strong and urged her with him. "There are things you need to know." His deep voice was soft, but implacable. He drew her to the front door and led her down the steps and around the side of the house towards the rose garden. Their footsteps crunched on the raked gravel pathway.

"You are not cold?"

She shook her head, her mind spinning with questions.

They reached Lady Marsden's romantic rose arbour and he led her straight to the pavilion. The roses blooming in the morning sunshine released their perfume into the warm air.

He came straight to the point. "It is astonishing

timing, but this is the last part of the mystery—the part Sir William did not care to explain last night. He thought to spare you any more distress."

Kit stared at him, puzzled.

"Cranmore was not simply your father's friend," said Hugo. "He was your aunt's fiancé."

"You mean back when it all happened, when Papa… The woman Mr Cranmore was to marry in two weeks was…was Rose?"

Hugo nodded.

Kit felt sick. She thought she'd heard the worst last night, but this—this was more than devastating. Not only had her father cheated his friend, he'd destituted the man his only sister was about to marry. She thought back to the scene just enacted in the sitting room, the way Mr Cranmore had scooped up Rose against his heart, the expression in Rose's eyes as she looked up into his face.

"It was not a match of convenience, was it?" she said sadly.

Hugo shook his head gently, "If they can look at each other like that after twenty-two years…"

"Twenty-two years apart…" Kit repeated. "All these years, she thought he was dead, and yet she never married."

Twenty-two years. Both Rose and Mr Cranmore had lived their lives in exile too. Her father had ruined so many lives…

She looked at Mr Devenish, who regarded her in such a solemn anxious way that, it was like to break her heart.

Her father had ruined her life as well. No, she could not blame her father for this. She'd ruined her own life. She'd known in her heart of hearts that what she was doing was wrong.

She had tried so hard, risked everything, deceived everyone, to prove herself worthy of her father's love. He was not worthy of such a sacrifice—he'd never been worthy of it.

But nor was she. She was cut from the same tree—stick, root and branch. And even when she'd had the choice, she'd chosen wrongly. She was not worthy of anyone's love or respect. She was a liar, a cheat, a thief. A person who would do such things, even for the sake of love, was not worthy of respect, let alone love.

Kit stood up and walked to the door of the pavilion. The scent of the roses made her feel sick at heart. The roses mocked her—there was no beauty left in her world. "Thank you for telling me, Mr Devenish," she said formally. "I am going to my room now."

Mr Cranmore stayed to dine with them. Kit could hardly believe the difference in the way he looked. A few short hours had taken years off his face. And as for Aunt Rose—she was positively lit from within. She ate almost nothing. She hardly took her eyes off her beloved Donald and his gaze kept returning to her. Kit felt almost embarrassed to be present, only—how could such blatant happiness be embarrassing?

Donald Cranmore kept them all spellbound with the tales of his adventures of the last twenty-two years. He had been in India, they discovered, serving the Sultan of Kandahar, who had saved his life and had demanded his service in return.

"I did pretty well out of it in the end, so I shouldn't complain. But it prevented me leaving, you see," he explained.

"How is it you could leave now, after all this time?" asked Kit. "And return today—the very day after we had all been talking about you."

"It might seem sudden to you, Miss Kit, but from my point of view, the journey has been a very long one." Mr Cranmore took Rose's hand and smiled into her eyes. "I was only able to leave Kandahar six months ago, you see, after the old Sultan had died." He chuckled. "And as for coming here today—in fact, I was here several weeks back, at Gelliford House, but George Singleton sent me back to London."

"Why would you go to Gelliford House? Did you think my father would still be there?"

"It was my home too, over twenty years ago, Kit," said Rose softly.

Kit flushed. It was difficult to get the question of

revenge out of her mind. One look at Rose should remind her, she thought.

"When I heard my Rose had never married, I came straight to Gelliford."

Sir William snapped his fingers. "Of course! The foreign-looking chappy! George couldn't remember his name, d'ye recall, Rose?"

"You mean that was you?" asked Kit.

Mr Cranmore nodded. "I've traipsed up and down that road from London several times but I'll not complain. I'm well content to have ended up here. And here we'll stay, where Rose is close to friends and family."

Rose blushed, rapturously.

Kit gaped. She had never seen Rose so…so girlish. And happy. "You mean—?"

Mr Cranmore hesitated, glanced at Rose, then stood and announced with simple pride, "This afternoon, Miss Rose Singleton did me the singular honour of agreeing—again—to marry me. We shall be wed in the Gelliford chapel as soon as the banns have been called." He kissed Rose's hand, on the fourth finger of which sat a large, glittering diamond. He had indeed done well by the Sultan.

There was an instant chorus of congratulation and delight. Champagne was brought out and toasts were made. Kit was delighted for her aunt, but felt ill at the thoughts she'd had. She'd been expecting revenge from Mr Cranmore, but Mr Cranmore had come with only love in his heart.

Kit was the one steeped in revenge. Kit was the one who'd betrayed her friends.

In one moment, her whole life had been turned upside down.

It was destined to happen, she saw that now. Had they not made that fateful visit to her ancestral home of Gelliford House, the story would still have come out with the arrival of Mr Cranmore on the scene. He had probably left India the same time she and Maggie had left Java.

It was fated. And so was the rest to come.

She did not sleep, of course; she had not expected to. The hours crawled past. Never had hours moved so slowly. She counted them by the tolling of the hall clock.

Two…

Three…

Four… It was time.

Kit slipped out of bed with a heavy heart.

She went to the camphor wood chest and opened it. She took out the oiled silk parcel that contained the Chinese Burglar and weighed it in her hands, indecisively.

No, it was not the night for the Chinese Burglar. On the other hand, maybe it was best if he finished what he'd started. Kit slipped into the disguise. It was symbolic.

She would return all the things she had stolen, and then the Chinese Burglar would burn.

She lifted out the heavy box which contained Sir William's prized chess set and padded down the stairs towards the room in which he kept his safe, the green room.

The house was in darkness, but Kit's senses were attuned to the darkness, like a cat. Miss Kitty-cat, she thought miserably. And how had she repaid such kindness, such a welcome? Tears flooded her eyes and choked her breathing.

She eased open the door to the green room. The first time she had opened it, it had squeaked. She'd oiled it since then. The door opened soundlessly. She padded across the room and lifted down the gilt-framed painting that concealed Sir William's safe.

Using the skills she had been taught as a child, she opened the safe, picking the lock with a specially constructed length of wire.

She bent down to pick up the box containing the chess set.

"Gotcha!" The shout rang out, even as rough hands grabbed her from behind. Kit dropped the chess set and allowed her body to collapse bonelessly in a feint.

"Oy! The blighter's fainted!" The rough hands relaxed for a moment. It was her only opportunity.

Kit wiggled sideways, rolled away from her captor and turned to escape but a sudden heavy blow felled her from behind.

There were two of them, she realised dazedly as she collapsed. She was done for. It was all over.

The Chinese Burglar had been captured.

She came to slowly, to find Sir William and several of his servants standing over her. Kit struggled but it was no use. They had her hands and feet tied.

"Light some candles there, Dawkins, so we can get a little light on this scoundrel," said Sir William. "He's had half of London chasing him—what the devil he's doing all the way out here, I don't know."

"Your chess set, Sir William." Kit recognised the voice. It was Sir William's butler.

"Devil take you, so it is! My chess set, is it, you plaguey scoundrel! Caught in the act, by God! You'll swing for this, my bucko. If you've damaged it—no. All intact, thank Heavens." Sir William faced Kit again. "Now, fellow, let's have a look at you. Dawkins, take off that damned mask of his."

Rough hands ripped off the black skull cap. They tore away the black cotton scarf she'd wrapped around her face. The same rough hands had brought her tea and served her with muffins only the day before. Only they hadn't been rough then.

Kit didn't resist. There was no point.

As the black wrappings fell away from her face, the men exclaimed in surprise. Somebody swore, Kit wasn't sure who.

There was a sudden silence in the green room.

The hall clock tolled the half-hour. Half past four. An hour to dawn. Kit wished she never had to face it.

"Miss…Miss Kitty-cat?" Sir William sounded appalled.

Kit couldn't speak.

"Tell me it isn't true, lass."

Kit hung her head. She could not look him in the eye.

"What's happening William?" called Lady Marsden and came into the room. She stopped suddenly. "What on earth…?" Her voice trailed off as she took in the picture of Rose Singleton's long-lost niece dressed as a Chinaman, tied up on the floor. The safe door was open. Her husband stood over Kit, the box containing his precious chess set held in his hand.

The concern faded from her face. A cold, disdainful look replaced it. She glanced down at Kit. "So this is how you repay our hospitality."

Kit swallowed. There was nothing she could say. All the disgust Lady Marsden expressed could not equal the disgust Kit felt for herself. She wanted to explain that she had been trying to put the chess set back, but she knew nobody would believe her. And she had stolen it in the first place.

"It seems the apple didn't fall far from the tree after all," said Sir William. He sounded immensely weary. Utterly disappointed.

"Papa, what is happening? Nell says you have caught a wicked thief and I want to see him—" Little Sally's voice broke off, suddenly uncertain. She stared down at Kit, who was still on the floor. "Papa? It is Miss Kitty-cat! Why is she on the floor? And dressed like that?"

Nell tumbled into the room after her, followed by a nursemaid in a blue flannel gown, muttering dire threats.

"Papa, did you catch him? How monstrous excitin'—Papa!" The girl stopped, her face suddenly shocked. Her face ran over the ropes around Kit's wrists and ankles. "Miss Kitty-cat?" she whispered in distress. "You cannot be the wicked thief…can you?"

Kit closed her eyes.

"Come away, my darlings. This is no place for you," said Lady Marsden and gathered the children hurriedly out of the room.

"What the devil!" Mr Devenish burst into the room and took in the situation at a glance. "Why the devil have you got her tied up like a criminal?"

"She was caught in the act of stealing the chess set, sir," said the butler.

"Nonsense, I don't believe it! Get those ropes off

her now, before I do someone an injury—and it won't be her, you can rest assured!"

"But, Dev, old fellow, she did steal the chess set," Sir William said heavily. "Have to face it, old man. The girl deceived us all. She's the Chinese Burglar."

"I knew that!" snapped Hugo Devenish. "Now get these blasted ropes off her—ah, give me that!" He snatched a knife off one of the servants and sliced through the ropes binding her. Gently, solicitously, he lifted her to her feet. "Can you walk, sweetheart?" he said softly. He glared around at his stunned audience. "If you've harmed her, I'll have your heads for this, you misguided fools."

He helped her to a seat, supporting her with his hands and his voice. His body radiated rage and protectiveness.

He was going to take responsibility for her, Kit realised suddenly. He was standing up for her in the blackest of black situations. Never had anyone stood up for her like this.

She didn't deserve it.

She couldn't allow it.

She stood up and pushed his hands away from her. "It is nothing to do with him," she said. "*I* am nothing to do with him." She stepped pointedly aside.

"Dammit, Kit—" he growled.

"I am the Chinese Burglar and I did steal your chess set, Sir William," she said clearly. "It is nothing to do with anyone else, not my maid, not Mr Devenish—it was all my own doing." She raised her chin and tried to look Sir William in the face. His distress was more than she could bear. She hung her head again. "I'm sorry," she whispered.

There was a long silence.

"Take her up to her room," said Sir William at last. "I'll deal with this in the morning... somehow."

The servants led Kit away.

"And, Dawkins—"

They paused.

"Lock her in."

As she ascended the stair she heard Mr Devenish's voice saying angrily, "Dammit, Billy, I'll not allow you to turn her over to the authorities. They'll hang her, man!"

Kit did not hear Sir William's response. But she knew what it would be.

Sir William was a magistrate.

"She's gone!" Dawkins burst into Sir William's study. "I went to let her maid in as you instructed, sir, and the room was empty."

Sir William raised his brows in surprise.

"I did lock the door, sir, truly I did. And I kept the key by me all night, too—not trusting that maid of hers not to let her out," Dawkins assured him. "But the lass must have climbed out the window. Dunno how, sir. A fearful long way to the ground it is, and with the night being so damp, the slate would've been terrible slippery."

Sir William jumped to his feet, staring towards the garden, a worried expression on his face.

Dawkins anticipated his question. "No, sir. She ain't lyin' in the garden with a broken neck either. I checked. She got clean away, sir."

Sir William subsided into his chair with a sigh of relief. "Well, I have to say, I'm glad of it."

"Sir?"

"Come now, Dawkins, could you really see us taking that girl off to prison?"

Dawkins relaxed his stance a little. "Well, sir, we was all right unhappy about the idea. But a thief is a thief, I s'pose." His brow furrowed. "Didn't act like a thief, if you don't mind me saying so. We was all very fond of Miss Kit." He spoke for the servants' hall. "A bonny, sweet-natured lass, she were, sir."

Sir William sighed. "Yes, Dawkins. A lovely girl. Lady Marsden and I were very fond of her. And the girls too. The pity of it is…" He did not finish his sentence, but sat for a moment, looking miserable.

"You'd better fetch Mr Devenish then, Dawkins. Having bent my ear all night about the girl, he has gone upstairs to shave."

* * *

Hugo felt a cold fist close around his heart. "What do you mean, she's gone?"

"She's gone, sir," said Maggie Bone. "Climbed out the window and across the roof. She borrowed a horse from the stable—left a note in the stable to say it would be at the coaching inn."

"A note?"

"She left a letter addressed to you, sir. And a note for me. Yours is the biggest." She proffered a neatly folded square. Hugo almost snatched it. He carefully broke open the seal on the letter and read it hastily.

Dear Mr Devenish

I do not wish to be hanged and so I am leaving. Please convey my most abject and sincere apologies to Sir William and Lady Marsden. Please tell Sir William that I was, in fact, returning the chess set. I stole it on the first night of my arrival—the night we made toast in the nursery. I repent it most bitterly.

My entire purpose in visiting England was based on the very worst of falsehoods and deception, but there is no point in excuses. I thought I was doing the right thing and that all the people I stole from had stolen those objects from my father. I was wrong. I didn't realise Papa would even lie to me on his deathbed.

Please ask Sir William not to report my crime, for Aunt Rose's sake. I will do my best to undo the harm I have done. There is a small risk I may be apprehended. If so, you may rest assured I will give a false name so that she shall not be tainted by the scandal. My family has caused Rose enough distress. Please, sir, protect her as best you can from the worst consequences of what I have done.

I also leave in your care my beloved and faithful companion, Maggie Bone. She is a loyal and hardworking servant and a woman of the highest moral calibre. Please, do not judge the servant by the mistress. Maggie has done her best these last six years to turn me into a respectable person. That her efforts were unsuccessful is not her fault, but the fault of my early upbringing. Also my blood. What I have learned in the last few days has convinced me of that.

If you could offer Maggie a position in your household, I would be eternally grateful. As well as securing the services of a first-rate maid, I hope you will thereby also promote the happiness of your groom, Griffin. He has been walking out with Maggie these last weeks and I believe their attachment is sincere and powerful. Maggie would never choose her own happiness over what she sees as my welfare. She will be hurt and distressed by my departure, but I want her to find joy and security on her own account with Griffin.

As for yourself, my dear sir, I must thank you for the friendship, forbearance and care you have shown me.

I also thank you for the offer you made at the opera, that night. It was the most wonderful offer I have ever had, much more than I could ever deserve. I shall never forget it, or you.

You will find another girl, sir. A girl much more deserving of such a magnificent offer, who will bring to her marriage honour and an un-stained past. You will find true happiness with a girl like that, I am sure of it. I will pray for you.

Had things been different—(This last was scratched out.)

Do not try to find me, I beg of you. It does me no credit to admit I have much experience in dis-appearing without trace. Please do not worry about me. I shall go to live with my mother's family.

Take care of yourself, dearest sir, and of Aunt Rose and Maggie Bone. Know that I leave behind me the three people in the world whom I love, with all my heart.

Yours forever, Kit

Hugo crushed the letter in his hand. There was a hard, bitter lump in his throat, so that he could not speak for a moment. He stared down at the crushed paper in his hand and with careful deliberation smoothed it out again.

Know that I leave behind me the three people in the world whom I love, with all my heart.

Three people? Her Aunt Rose and Maggie Bone. And...himself? ...*the three people in the world whom I love...* He was the third, *whom I love with all my heart.*

It was enough. He started to breathe again.

With slow precision, Hugo folded the letter along its original folds and slipped it into his shirt, against his heart.

"Where would she go, Maggie?"

If Maggie felt surprise at his informal use of her first name, she didn't show it. "I don't know. It's hard to tell, sir. She's tricky, Miss Kit."

"Which part of Ireland?"

Maggie stared. "Ireland? Whatever would she go to Ireland for, sir?"

Hugo frowned. He touched his hand to his chest, hearing the faint crackle of paper. "She said she would go to her mother's family. They are in Ireland, are they not?"

Maggie shrugged. "Her mam may have come from Ireland, but Miss Kit ain't got a relative in the world that she knows of. No, I reckon she'd make for Italy— leastways, that's what her plan used to be." Her stoic demeanour collapsed suddenly. "She's taken herself off, sir, all alone in the world as she is! And without no one to care for her!" She burst into tears. "Oh, why did she do it? Why leave me behind?"

"Italy," interrupted Rose, confused. "I don't understand. Why would she go to Italy? I don't understand. Why would she steal from Sir William? I thought she'd come home to live, here in England." She looked from Maggie to Hugo in distress. "I don't understand anything at all."

Hugo regarded Rose sombrely. "She didn't know she was your real niece, Rose. She thought it was some masquerade her father had cooked up with you."

Rose looked puzzled. "A masquerade? But why?"

"'Twas a promise she made him, Miss Rose, ma'am—her father," said Maggie, wiping her eyes. "When he was dying. Asked her to take care of…some unfinished business of his. Miss Kit has never broken a promise yet."

"But why would she not know I was her aunt? I don't understand. She must have known. She called me Aunt, from the beginning."

"Fact is, ma'am," said Maggie grimly, "that girl has never known who she is. Her whole life with His Nibs—your brother, ma'am—has been one long masquerade after another. Miss Kit never knew she was a true Singleton. In all her life with him, she's had that many names and played that many parts it's been a wonder to me she could ever keep up with them." Maggie looked bleak. "He lied to her, ma'am. Lied to her all the time. Sent her to London with a dangerous job to do and his own version of the truth—which was all rubbish, as it turns out! Miss Kit thought you were an old, er, friend of his."

Hugo frowned. He hadn't missed the hesitation before the word friend. What a life the girl must have led, to accept a mistress more readily than an aunt.

"But—"

"Fact is, Miss Rose, it didn't help matters that ye never did reminisce about her father to her. I understand why, now, o' course, with Mr Cranmore coming back and all—" Maggie looked a little self-conscious as a blush coloured Rose's cheeks. "Sorry ma'am, but servants will talk. And I don't blame ye, ma'am, for not wanting to speak of such matters. But ye see why Miss Kit might've thought ye weren't truly her blood relation—that ye were playing a part too. Fer the sake of His Nibs."

Rose bit her lip, looking troubled. "Oh, yes, I suppose I can see that now. Oh dear, oh dear, what a frightful mess it all is." She sighed. "James always did leave a trail of damage behind him."

Hugo said decisively, "Well, there is no reason why that should happen any longer. We'll fetch her back,

Rose, do not fear. Maggie, will you come with me? The coach goes to London, so we'll try there first."

Maggie looked at him steadily a moment as if assessing his motives. "You're not fixin' to hang Miss Kit, are ye?"

"What?" exclaimed Rose, horrified.

Hugo looked calmly back at Maggie. "Sir William will explain everything to you, Rose. And no one is going to hang Miss Kit, Maggie. I promise you that. And I don't break my promises, either."

Maggie smiled suddenly and jumped to her feet with new spirit. "Then I'll come with you, sir, and right gladly."

As the fast travelling chaise raced and bounced along the road to London, Maggie filled Mr Devenish in on all the information she felt he ought to know about Kit.

"He was a scoundrel, through and through, her father, but charming with it, you know?" She snorted derisively. "Not that I ever felt the charm, mind, but I saw enough people fall for it—men as well as women. And Miss Kit, she 'ad a real blind spot where he was concerned. Loved him, despite all he did. It's her weakness that—she'll do anything for those she loves." Maggie gave him a thoughtful look and added, "You'll need to be careful of that."

Hugo stared straight ahead, unwilling to put the idea of Kit loving him any more firmly in his head, in case he was wrong. He couldn't bear it if he was wrong. Now that he'd absorbed the notion that perhaps she loved him a little, he was like a man paused high on a wire, over a precipice, waiting to find out, for sure.

"Miss Kit, she's got a soft heart and more courage than is good for any woman. Those what loves her ought to take care of her. But that man played 'er like a dratted violin. And he had no scruples about using her for his purposes."

Hugo shot her a quick, hard look, which Rose interpreted correctly.

"No, not that, sir. At least he spared her that, though he nearly did sell her to an Indian prince once, for to be his heathen princess. But Miss Kit, she ran away and hid, so she told me, and it all fell through." She added, "But that was before my time. And I really don't know as how her pa would actually have sold her, or whether he was just planning to swindle the prince out of a small fortune in jewels. He were bad, but he weren't evil."

"Before your time? When did you come into her life, Maggie?"

Maggie clucked and shook her head disapprovingly. "I dunno as I ought to tell you that tale. But I suppose, since you're a going to—" She frowned suddenly and leaned forward to scrutinise his face. "What are ye planning to do with Miss Kit if—?"

"When."

Maggie's face softened at his implacable refusal to consider defeat.

"All right, then, *when* we find her. What are ye planning to do with her, sir?"

"Marry her."

Maggie sat back in her seat in a bustle of relieved bombazine. "Oh sir, I'd hoped...I never dreamed..." Tears began to roll down her cheek and she began to grope around in her reticule. "Oh, drat it, where is that handkerchief!" She sniffled and smiled at him mistily, the tears pouring down her cheeks. "I'm that glad, sir. I used to worry that she'd never...oh dear, where is that dratted thing? Miss Kit, she's...she's a real darlin', you know."

He smiled, leaned forward, handed her a folded white handkerchief and said softly, "Yes, Maggie, I do know."

After some time, when Maggie had composed herself, Hugo leaned back against the cushions, crossed one long leg over the other, and said, "Now, Maggie, I would like to hear how you met Kit, when she was thirteen, I believe."

"She really ought to tell you herself..."

Hugo smiled. "She will. After we are married, no doubt."

Maggie conceded. "Very well. I'd been sent out to be a maidservant, a nanny, really, to an English family in India. Only when I got there, it was to find that every poor blessed soul in the family, even the kiddies, had died of the yellow fever. So, of course, there wasn't no job for me. Somebody from the Company did offer me a job, mind, but with all that disease, and the dirt, sir! Well, I didn't want to stay, and since they'd offered to pay my way home again…"

She shrugged. "So there I was, staying in a little hotel in Calcutta, waiting for the next English ship to come to take me back home. Days, I waited. And one day, well, night, it was, something woke me, a noise. I got up, and investigated. I had one of those elephant-foot umbrella stands—bought it for me Da—and I waved it about, thinkin' to hit the intruder over the head with it. Well, to cut a long story short, I found myself waving the elephant's foot at this skinny, dirty little Indian boy, doubled up in the corner of my bedroom. Clutching his stomach, and in a panic."

She watched his face as she spoke. "O' course, I yelled at 'im good and loud, just to frighten him off, not expecting him to understand, of course—I'd yelled at him in English, naturally. Well! You coulda knocked me over with a feather because he answered me—in English!"

He frowned, not seeing quite where this would lead.

Maggie continued. "And it weren't no pidgin English, either. Nor any learnt from sailors or such. Nor was it my sort of English, either, ordinary folks'

English." She paused. "It was the sort of English spoke by the gentry."

He made a sudden stifled sound as he realised what she was about to say.

"Well, to cut a long story short, it weren't no boy and it weren't no Indian—it was Miss Kit."

"Why was she clutching her stomach? Was she ill?"

Maggie blushed furiously and stared out the window at the fields rushing by, as she explained. "No, sir, she…she said she was…bleeding. I checked her over for injuries and that's when I discovered she was a girl. She were having her first attack of the cramps some women get with their monthly time. She, er…no one had told her about bein' a girl and what to expect, sir. He—her Pa—had dressed her as a boy most of her life. And treated her as a boy, too. So when she started having these pains, and found she was, er, bleeding from the inside, she thought she was dying, poor little soul."

Hugo swallowed, imagining the scene. He didn't know much about female society, but he imagined most girls would come to womanhood with the support of their older female relatives. His little Kit had been quite alone. She had spent too much time alone, coping with problems that he could only imagine…

"She told me later her mother had died like that, bled and bled from the inside, after havin' a baby. The baby died too, poor little soul." Maggie heaved a sigh. "And Miss Kit, poor little tyke, were in a panic, because she knew she'd been caught thievin' and didn't know which was worse—a thief's punishment—that's havin your hand cut off—or bleedin' to death like her ma."

Hugo closed his eyes for a moment, his fists clenched. "That swine of a father of hers should rot in Hell for his neglect. What the devil was he doing, letting her go out stealing?"

Maggie's face soured. "Letting her? Had her taught to do it, didn't he? Like a little apprentice. From an early age. He couldn't earn a good enough living with the cards, and God forbid that a gentleman like him would lower himself to work!"

"So he taught his child—his daughter—to steal?"

"Not a pretty tale, is it?" agreed Maggie grimly. "But as an English gentleman, he ran tame in all the nobs' houses and palaces, and his innocent little 'son' too, going where they pleased, and learning the lay of the land. And then later, little Miss Kit would get into native dress and go back and thieve for him."

"I put a stop to all that, mind. It weren't decent. I had Miss Kit into a bath and a nightgown as quick as you could say Jack Robinson. And by the time her worthless pa came a lookin' for her, I'd decided to stay with her and teach her right from wrong, seein' as nobody else had seen fit, and so I told him. And so he was stuck with me, and she became a girl instead of a boy for the first time in her life."

"I begin to see why Kit said she would do anything for Maggie Bone," Hugo said softly.

Maggie blushed. He leaned forward in the coach, took Maggie's hand and kissed it, quite as if she was a duchess or a queen.

"Miss Bone, I thank you," he said formally. "If there is anything I can do for you, at any time, you need only ask."

"Oh, pshaw!" Maggie said gruffly, puce with embarrassment and pleasure. "Anyone would've done the same. She were a grand little girl, so warmhearted and good inside, for all the bad habits she'd been taught. She's not hard to love, Miss Kit."

"No, indeed," he agreed softly, which set Maggie groping for the handkerchief again.

She snuffled a moment, blew her nose and added in a watery voice, "And she never did steal so much as a pin from then on, until he got her to promise him on his deathbed that she would come here and get all those things from those gentlemen. Oh, Mr Devenish, sir, I couldn't bear it if Miss Kit was to hang or get transported."

"She won't," he said simply. "I won't allow it. We will sort everything out, Maggie, I promise you."

"But how will we find her, sir? Miss Kit is very good at fading into the shadows and disappearing."

"As long as she goes to London first, we have an excellent chance of finding her. If you are wrong about Ireland, and she goes there, then we will have more difficulty. But if she plans to leave from London and go to the continent, I have the port of London well covered. I have men, too, in Dover and at Southampton."

Maggie looked at him in surprise. "You knew, then, that she would run away? But how could you know a thing like that?"

"No," he corrected her. "I thought she might need to flee—from the authorities. I took steps so ensure that if she was pursued, there would be a ship available to her—one of my ships, so that I would know where she went." He smiled faintly. "I have no intention of losing her, you understand."

A few moments later he said, "I might have to go abroad for a short time. I trust you will remain with Griffin?"

Maggie blushed. Hugo glanced forward, at his groom. Griffin's ears had gone bright red. They almost matched Maggie's cheeks.

"Yes sir," mumbled Maggie.

"You'll take good care of Miss Bone in my absence, Griffin?"

Griffin turned around. His face split in a grin. "I will indeed, sir. I'll not let her out of me sight one minute."

Scarlet-faced, Maggie tossed her head. "I'm a decent woman, I'll have you know."

"Aye," said Griffin. "I wouldn't marry any other."

Maggie sniffed. But a smile grew on her face to match the one on Griffin's.

It was a good omen, thought Hugo.

Chapter Twelve

Kit paced the small cabin. Oh, when would this wretched ship leave? Each small delay was unendurable. Once she had decided to leave, she wished to be gone. It was unbearable, waiting, gazing out of the tiny porthole at what would be her last sight of England. England, the land she had spent only a few short months in but which had come to feel like home.

If she craned her neck and peered from the side of the porthole, she could see the prison hulks moored on the river, rotting low in the water, their cargo one of misery and wretchedness. From time to time a scream or a moan or a coarse, brutal shout wafted across the water to her ears and she shivered. If she didn't get out of England soon, she may well end up there. If she was lucky, that is. If her luck failed her, as it had so far, she would end up at Tyburn. On the gallows.

Every hour that passed and the ship failed to depart chafed at her nerves. Her helplessness gnawed at her. First, the captain had said he had to wait for the tides. But the tide came and went, and still the ship didn't leave. Then he said the wind was in the wrong direction, and only an hour or two later, the wind had changed and freshened and she'd expected that any moment she would see the wharf drifting away, as they moved off down towards the sea.

But no! She'd gone up on deck and found the captain and asked him what the delay was this time! And he'd shrugged his shoulders and apologised profusely and explained that he'd received a message from the ship's owner, who was sending an important package for delivery. "Only a short wait longer, Miss Smith," he'd said, as he'd said to her at least a dozen times previously. "Only a short wait."

Fuming with impatience and anxiety, Kit had returned to her cabin. For two pins she'd have marched down the gangway and boarded the next departing ship, but she'd already tried and she hadn't been able to get passage on any other ship currently in port. Not one single ship's master had been able to squeeze her in. So she was stuck with this wretched ship and Captain Short-wait!

She heard some church bells chime and gazed out of the porthole again, listening to the mellow golden notes. Home. What was home anyway? Any place could become a home; you just had to make up your mind to it.

What was that English proverb about home? Home was where the heart— No, she wasn't going to think about hearts. She was leaving hers behind, with the ones she loved. Maggie, and Aunt Rose. And him…

He'd offered her marriage…and money, as much as she'd wanted. It had not been too difficult to refuse that.

He hadn't spoken of love.

She told herself she was glad he hadn't. If he'd spoken of love, it would have been that much more impossible to refuse him, and she had to refuse him, because she wasn't the right sort of girl to marry any honest man, let alone a fine, honourable gentleman like Hugo. She couldn't bear to drag him down to the gutter she'd spent her life managing—just—to stay out of.

There was that look in his eyes some times when she caught him watching her…

Oh, it wasn't significant, he didn't mean anything by it, he was just trying to keep her honest.

She could make a home in Italy. Italy was beautiful, the weather was warm and the Italian people were very friendly. She had vague memories of it from when she was a small child, before Mama had died. Yes, Italy, where Mama and little Jamie were buried. She could make a perfectly satisfactory home there, if only this wretched ship would move!

Time spent waiting meant time available to think, and she didn't want to think any more about anything, or she'd weaken and change her mind and

then where would she be? In a mess, that's where.
Ruining more people's lives.

There was a sudden knock at her cabin door.

Kit froze. "Who is it?"

"It's the captain, Miss Smith."

"Oh." Kit slipped off her narrow bunk and
opened the door.

The captain stood in the doorway, an odd look on
his face. "It seems you're wanted, Miss Smith.
There's someone here for you." He stepped aside.

Kit panicked. It was the Runners come to take her to
prison. She glanced wildly at the porthole. Too small!

"Miss Singleton, I believe," said a deep voice.

Kit froze. She turned. "Mr...Mr Devenish," she
managed.

"Thank you, Captain. I'll take her into custody now."

Custody! "No!" she flashed. "You cannot let him
take me, Captain. He—he has no authority over
anyone and especially not me. He—he is a vile
kidnapper, trying to kidnap me! Please, I beg of
you, Captain."

The captain gave Mr Devenish a searching glance.
"I dunno, miss, he don't look like a kidnapper. He
looks uncommon like a gentleman to me."

"Oh, that is just a disguise," she said desperately. "He is a dreadful man. He wants to steal me
away, for... for—"

"For your inheritance?" suggested Hugo drily.

"Yes, for my inheritance. And who knows what else?" she added wildly, sending a pleading look in the captain's direction.

Hugo shrugged, looking every inch the respectable man. "In fact, Captain Patchett, she has taken something which belongs to me. She is a wanted woman."

"Has she now, sir? Well, I can't say that surprises me, now I come to look at her…"

"I'm not," said Kit in a small, desperate voice. "I haven't got anything that is not truly mine, honestly I haven't. You can search, Captain. Anything that was stolen has been returned, I promise you. Send a message to your home, Mr Devenish. You will find your tie-pin there."

The captain looked doubtfully at her. She could understand why. Hugo just stood there, positively exuding respectability and authority.

"Sorry, miss, I reckon I'll have to hand you over to him."

Kit's heart plummeted. "But he has no authority over you! You are the captain—on this ship, you make all the decisions. No one can *make* you do anything!"

The Captain shrugged, a glint of amusement in his eyes. "Got no choice, miss. Mr Devenish here owns this ship. I been waiting all day for him to get here. Sorry, miss." He patted her hand and left, closing the cabin door behind him.

Defeated, Kit subsided onto her bunk. She could

feel the faint breeze through the open porthole. It brought an echo of the stench of the prison hulks.

The wages of sin.

She could not complain that it was not just. But why, oh, why did her captor have to be him? The one man in the world whom she could not bear to face. The one man in the world whom she loved with all her heart.

She swallowed convulsively. He'd called her a thief. It was true. He was come to take her into custody. He'd said so. He'd called her a wanted woman.

Would he take her to Bow Street first? Or straight to prison? She wasn't sure of the procedure here. She swallowed again. She knew one thing about English justice. They hanged people. A petty thief might get transportation, but a jewel thief…

It was justice, after all.

Kit took a deep breath and stood up to face her fate. She forced herself to look him in the eye. He had the oddest look on his face.

Hugo stared at her. "You will not deny, I hope, that you've taken something of mine."

Her eyes were huge and miserable, her face chalky white, her firm little chin set to take her punishment.

"Your beautiful phoenix tie-pin," she whispered. "But I did return it—it is at your town house, I promise you." She looked up at him beseechingly. And then bit her lip. "I know you think my promise is worthless, but indeed it is—"

"I'm not talking about my phoenix tie-pin," he said gruffly. "I have it here." He took it from his pocket and handed it to her. "It is yours. And your promise is not worthless. Your promise is the most precious thing in the world to me."

Hot dry sobs threatened to choke her. She forced them back.

"No, no. I don't want it." She refused to take it from him and after a moment he pocketed the pin again.

"You say you believe my promise; I promise you, I have stolen nothing else of yours—of anyone's. I gave back everything I took, truly I did."

"No. There is one more thing. A small hardened lump of rock, worthless to most, but still…"

She looked at him bewildered, distressed. "But I didn't—"

"My heart," he said. "You have stolen my heart."

She stared at him for a long long moment. The silence stretched between them. Then her face suddenly crumpled.

"Do not make sport of me, I beg you, for I cannot bear it."

"Oh, my poor darling," he said, crossing the cabin in two great strides and taking her into his arms. "I am sorry. I did not mean to make sport of you. You have led me on such a dance, I could not resist teasing you a little. But now I've found you, minx, and I'm giving you fair warning, I will never let you go."

He cupped her firm little chin in his hand and raised her face to his. "You have stolen my heart, Kit Singleton, and I offer you the complete set: my heart, my body and my soul. Marry me." His voice cracked with emotion and he lowered his mouth to hers in a brief, tender kiss.

She half-heartedly pushed him away, her face crumpled. "Oh, no, you must not. I am all wrong for you. I am more like my father than you could possibly imagine. I have been a thief most of my life. I lie, I cheat, I steal, I deceive."

"Hush." He kissed her again. "You have a beautiful, loving heart and you are the bravest, most honourable person I have ever known."

"Oh, no," she wailed. Tears spilled down her cheeks. "You must not say such terrible lies."

He kissed her tears away. "They are not lies. I do not care what you were made to do as a child—"

"Oh, but—"

"—nor what you were tricked into doing as an adult. The past is full of pain, most of which neither you nor I could help. We can dwell amongst the ashes of the past and be miserable, or we can rise up and build the future we choose, together. Which is it to be for us, Kit?"

She gazed up into his eyes, her face wet with tears, her eyes shining.

"You truly want to marry me?"

"I truly do, more than anything in the world." He accompanied his words with a rib-crushing embrace and a series of tender kisses beginning with the tears spilling from her eyes and ending in the searing possession of her mouth.

"Oh. Oh, dear, what a lovely thing to say to me," she sobbed, kissing him back. Then she pulled away, dolefully. "Of course, I cannot marry you. But, oh! I do thank you for asking me."

"What the devil do you mean, you cannot marry me? Of course you can marry me!" Hugo growled, pulling her back against his chest.

She pulled away, a determined set to her jaws. "No. No—please, Hugo, do not make it any harder than it is for me. You know it as well as I do. All chance of marriage was ruined when I was caught with Sir William's chess set." She touched him on the cheek, softly. "The future Mrs Devenish must bring her husband and children honour, not a tarnished past, full of shameful secrets." She turned away from him and walked to the porthole.

"You will bring me hono—"

"No!" She shook her head and stared out the tiny porthole, fighting for composure. The grey oily water slapped, listless and regular against the hull of the ship. Seabirds circled and called on the grimy air, their cries piercing and mournful, like souls risen from their bodies, stranded forever in limbo.

A long moment passed. Hugo watched her silhouetted in the circle of light. His one particular woman, fighting herself, fighting him. Finally he said, "You said in your letter that you left behind you the three people you loved most in all the world."

She stilled.

"Did you mean that I was one of the three?" he said, his voice low.

She said in a low, intense voice, "How can you even ask such a thing? Do you not know? You are the best of the three. I love you with all my heart, more than anyone or anything in the world. You are everything to me, and that is why I cannot—"

"Turn around, minx."

Slowly she turned.

"Come here." He held out his arms to her.

She came, flying across the cabin like an arrow. His arms closed around her and the force of her flight sent them tumbling back on to the cabin bunk. They did not notice; their lips met in desperation and passion. She closed her eyes and simply gave herself up to the moment, the man.

His mouth moved over hers, pouring into her the words he could not say; his passion, his desire, his possession. They engulfed her like flames devouring tinder. The knowledge burned through her, leaving her changed forever in her understanding of what is a man, what is love.

His arms embraced her, holding, enfolding, staking his claim.

She relished the power of the body that cradled her against him, the long hard limbs lying hot and heavy across hers, holding her with a leashed strength. In his arms she felt cherished, wanted, protected, loved. There was pleasure even in the slightly scratchy fabric of his coat against her skin, the damp woolly smell of it. She learned the scent of his skin, the texture of his hair. And the feel of his mouth fitted to hers in a way she had never believed possible.

His strength, his tenderness, his open satisfaction and delight at every small tender gesture she made; all these were a balm to her lacerated sense of self, her crushed feeling of worth. His every touch soothed away the shame and the fear and the endless prospect of loneliness she had faced. And she poured out all the love she felt, in every way she could, returning embrace for embrace, kiss for kiss, caress for caress. Hoping it would be enough. And knowing it could never be.

After a time, he slowed, pulled back slightly. She opened her eyes and found him staring at her. She opened her mouth to ask him what was wrong, but his hands cupped her face as if they held something infinitely precious cradled between them. He simply held her, his thumbs smoothing back and forth along her jawline, tenderly, staring into her eyes.

"I need to make you mine," he said quietly. "If you do not wish it to happen now, Kit, say so and I shall stop."

Kit saw the need, the pride, the quiet, desperate hunger and felt her heart shatter with love anew. How could anyone not love this big, gentle, passionate man? She certainly could not help herself. She was his forever, even if they were together only this one last time.

It must happen. She was an innocent in these matters, but when a man and a woman lay down on a bed, and with such feelings within them that they must explode to be let out somehow…

She wanted it to happen. So very, very much.

Like a squirrel, she had hoarded up moments of joy throughout her life. They didn't come often; she treasured them when they did. And this, to lie down with the man she loved more than life itself, to become one with him… This would be the greatest moment of joy in her life. She wanted it—every moment, every gesture, every touch.

While they were here, together in the tiny cabin, it was as if the world did not exist. It was only they two: one man, one woman, one love. One great, splendid, conflagration of joy to last her the rest of her life.

Oh, yes, she wanted it.

For outside, winter was coming. And she knew it

would be the coldest, bitterest one yet. Even worse than when Mama and little Jamie had died.

She reached up and traced his mouth lightly. "I need you too, my dearest love."

His eyes flamed with—what? Relief, triumph, exultation? And then his mouth lowered to hers and she felt as though her heart must burst, to feel so much, all at once.

He carefully peeled away the many layers of her clothing. And if there was shyness in her response, if there was hesitance in this, her first experience of nakedness with a man, there was also a tentative, joyous blossoming of pride in his response to her.

It was probably sinful to feel so…so worshipped, but, oh, she gloried in it. Every look, every touch. Tender. Needy. Loving.

She watched, wide-eyed and enthralled as he shrugged himself out of his coat and shirt. His shoulders were magnificent.

"I fell in love with your shoulders the first time we met."

"My shoulders?" He looked down at them doubtfully. "You don't mind them being so…big, then?"

She smiled and it was the smile of Eve. Pure feminine appreciation. She reached out and stroked her hands over the broad muscled strength of him and a tremulous shiver passed though her whole body. He felt his own response surge, deep in his loins. Desire. Passion. He gazed into her eyes as she pulled his mouth down to hers. Love.

And then she learned him anew, learned the difference between lying with a man fully clothed and lying with him naked, skin to skin, mouth to mouth, heat to heat.

She gloried in the sensation, of the feeling of him tasting her as she tasted him, learning each other in ways she had never known before. His warm, calloused hands moved across her skin: over, around, beneath, between, leaving trails of shivering sensation...

She stored up every tiny sensation, each splendid golden acorn, against the long winter, a bittersweet memory for the future.

His possession of her. Heat and pleasure and passion spiralling, speared with a single sharp instant of pain. It was the pain which told her it was real, it was true; the very heart of exultation.

Her possession of him. He was at the core of her now, deep within her heat, lost on a pounding tide of sensation...unto oblivion.

Afterwards they lay on the small, narrow bunk, their breathing slowing, their hearts full, gazing into each others eyes. Skin to skin, limbs entangled, unable still to stop touching. Wonderment. Joy. Passion only slightly slaked. A new world of sensation and intimacy.

"Are you all right, love?" His deep voice cracked as he spoke. His big square hands caressed her.

She nodded, tremulously. "Never better." It was the truth, and yet the concern and love she could see in his eyes undid her, and her tears spilled over. "Never better," she sobbed and he gathered her to his warm broad chest and let her weep. And when the storm was over, she lay against his long hard body and explored him dreamily, finding him endlessly fascinating. The hard, the soft, the smooth, the hairy, the strong, the tender…

And he explored in return. "Your skin is like silk," he murmured in wonderment.

She ran a finger along his beautifully sculpted jawline. "Yours is like sandpaper."

He drew back. "I'm sorry. I did not think—"

She smiled and pulled his head back. "Oh, but I like it," she whispered softly and butted her face gently along his jaw, like a cat.

And so, they loved again.

"You will have to marry me now," he said much later, sitting up on the bunk and reaching for his breeches.

"You know I cannot."

He turned back and kissed her possessively. "My dearest girl, I know nothing of the sort. We shall be married as soon as possible."

She twisted away from his embrace and with

clumsy hands jerked her chemise on over her head. She felt at a disadvantage without her clothes on. He had only to look at her and she melted. It had been difficult enough to stand against him before. Now, after what they had shared, opposing him was infinitely harder. But she had to oppose him.

She could not marry him. She would not shame him so.

"Do you care to be married in London, or would you prefer to be married from Gelliford House?"

"I do not care to be married at all!" Kit said. "If you are feeling guilty because of…of what just happened, then there is no need to be. I wanted it as much as you did."

At this last sentence, the anger on his face softened a little.

Kit did not think she could bear to see that tender, possessive expression in his eyes. She hurried on, "Men tumble women all the time. It does not have to lead to marria—"

Hugo smashed a fist against the cabin wall. "I did not *tumble* you! We made love! And we shall do so again and again, as often as we want for the rest of our lives! In our marriage bed and wherever else we—" He broke off. He must have seen something in her face of the distress she was feeling, for his tone moderated. "I am forgetting your inexperience, my love. This was no mere coupling of a man and woman. It was a…a—"

She wrapped her arms around herself, defensively. She had to keep herself separate from him. It was almost impossible to refuse him while her body hearkened unto him.

His voice was deep, vibrating with emotion. "It was a plighting of troth. Yes, that's what it was. We plighted out troth, my love. With my body, I thee worshipped. And…" he fished in the pocket of his coat, hanging on a peg, and took something out "…with all my worldly goods I thee endow." And he crossed the tiny cabin in two steps and carefully pinned the small gold phoenix tie-pin to the bodice of her gown. "The ashes of the past, love, or a golden future?"

Two tears spilled down her cheeks. She dashed them away. His words, his actions, had torn her in two. She wanted, so badly to say yes to him, to let him marry her and take her away to his home and dwell with him forever, but the knowledge of her shame, her disgrace, held her silent. He was such a good man, a generous, decent, beautiful man.

She had not been unaware of the slights he'd faced in society, because of his mother's background, his own years of menial labour and his current activities in trade. Even if he managed to keep her from prose-cution by the law—and she trusted he could do it—the scandal would still be whispered about. She was sure that by now, Lady Marsden would have informed all her friends of that frightful scene in the green room at Woodsden Lodge; the *ton* would be gossiping about how Rose Singleton introduced a thief into society.

Bad enough the damage Kit had done to Rose. Rose would eventually be seen to have been duped. But there would be no question of Hugo Devenish being duped. If she married him, all she would be doing is giving the cats of society just one more weapon to wound him. She could just imagine it: *Devenish? In Trade, you know—well, blood will out, my deah. And married to a thief—yes, really. The Chinese Burglar turned out to be a woman. And he married her. Well, my deah, all tradesmen are thieves at heart, are they not?* Accompanied by genteel, spiteful tittering.

"No," she said and stepped away from him. "I will not marry you." She fumbled at the phoenix pin, but her hands were shaking and she could not undo it.

"Keep it," he growled. "If you try to give it back to me again, I will not be responsible for my actions." A small nerve twitched in his clenched jaw.

There was a silence as she finished dressing. He watched her with bleak, angry eyes. She ought to have been embarrassed by putting on her stockings with a man watching, but this was the first, the last, the only time it would happen, and she was storing up the memory. There was something wonderfully intimate in putting on a pair of stockings in front of the man who had earlier removed them, stroking down her legs with warm, shaking, rough-skinned hands. She shivered as she thought about it. Even if he was now hurt and furious.

"What if we made a child today?" His deep voice broke into her thoughts.

She stilled, then touched her belly, wonderingly. "Then I shall love it with all my heart."

"And yet you would deny it a name, a father, a heritage. And you would deny me my child."

She was mute, unable to answer him. What he said was true. Which would be worse, the shame of a mother who was a known thief, or—?

"This is nonsense!" he exploded. "I shall have Captain Patchett marry us here and now and that will be an end to it!"

"No, Hugo, I won't marry you. I mean it."

He clenched his fists. "But you said you loved me, dammit. Was it a lie?"

She shook her head, miserably. "No. I do love you. Too much to see you shamed by a wife who is known to be a thie—"

"Known to be a thief! What rubbish! Nobody knows. The *ton* loves a mystery and what better than that of the Chinese Burglar who mysteriously appeared on the scene one year, stole a series of fabulous treasures, returned them just as mysteriously and then—pouff! He disappeared!"

"Nobody knows, you say? What of Sir William and Lady Marsden?"

"They will say nothing."

"Oh, indeed, even though Sir William is a magistrate and Lady Marsden despises me!"

"She doesn't—" Kit gave him a disbelieving look and he added, "Or if she does, she'll come around."

"And what of Rose and Mr Cranmore?"

"Rose will say nothing of—"

"And the butler who tied me up?"

"A sum of money will shut—"

"And will you also bribe the footmen who locked me away and the maidservants and—?"

"Enough, dammit! None of these people will blab!"

"How can you know that?"

"Because they *like* you, you thick-headed, stubborn little mule! You don't believe me? Very well, let's put it to the test! Let us return to Woodsden Lodge and see exactly how everyone there reacts to you."

"And when Sir William has me arrested?"

"Confound it, Kit, he won't. I know him." Hugo held up his hand to stop her flow of argument. "And if he does look like doing any such thing—which he won't!—I'll get you away and onto the nearest ship. I'll have one waiting at the closest port. But he *won't* have you arrested!"

Kit took a deep breath and glanced out at the sullen grey sky beyond the porthole. There was only one way Hugo would accept that a marriage between them was impossible. She would have to prove it to him. But the thought of going back, back to where she had betrayed her friends, back to where they had stared at her with hurt and contempt… The thought of doing that chilled her to her bones.

"Very well, I agree to return to Woodsden Lodge and…and face whatever happens."

"What will happen, my stubborn little love, is a wedding! And I'll have your promise on that, if you don't mind."

"I…I…"

"Your promise, Kit, or I fetch Captain Patchett to wed us here and now!"

"Very well, if the scandal has not spread and Rose and the Marsdens forgive me, I will marry you." She knew it was impossible.

"Aha!" he began triumphantly.

"But if they react as I know they will, with anger and disgust…" she closed her eyes, recalling the scene in the green room "…if they despise me, and… Then I shall leave England immediately and you'll not stop me. Agreed?"

"Agreed."

She was a little stunned by his easy capitulation. And a little suspicious. "So you'll allow me to leave without argument?"

"Yes, of course. We shall depart the instant you feel

the slightest discomfort. We shall then be married by Patchett and sail away to live in—Italy, was it? Or Ireland? Whichever you prefer."

Kit gasped at the generosity of his offer, but shook her head. "I lived with an exile all my life, Hugo. I could not bear to watch you become more and more embittered as the years passed. You might agree to it now, but in the end you would come to resent it. And to blame me for it."

He gestured to the ship surrounding them. "You forget, I have already been an exile. I was sent far away from this country as a young boy. And my loving family certainly hoped I would never return."

"But you did return."

He inclined his head.

"And you carved a place here for yourself and against all odds found acceptance in society. I have some idea of how difficult that must have been. Do you think I would let you throw it all away—for me?"

He shrugged. "I am a man with a reputation for knowing a good bargain when I see one. How did the poet put it?—'To count the world well lost for love.' If it was a choice between you and the world, my dearest, stubborn love, I would take you every time. For the world is fickle and faithless and cares not the snap of its finger for Hugo Devenish. But Kit Singleton, ahh, she loves me. She told me so, and she is not a liar."

"No. Only a thief," she said in a desolate voice.

He smiled, took her face in his hands and said in a deep, soft voice, "Make up your mind to it, my love. You cannot tell me you love me one moment, take me to paradise the next and think I will just tamely let you walk away afterwards. One way or another, you're going to marry me, my girl, and you have *my* promise on that!" And he kissed her, a hard, possessive kiss.

And he called her stubborn! Surrendering temporarily, she kissed him back, twining her hands into his short cropped hair, for there was a limit on how much you could reject a man for his own good and Kit had reached it.

She would regain her strength of purpose later, at Woodsden Lodge.

Chapter Thirteen

Kit's heartbeat quickened as the travelling carriage turned off the road between the stone-mounted gates of Woodsden Lodge. She felt ill; she had been able to eat nothing all day. She listened to the wheels crunching the gravel of the long winding drive which led to the house, carrying her ever closer.

She had always assumed she had at least a little courage. She knew better now. The risks she had taken so light-heartedly in the past were not courage, but foolishness. She'd always been able to run away from the consequences before. This time, the consequences had faces—beloved faces. And feelings. Feelings which she had trampled on.

She did not want to face them.

The carriage turned a curve and there stood the beautiful old Elizabethan house. The late afternoon sun glinted on the mullioned windows and the waters of the lake. Kit shivered. The dark stone of the house, the walled stone terraces and the deep, shadowed valley looked more and more like a prison to her.

She had decided what she would do.

There was no possibility of the Marsdens and Aunt Rose forgiving her betrayal of their friendship. She would never marry Hugo Devenish. She would face them, apologise and be off out of the country as quickly and stealthily as she could manage it, leaving Hugo behind in the world he had fought so hard to find a place in.

It was all very romantic to count the world well lost for love, but Kit *knew* what an exile's life was like. She knew what it was like never to belong, never to be able to mix freely with English visitors for fear that they would learn she was the child of an outcast. Even the locals knew they were not welcome in their own country. And once you had been thrown out of your own country, you could be tossed out of any country. Kit had experienced it often.

She did not want that life for him; she did not want it for their children.

The carriage drew into the courtyard. Her palms felt clammy. She did not want to face Rose, Sir William, Lady Marsden and the little girls. Especially the little girls…

"Please do not make me do this, Hugo," she said in a low, shaking voice.

He looked at her white, set face. He reached across

and took her hands in his. They were cold and shaking. "I am not making you do anything, love. This was your choice. I will marry you, no matter what, you know that."

"I do not know if I can bear…" She bit her lip agonizingly. "The little girls."

His face softened and his warm grip on her hands soothed. "Have faith, love."

This time no servants ran out to greet them as the carriage pulled up at the front entrance. Griffin stepped down and lowered the carriage steps. Hugo held out his hand to assist Kit down. She shook her head. "Griffin, would you please inform Sir William and Lady Marsden that we—that I have arrived." Hugo made a small sound and she whirled on him. "I will not gain entry to their home on false pretences again. They must know I am here. They may invite me in, or not. Then I will know how I stand."

Griffin headed off, and Kit slowly descended from the carriage. She would not allow Hugo to come with her; she made him wait in the carriage. "I must do this by myself." The sweet scent of the roses wafted to her on the evening breeze. She felt sick. Her legs were trembling. She stiffened her knees and waited.

Sir William came out first. He saw her standing alone in the paved courtyard and stopped still. His wife followed a moment later. There was no sign of Rose.

Sir William and Lady Marsden stared across at Kit. Kit lifted her chin and waited. Sir William was a magistrate: it was his clear duty to have her arrested. Kit braced herself.

There was a sudden flurry at Lady Marsden's skirts, and three small heads peered around their mother's body. "Miss Kitty-cat" she heard Sally say. She was quickly hushed.

"Go back inside, children," said Lady Marsden coolly. "It is chilly out here."

It certainly was. Kit swallowed. She knew what she faced now; they had made their decision. But now that she had come, she was determined to apologise to them, even if they refused to listen. She opened her mouth to speak.

"Kit, my dear, whatever are you standing out there for?" called Lady Marsden. "Come in, child, before you catch your death."

Kit blinked. It didn't sound like the sort of thing a woman would say if her husband intended to hang you.

Lady Marsden hurried forward. "My dear, I'm so glad you've come back to us. And I am so sorry about that dreadful misunderstanding. Come inside. We have been up in the nursery, making toast, and the children have missed you."

Kit blinked harder.

Sir William strode forward and put an arm around her. "You're frozen solid, girl. Let's get you inside and get you in front of a fire. I'm very cross with you, you know."

Kit braced herself again.

"We were all so worried when you ran off like that. For Heaven's sake—why did you not explain that you were putting the wretched chess-set back?"

"Not now, William," said Lady Marsden.

Kit stopped. "Yes, now, please. I need to explain, and to know."

"Yes, my dear, and so you shall. But first you must come inside and warm yourself—poor child, you are shivering." Lady Marsden and Sir William escorted her inside. Kit glanced back and saw Hugo descend from the carriage, a faint smug smile hovering about his mouth.

By the time Hugo entered the house, Kit was ensconced in a comfortable chair with a rug around her and a glass of wine clutched in her hand. Lady Marsden hovered, the little girls were clustered around Kit's feet and Sir William was leaning against the mantelpiece, observing the whole with a benevolent eye.

"Where is Rose?" asked Kit. She wanted to explain, but it didn't feel right without Rose present.

Lady Marsden smiled. "She and Mr Cranmore are dining with the vicar tonight. Their wedding will be in three weeks' time."

"Oh, very well." Kit swallowed and took a deep breath. "I must tell—"

"Oh, you don't need to worry about all that, Miss Kitty-cat," interrupted Sir William. "Big misunderstanding, easily sorted out."

"But I—"

"My dear girl, you were a victim of your father's dishonesty, as much as any one. Dev here explained what you'd promised to do and I presume that once you found out it was all a pack of lies, you gave back the, er—" he glanced at the little girls "—items you had acquired."

"Yes," said Kit in amazement. "But how could you know that?" She glanced at Hugo. "You didn't tell them, did you?"

Hugo shook his head.

"My dear girl," said Sir William, "you don't think I've been a magistrate for more than ten years without learning something about human nature, do you? You're as true an arrow as ever has flown. There's not a bent fibre in you! Brave and true…" he bent over her and flicked her chin affectionately "…and bonny, too. Now, what's happened to all that toast we were going to make, eh, girls? You take Miss Kitty-cat up to the nursery and give her a toasting fork. I shall fetch the marmalade."

Dazed, Kit allowed the eager little hands to lead her up the stairs to the nursery.

To be forgiven so easily—it was beyond her experience, beyond her understanding. To be accepted back into the fold, after such a betrayal. It was a gift greater than any she had ever imagined. She couldn't quite believe it.

She glanced behind her, to where Hugo was mounting the steps, with tiny Molly Marsden energetically riding his shoulders and clinging fiercely to his hair. He saw the stunned bewilderment in her eyes and smiled. "I said have faith, love, did I not? Faith in your friends. And faith in yourself."

Kit could not speak: her heart was too full.

Soon she was settled in front of the nursery fire, the children clustered around her and a toasting fork in her hand. Hugo sat beside her, his long legs stretched out in front of him, touching hers.

Nell had been watching her solemnly. Suddenly she hugged Kit convulsively. "Papa said you were a good girl—a daughter any man would be proud of, Miss Kitty-cat. He said your papa made you promise to do a bad thing. He shouldn't have done that, should he?"

Kit couldn't answer. She pressed her trembling lips together and shook her head. Hugo put his arm around her.

Nell said, "Our papa wouldn't do that, would he?"

Kit shook her head again. "No, darling," she said softly, her voice ragged with emotion. "Your papa would never ask you to do anything that was wrong." She hugged the child to her, blinking hard, keeping the tears at bay.

Sir William stood in the doorway, a pot of orange marmalade in his hand, staring at the little tableau in front of the fire. It was obvious he had heard the conversation. He put the pot down and fished out a large white handkerchief. He blew his nose noisily, then sat down. "Now, about this wedding," he said.

"You mean Rose's," Kit began.

"Lord, no—that's all organised. No, I meant yours and Hugo's." He glanced at each of them, and frowned suddenly. "There is going to be a wedding, isn't there? My wife said there was."

Hugo nodded and took Kit's hand possessively. "Yes, there is most definitely going to be a wedding. Agreed, my love?"

Kit's eyes misted again. She nodded.

"Excellent," said Sir William. "Now, what we had thought, if you don't mind, Miss Kitty-cat, is that since Rose and Cranmore are to be married from Gelliford House, you might like to be married from here."

Kit was startled. "From here?"

Sir William hurried on. "Yes, the lady wife would be in her element having all the fuss and botheration of a wedding, and besides, she'd like to make it up for…you know what." He cleared his throat violently and hurried on, "And I know that old George Singleton is the head of your family, but…just thought…if you needed a volunteer to give away the bride…you know. Happy to oblige. If you wanted me, that is."

Kit just looked at him, then her face crumpled and the tears spilled over.

Hugo leaned across and pulled her gently back against his chest. He thrust a white handkerchief into her hands and smiled over her head at Sir William, who was looking horrified. As were the little girls. "I think you can take that as a 'Yes, please, Sir William.'"

"Oh, I say! I didn't mean to upset—'

"No, no. She's not upset. Thing is, she expected you to clamp a pair of leg-irons on her, not offer to walk her down the aisle."

"Clamp a pair of—?"

"She's been a little emotional lately, that's all. Rather a lot happening in her life. Bound to catch up on her. A temporary state of affairs—I hope."

In the circle of his arms, Kit stopped on a gulp.

Hugo winked at Sir William and added, "I'm running out of handkerchiefs. She's turned into a regular watering pot!—oof!"

Kit had thumped him in the ribs. "I am not a watering pot," she muttered.

"Ahh," said Hugo, his eyes gleaming with wicked humour. "Reminds me of our very first meeting, love. Very—oof!—romantic."

Kit, remembering how the Chinese Burglar had trounced him, blushed. Hugo, having achieved the result he had wanted, grinned unrepentantly.

"You were saying, Marsden, old fellow? You're going to walk Kit down the aisle and…?"

"Oh, yes, what was the other thing?" Sir William glanced down at the two elder girls who'd been watching the interplay between Kit and Hugo with great interest, but now were jiggling up and down with suppressed excitement, and grinned. "Oh, that's it. There are a couple of young ladies here who have been pestering their mother for days about whether Miss Kitty-cat would need any rather short brides-maids? What do you say?"

Kit looked at the little girls, and her heart filled again. Sally's small sticky hand stole into hers.

"Could we, Miss Kitty-cat? Please?"

There was a huge lump in Kit's throat. She nodded and Nell and Sally squealed with delight. "Mama, Mama! Miss Kitty-cat said yes! We can be her bridesmaids, even though we're little!"

Lady Marsden, who had just entered the room, hushed them indulgently. "Now, Kit, don't let these young hoydens push you into anything you don't want. It is your wedding, my dear. It must be just as you would like it. And if you don't want to have it here, you must say so. We shall not mind in the least, shall we, William?"

"Says the woman who has spent the last week alternatively fretting over Kit's whereabouts and poring over designs for wedding gowns," agreed Sir William.

Lady Marsden blushed. "Oh, hush. It is all up to Kit. What do you say, my dear?"

Kit swallowed the lump in her throat. "Are you sure of this, Lady Marsden?" She was not asking about a wedding.

Lady Marsden embraced her. "Quite, quite sure, my dear girl."

There was a short silence in the room.

"Papa, Miss Kitty-cat is crying again and now Mama is too!"

"It is because of the weddings, my dear," explained Sir William gently. "Ladies always cry at weddings."

There was a hush in the ancient chapel which stood in the grounds of Woodsden Lodge. The smooth oaken pews were polished to a shine with age and with beeswax. It was a small wedding by society standards, but as far as Kit was concerned, the cream of society was there.

There was Maggie, and her proud new husband, Griffin. There was Rose and her equally proud husband, Donald Cranmore. There was the entire Marsden household, even down to the scullery maid. There was the groom's nephew, Lord Norwood, his betrothed, Miss Libby Lutens, and Miss Lutens's mama. There was even Lord Norwood's mother, sitting scowling in a pew at the back of the church, still convinced Hugo had stolen the heiress. Cousin

George Singleton oversaw the whole affair from the traditional Singleton family private pew. And Captain Patchett had arrived a short time earlier, looking splendidly nautical in a blue coat with enormous, shiny brass buttons. He was going to sail the married couple to Italy for the honeymoon.

And to everyone's amazement, three immensely modish old ladies had arrived, unannounced and uninvited: Lady Gosper, Lady Hester Horton and the Honourable Pearl Hamnet. They had loudly announced they were sitting on the bride's side of the church.

The organ pipes surged with music, filling the church with ageless beauty. The bride stepped into the aisle on the arm of a distinguished-looking gentleman; Sir William giving the bride away.

The bride began her slow march down the aisle, her eyes fixed on the tall, ruggedly handsome man who awaited her by the altar. Two immensely solemn little girls, their hair braided with the palest pink roses, carried the bride's train, their small sweet faces frowning in fierce concentration. As well as the two diminutive bridesmaids, the bride was accompanied by three attendants: Maggie, Rose and Lady Marsden. Each lady's eyes were moist with tears.

Hugo waited, his nephew Thomas and Captain Patchett by his side, watching his love come to him. She smiled as soon as she saw him waiting, her mouth a little tremulous but her eyes were incandescent with joy. His heart filled as he never thought possible. He was trembling. He could see by the way she was walking that she was shaking too. He wanted to stride up the aisle, snatch her up and hold her hard against him, to know, to feel it was real, that she was real. The long moments of the bridal march passed and at last he could take her by the hand. The relief of it passed through him like a shock. This was his love, his woman, his own bright, particular star.

"You'll not run from me now, Kit, will you?" he murmured.

She shook her head, her eyes luminous with love and happiness. "Never," she answered him. "I have everything in the world I've ever dreamed of, and more, right here before me."

And she was looking only at him.

She touched the bright phoenix pin which she wore at her throat. "You have brought me out of the ashes of my past, my dearest love. I do not care if the future is golden or not, as long as I am with you."

He drew her hard against him and oblivious of convention, kissed the bride before the ceremony had begun. "If you and I are together, love, how can it be anything else?"

* * * * *

NEATH PORT TALBOT LIBRARY
AND INFORMATION SERVICES

1	4/19	25		49		73		
2		26		50		74		
3		27		51		75		
4		28		52		76		
5		29		53		77		
6		30		54		78		
7		31		55		79		
8		32		56		80		
9		33		57		81		
10		34		58		82		
11		35		59		83		
12		36		60		84		
13		37		61		85		
14		38		62		86		
15		39		63		87		
16		40		64		88		
17		41		65		89		
18		42		66		90		
19		43		67		91		
20		44		68		92		
21		45		69		COMMUNITY SERVICES		
22		46		70				
23		47		71		NPT/111		
24		48		72